"We've all met [Peter Benchley's] hero, likable, pitiable Scott Preston. We recognize him the moment Mr. Benchley brilliantly gets us inside his befogged head." *The New York Times Book Review*

"Insightful . . . [RUMMIES] proves that there are far stranger creatures lurking in American drug and alcohol rehabilitation clinics than in the vasty deeps of the ocean." Paul Theroux

"Peter Benchley has submerged himself again, not in the sea, but in the lower depths of alcoholism, where the defiant denizens must dry out or die. From the mire of addiction, the author of *Jaws* launches a geyser of suspense and raw humor." *Atlanta Journal & Constitution*

"Peter Benchley addresses himself to a serious subject, lacing it with considerable humor. The book has elements of mystery, intrigue and adventure. . . . RUMMIES is a story of considerable strength and immediacy." *The Chattanooga Times*

"This may be Benchley's best-written, tightest novel." *The Kirkus Reviews*

"Fascinating . . . Fast moving . . . Benchley moves from the deep of the ocean into the depths of the psyche."

The Grand Rapids Press

"Benchley's story-telling skills make a 'lush tank' seem as fascinating and as frightening as the shark-populated waters he wrote of in *Jaws*."

The Dallas Morning News

"A murder mystery, a comic piece, a treatise on alcoholism, an inspirational tract. Benchley, like a bartender with a pen, mixes them together and pours out a smooth blend of a novel."

The Sunday Oklahoman

"*The Lost Weekend* served for years as the classic portrait of an alcoholic. . . . [RUMMIES] updates the whole picture, showing that alcoholism has proven equal opportunity for women, but still, the first step toward a cure is the alcoholic's admission there is a problem."

Southern Statesman

Also by Peter Benchley:

TIME & A TICKET
JAWS
THE DEEP
THE ISLAND
THE GIRL OF THE SEA OF CORTEZ
Q CLEARANCE

RUMMIES

PETER BENCHLEY

FAWCETT CREST · NEW YORK

A Fawcett Crest Book
Published by Ballantine Books
Copyright © 1989 by Peter Benchley

Grateful acknowledgment is made to the following for permission to reprint previously published material:

Macmillan Publishing Company and A. P. Watt Ltd.: 5 lines from the poem "For Anne Gregory" by William Butler Yeats, from *The Poems of W. B. Yeats: A New Edition*, edited by Richard J. Finneran (British title: *The Collected Poems of W. B. Yeats*). Copyright 1933 by Macmillan Publishing Company. Renewed 1961 by Bertha Georgie Yeats. Reprinted by permission of Macmillan Publishing Company and A. P. Watt Ltd. on behalf of Michael B. Yeats and Macmillan London Ltd.

The Songwriters Guild of America: Excerpt from the lyrics to "Whatever Lola Wants (Lola Gets)" by Richard Adler and Jerry Ross. Copyright © 1955, 1957 by Frank Music Corp. Copyright renewed 1983 by Richard Adler Music and J & J Ross Company. All rights administered by The Songwriters Guild of America.

This is a work of fiction and all the names, characters and events portrayed in this book are invented.

Library of Congress Catalog Card Number: 89-3997

ISBN 0-449-21945-3

This edition published by arrangement with Random House, Inc.

Manufactured in the United States of America

First Ballantine Books Edition: December 1990

For Nat and Márika

All envy would be extinguished if it were universally known that there are none to be envied, and surely none can be much envied who are not pleased with themselves. . . . Such is our desire of abstraction from ourselves, that very few are satisfied with the quantity of stupefaction which the needs of the body force upon the mind. Alexander himself added intemperance to sleep, and solaced with the fumes of wine the sovereignty of the world. And almost every man has some art, by which he steals his thoughts away from his present state.

—SAMUEL JOHNSON
Idler 32

PART ONE

1

I⟋T MUST BE a metabolic thing, this sweating. Like some people gain weight on a diet of arugula and Yoplait while others gobble nesselrode pie and *crème fraîche* and look like Twiggy. He wasn't fat, didn't overdose B vitamins. It had to be metabolic. Because on a day like this, here on the yuppie version of the Murmansk Run, nobody else was sweating. The March wind slashed across the Jersey Meadowlands, churning chemical whitecaps on the marsh scum. Smears of acid ice streaked the windows of the New Jersey Transit train car, inside which the air-conditioning blasted away with perverse efficiency. Captains of industry were huddled in their Tripler overcoats, turning the pages of the *Times* with fleece-swaddled fingers.

And Scott Preston sat there, in nothing but a light-weight suit, sweating.

He was having trouble concentrating on the *Times*. He read one paragraph, and by the time he had started on the second, he had forgotten what the first one said. So he turned to the crossword puzzle: nothing to remember, all there in one glance. But today was a Friday, usually the hardest puzzle of the week, and the first two clues he saw were "Babylonian stringed instrument" and "Hebrew pastry." He dropped the paper under the seat and stared out the window, wiping beads of sweat off his upper lip with the back of his hand.

The train slowed, stuttered and sighed to a stop. In the middle of nowhere. He didn't like it when this happened, didn't like being trapped in a steel tube on a frozen desert. He looked to the door at the end of the car, expecting to see the conductor burst through, maybe wearing a gas mask, shouting something like "It's gonna blow!" None of the other passengers even glanced up from their papers. Sheep, all sheep, conditioned to mindless resignation by years of debasing routine.

Not Preston. He was getting *out* of here.

No! Stop it! Nothing's wrong. Take a deep breath.

He gripped the back of the seat in front of him. His palms were slimy.

Count one tiny blessing: No one was sitting next to him. He couldn't stand being crowded, especially by strangers, especially in emergencies like this.

So of course just then some sonofabitch had to sit down next to him. Preston felt him rather than saw him, for Preston had his face pressed to the window.

"It's like an oven back there," said the intruder. "This railroad's got two classes of service: bake and freeze."

Damn! He recognized the voice. Of all the four billion people on the planet Earth, all the mutes and Lithuanians, bail-jumpers and illegal aliens—people who would not conceive of engaging Preston in idle chatter—the guy who took this last seat in this frigid coffin had to be someone he knew. Not only knew but worked with! Just his luck. He had sensed it since the first blades of light had pierced his eyelids this morning: Today would not be a good day. If his atavistic sensibilities had been more finely tuned, he would have read the omens, chucked his spear into the dirt and turned back into his cave to await more favorable signs.

He hunched his shoulders and ducked his head, pretending to count dirt balls on the windowsill.

"Scott! . . . Hey, Scott!"

With a phony yawn and an elaborate stretch, Preston turned away from the window. "Oh, hi, Dave."

"I thought you always took the seven-fifty."

"Overslept."

"I had root canal. I think my dentist was the guy in *Marathon Man*." Dave Diamond slapped his *Times* on his lap, folded it open to the advertising section. "We can split a cab."

The train jolted, lurched a couple of times and gathered speed. Preston wiped his hands on his trousers, squeezed droplets of sweat out of his eyebrows and forced his mind to focus on devising a plausible reason for not sharing a cab to the office.

Sharing a cab was a commitment, and he was not ready to make a commitment. Not today. Today was going to be a day to get through, to survive. All bets were off, all promises on hold. It was weird how days like this crept up on him without warning. He had been having more and more of them lately.

But he could deal with them. The tools were at hand. Or they would be. He smiled as the train plunged into the darkness of the tunnel.

He felt better already, now that the decision had been made.

When they reached the top of the stairs in the main concourse of Penn Station, Diamond pointed to the Eighth Avenue exit. Preston shook his head: no.

"What's the matter?"

Affecting a stricken look, Preston said, "I have to stop at the john."

"I'll wait."

"No, don't." He clutched his stomach. "Something tells me this'll be a long one. I'll catch you later."

"No sweat. I wait five minutes, I still save time taking a cab."

"No!" Panic. He hadn't thought it through. "I could be an hour. *Two* hours." Preston reached for his wallet, pressed a few dollar bills into Diamond's hand. "Here. My share." He scurried away before Diamond could think up some other stupid argument. He didn't look back but imagined Diamond standing there, bewildered, as if thinking: This isn't right, this isn't the way things go.

Screw him. Preston didn't owe him an explanation. Some people think that because they suggest something that on the surface makes sense, like sharing a cab, if you don't go along with it there's got to be something wrong with you and they have a right to know what it is. Well, they don't. Everybody has their own imperatives, and they handle them in their own ways, and

Preston wasn't about to tell him what was going on beneath *his* surface. The man wouldn't understand. People always think they'd understand, but they never do. Sometimes they pretend to, but they don't really. Because they can't.

About fifty yards down the concourse, Preston did turn back, to make sure Diamond wasn't following him. Not that he should be, but it never hurt to be careful. He could see Diamond riding the escalator up to Eighth Avenue.

The restaurant at the end of the concourse was opening up. A waitress was swabbing tables, the bartender slicing lemon peels into a bowl.

Preston walked back to the far end of the bar and sat on a stool in the shadows. He sighed. Almost home.

The bartender did not look up, just kept slicing his lemon. Preston's mouth was dry, his palms sweating again, but he said nothing. Don't be impatient. Be casual.

The bartender sliced the last scintilla of peel off the lemon and dropped the bald white ball into the steel sink.

Now he would turn to take Preston's order. Preston forced a smile, started to speak.

The bartender picked up another lemon and started to flay it.

Preston's smile froze. *Jesus Christ! What does he want? An engraved invitation?*

He cleared his throat.

The bartender ignored him.

He said, ''Excuse me?''

"What for?" the bartender said without missing a slice.

Now Preston knew. The man was a sadist. The cardboard landscape of this man's day was brightened by inflicting pain on strangers. The kind of man whose car sported a bumper sticker reading, "Hire the handicapped. They're fun to watch."

Preston didn't need this. Not today. He'd take his trade elsewhere. He looked at his watch. Nine forty-five. No time to seek out another oasis.

He slid off the stool, walked down the bar and stood before the bartender, who, head bent to his sacred lemons, presented to Preston a tonsure in the center of which a scaly substance was thriving. A molting snake.

"I have just had root-canal work," he said as calmly as he could through a throat whose tendons were as tight as violin strings. "I am in agony. May I please have a double vodka on the rocks?"

"Twist?"

"Please." He returned to his stool in the shadows.

The waitress ambled by and placed an ashtray before him, letting her gaze linger on him for a second. A bony, angular woman whose canine teeth were missing, she looked fifty and was probably thirty.

Preston touched his cheek and said, "Talk about *pain.*"

"Sure, honey."

The bartender set the drink before him and took the twenty Preston had tucked under the ashtray. He retreated to his station, where the waitress stood smoking a cigarette. Preston noticed that they were both smiling and stealing glances at him, and for a moment he wondered why.

Then he reached for his glass.

The glass was full, brimful, a few molecules from overflowing, the liquid contained only by surface tension. And Preston's hand—as he approached the safe harbor of relief from this most hideous of mornings, as he instinctively tasted the succor waiting in the glass—was palsied. It trembled so much that had his fingers not been padded with flesh, they would have rattled together like castanets. He could not touch the glass without slopping vodka all over the bar, could not lift the nectar to his lips without soaking his shirt.

This was no accident. The bartender had done it on purpose. Preston looked at the vile, sniggering couple huddled in a miasma of toxic fumes over a pile of mutilated fruit, and he knew that they were waiting to see him abase himself, hoping he would lean forward and bury his muzzle in the glass like a dog in his water dish or—better still—that he would attempt to hoist the glass and would spill it and, in desperation, would lick the liquid from puddles on the bar.

As ghastly as this day had been, as compelling as his need now was, he resolved that he would not be the butt of their cruel game. He felt like a captive member of the Maquis, determined not only to endure Gestapo torture and deny his interrogators the nuggets of intelligence they sought, but also to outwit them at their own game and escape to sunlit uplands, singing *"le jour de gloire est arrivé. . . ."*

He took his handkerchief from his pocket and unfolded it. Holding it beneath the level of the bar, he twirled it into a length of linen rope. His left fist gripped one end of the rope. The middle fingers of his right hand pressed the other end to his palm, leaving his right thumb and forefinger free.

Then he sat and waited, watching the vicious duo watching him, pleased that he knew what they were doing but that they did not know he knew, anticipating the triumph of proving to them that he was not one of the helpless rummies they were accustomed to tormenting.

Outside, in the concourse, commuters hurried by, unaware of the heroic test of wills being fought here in the dim cocoon. The stationmaster announced the arrival of a train from Boston.

Preston could hear his heart beating, could taste a dusty gum like plaster on his teeth. *Come on, damn you! Get bored. Slice a lemon!*

A homeless man reeled into the bar, dragging a fur coat on the floor behind him.

"Hey, man . . . gizabeah. . . ."

"Beat it, Jasper."

"Igotafuckinbread . . . gizabeah. . . ."

"I said beat it!" The bartender pointed at the door.

The waitress reached for a cigarette.

Now!

Fast as a cat, Preston looped the handkerchief around his neck. He dipped his right shoulder far enough for his right thumb and forefinger to lift the glass. Then he pulled with his left hand, and the glass rose—smoothly, without a quiver, without spilling so much as an atom—to his lips.

He drained it in a single swallow.

He closed his eyes and held the glass aloft as the precious lubricant coursed through his pipes and pooled warmly in his stomach. A delicious shudder traveled across his shoulders and lifted the hair on the back of his neck. He balled the handkerchief and stuffed it in his jacket pocket.

The warmth rippled outward, sending messages of peace to the sentinels at the farthest reaches of his body.

He opened his eyes and set the glass down on the lacquered bar. At the sound the bartender wheeled. His face betrayed nothing, but Preston knew he was dumbfounded.

Preston said pleasantly, "The other half, if you please."

One more, two at the most, would keep the peace till lunchtime.

As Preston awaited the refill, a vague spectre of disappointment fluttered by. He had promised himself that today would be the day. He had finished the last of the scotch last night before supper and, to banish temptation, had drunk at midnight the final four fingers of Stolichnaya from the bottle in the freezer. All that remained in the house now was cooking sherry, and he'd have to have a real problem before he'd drink that sewage.

Today was the first of the month, and he had found that it was good to quit on such signal days. It gave him landmarks to measure his progress against.

But how could he have known what today would be like? First Margaret forgot to wake him. Then the coffee machine went berserk and produced nothing but black sludge. Then the car was so low on gas that he had to fill it on the way to the station, which meant that he had to sprint for the train, ending up sweating like a longshoreman and having to stand all the way to Newark. Then the goddam train broke down somewhere in the tundra, which gave him a bad anxiety flash, and finally Dave Diamond had to sit next to him and babble like a fishwife all the way to Penn Station, which capped the morning with shit.

Perhaps there were Pollyannas who could deal with a day like this without a little help from their friends. Not Preston. He was a human being, not one of your high-performance robots. What was it Doctor Johnson said? "Life is a pill which none of us can bear to swallow without gilding." Amen.

The bartender put the refill before Preston and cut six more dollars from the twenty. There was no sneer on his face now, no holier-than-thou attitude. Preston decided that he wasn't such a bad guy.

Preston didn't gulp this one. He didn't have to. He sipped it, savoring the feeling of the icy silk as it coated his tongue and flushed all the gloom away. There was hope for today after all.

And tomorrow? Would tomorrow be the day? No. Forget it. Don't even think about quitting on a weekend. People who try to quit on weekends are kidding themselves. It can't be done. The pressures are too great: lunches, dinners, cocktail parties. What happens is, you promise yourself that you're going to quit on the weekend, and when you don't, you go into a funk of self-loathing for breaking your promise, and the only way out of the funk is . . . well, it's obvious.

Mondays were the best days. Clean slate. No social commitments. Early supper, a little television, read a book, go to bed. Once you have a whole day under your belt, the next day's easier and the next even easier, and so on. You can build momentum if you stop on a Monday.

Monday, Preston vowed. I'll quit Monday.

2

$\bigcap$S THE ELEVATOR opened onto the reception area of Mason & Storrow, Preston mashed the last of a Lifesaver between his molars and swallowed the crumbs. He exhaled into his palm: pure mint.

This reception area was famous in publishing. It had been featured in *Architectural Digest* and had been used as a set in half a dozen movies and television shows. It was decorated like the library of an Edwardian men's club, furnished with leather couches and armchairs, standing brass ashtrays and floor-to-ceiling bookcases packed with every book published by M&S in 103 years in the business, including (most prominently displayed) those by the winners of two Nobel Prizes, sixteen Pulitzers, a gaggle of National Book Awards, Newberys and Caldecotts too numerous to count and assorted Edgars and science-fiction citations.

To established authors, the reception area of Mason & Storrow was warm and welcoming, an affirmation of their accomplishment. To ambitious unpublished authors, it was inspiring but frightening, seeming to cry out to them, "Abandon hope, all hacks who enter here, for this is a class house."

To Preston, it was home. More than his house in Hopewell, more than his cottage in Maine, more than the house in which he had grown up in New Canaan, this imposing but cozy room represented support and security, long-term care for himself, his career, his retirement, his family. Even his teeth.

It was also home, from nine to five, to the finest-looking receptionist in all of publishing, one Sharon Prinze. Preston was fond of telling a story (apocryphal, perhaps; embroidered, certainly) about Styron and Mailer stopping by one day to see Warren Storrow and becoming so smitten by Sharon Prinze that they absconded with her to Elaine's and imprisoned her there until she consented to spend the rest of her natural life shuttling between Provincetown and Martha's Vineyard to serve each, in turn, as muse and boon companion.

What was particularly tantalizing about Sharon Prinze was that her formidable battlements had so far proven to be unscalable by anyone at M&S. She was congenial, efficient, respectful, breathtakingly beautiful and utterly unattainable.

This morning, Preston thought, she looked especially heartstopping, and it occurred to him that she might be susceptible to a subtle overture—say, a luncheon invitation tendered under the guise of seeking help with a difficult manuscript that dealt with the aspirations of single young women struggling against the anomie of the Big Apple.

But one of Preston's spiritual lifeguards had escaped drowning in the sea of four double vodkas, and now it called out to him from a remote beach in the back of his brain, "Don't be an imbecile!"

So he restricted himself to a cordial "Morning, Miss Prinze" and turned to the corridor that led to his office.

He collided with Dave Diamond, who was coming to retrieve a delivery from Miss Prinze.

"Hey, buddy," said Diamond. "How you feeling? You look better."

"Great!" Preston replied truthfully. "Just what I needed." He marched off to his office without stopping to decipher Diamond's look of vague distaste—as if he had swallowed a tainted clam.

Preston's office looked down on Park Avenue. The door was always left open so that his secretary (she preferred "editorial assistant"), Debbie Browning, whose workstation was a closet in a fetid corridor, could reassure herself that there existed a world without ducts. Now, for some reason, the door was closed.

Debbie looked like a young Margaret Thatcher, and indeed around M&S she was known as the Iron Maiden. She intended to be an editor—no, she intended to be *the* editor—and her work was her life. Preston assumed that she slept on the crosstown bus, because in addition to her forty-hour week for him, she worked on nights and weekends as a free-lance copy editor, read every esoteric quarterly in the land and clipped promising poems and stories, with which she besieged him each morning, and not only read every manuscript he edited but offered gratuitous detailed critiques of the writing, the editing and the typesetting.

She was a royal pain in the ass.

"Hi, Deb," Preston said. "Anything cooking?"

He expected to be handed a stack of phone messages and slapped with a sly rebuke about lax work habits.

Instead, this woman who believed that direct eye contact was a key to success, this paragon who could stare down a cobra, refused to look at him and said only, "Mr. Preston, I'm truly sorry."

"What?"

"I wish you the best of luck." She sniffled and sprang to her feet. "I mean that sincerely."

"That's very nice of you, but—"

She scuttled off toward the ladies' room, making a sound—*whuck whuck whuck*—like a dog with a bone in its craw.

Metabolic, Preston concluded. It must be a metabolic thing, like his sweating. She should consider taking Tryptophane. These mood swings weren't healthy.

He opened the door to his office.

Weeks later, from a prospect of some serenity, Preston would recall with amazement the speed with which his mind had received, dissected, interpreted and reacted to the sudden flood of unexpected information that greeted him when he opened the door. The concept of a nanosecond had always struck him as being as boggling as the concept of infinity—something that Man is not really meant to grasp, that doesn't exist except as an excuse for the endowment of highly paid chairs at Ivy League universities—and yet it seemed that in less than a nanosecond he was able to determine that: his parents had died, Margaret's parents had died, Kimberly had been expelled from Princeton Day School, Margaret was divorcing him to marry Warren Storrow, Kimberly had been arrested for selling cocaine, Mason & Storrow was going out of business, and he was being replaced as executive vice president and senior editor by Chris Evert.

Four people were in his office: Margaret, Kimberly, Warren and a woman who, on second glance, was older and flintier than Chris Evert. They sat in straight-backed chairs arrayed in a semicircle with their backs to his desk. A fifth chair had been placed at the focus of the semicircle.

They did not look happy. Margaret, in fact, appeared to be possessed by a fulminating, barely controlled fury Preston had seen but a few times before in his seventeen years of marriage, most recently late in the evening of her parents' thirty-fifth-wedding-anniversary celebration when her father had launched into one of his litanies of kike jokes and Gullah stories and Preston had called him a troglodyte asshole.

Kimberly looked nauseated. Warren looked gorgeous, as always, with his Tiffany collar pin perfectly straight and his helmet of Leslie Nielsen hair perfectly sculpted, but Preston could tell he was uncomfortable by the way his thumbs were exploring his cuticles. Chris Evert looked as impassive as Torquemada at an auto-da-fé.

"Come in, Scott," Warren said. "Shut the door." He pointed to the empty chair.

"What have we here?" Preston said because he felt he had to say something. *"This Is Your Life?"* No one smiled. "What's going on? Somebody hurt?"

Chris Evert said, "A lot of people, Scott."

"Who're you?"

"Her name is Dolores Stark, Scott," said Warren. "We asked her here to help you . . . to help us."

"Help us what?" Preston tossed his briefcase onto his desk and went to one of the windows overlooking Park Avenue. It was hot in here. He was starting to sweat again. He opened the window a few inches and turned around and leaned on the sill. He was damned if he would sit in that chair and be a bull's-eye. As long as he was standing, he retained a measure of control.

Dolores Stark said, "Sit down, Scott," and she pointed at the chair.

"I'm fine here. No problem. Now tell me—"

"Scott!" Warren barked. Preston had never before heard Warren bark, had thought him to be—like many WASPs, like himself—incapable of raising his voice, lacking the barking chromosome. "Sit down!"

Stunned, Preston walked meekly to the chair and sat. He could think of no jocular crack. Besides, Warren's Doberman tones had told him two important things: This little get-together was about him, and it was serious. *What have I done?* He revved his mental motor and tried to anticipate their complaints. *I am an extremely careful person—thoughtful, even. I do not insult strangers, I do not belittle waiters, I do not browbeat subordinates. On those rare occasions when I take afternoon naps in the office after wooing bibulous authors at lunch, I cover my tracks like an Apache. I do my work conscientiously and well. Authors ask for me to be assigned to them.*

Dolores Stark said, "How many drinks did you have on the way in this morning?"

Preston froze. His heart may have stopped, and surely his breath did. A bizarre recollection commandeered his mind. A year ago, one of his younger authors, a gifted storyteller but afflicted with a chronic compulsion to articulate the abysses of human experience that even Saul Bellow hadn't plumbed, had written a sentence that Preston excised as pretentious bushwa: "I felt as if he had punched me in the soul."

Preston owed the lad an apology. Dolores Stark had just punched him in the soul.

All he said was "I over*slept*!"

Margaret exploded. "Like hell! You were passed out in the living room. I left you lying there."

"I was *not* passed out. I was asleep because . . ." *Think! Think!* ". . . because when I went to bed you were snoring so badly that—" "Bull*shit*!" Margaret never said words like "bullshit." Ever. "On the floor? With all your clothes on?"

Preston expected Margaret to come out of her seat like a pilot ejecting from a burning plane, until Dolores Stark leaned over and touched Margaret's knee and turned to Preston and said, in a voice as calm as a windless sea, "How many, Scott? How many drinks this morning?"

She thinks she's got me. But I will become a handful of eels. Maybe the building will catch fire. Maybe an earthquake will strike.

"Look, the train broke down in the Meadowlands. . . ." As if that explained it all. As if he expected her to lean back and say, "Oh, no wonder! Then I guess we can adjourn. Sorry to bother you."

Preston wondered if perhaps he was going mad.

"Are you trying to tell me you didn't have any drinks this morning, Scott?"

"I'm not trying to tell you anyth—"

"Because you smell like a distillery."

"I do not! That's . . . that's . . ."

"Impossible? Were you going to say 'impossible'?" Dolores Stark smiled, not unkindly. "Because you ate a bunch of mints? Come on, Scott. Never try to shit a shitter."

Sweat coursed down Preston's scalp, dripped off his hair and into his ears. He opened his collar button, loosened his tie. He turned to Warren, who was examining his knuckles.

"Why are you doing this, Warren?"

Dolores Stark answered. "This is what we call an intervention, Scott."

"I'm not talking to you!"

"Fine, Scott. Talk to Warren, then." She shifted her gaze to Warren and locked it on him, as if injecting him with her strength.

Warren shot an angry glance at Dolores Stark. He probably hired her to be the assassin, Preston thought, and she put the knife in, but now she's forcing him to turn it.

"Scott . . ." Warren said. "We want to help you see what we see. We want to help you help yourself, before it's too late."

"I do my work. I do it damn well. And you know it." *Stupid! You've just begged him to find fault with you. He'll be on your back like a baboon looking for lice.*

Warren's jaw set and his skin tone darkened a shade as he looked directly into Preston's eyes.

"On February sixteenth at seven P.M., you called Paul Sanders in Pennsylvania and spoke with him about a proposal for a novel."

Warren paused, and Preston said, "Guilty."

"On February seventeenth at ten A.M., you called him again and began to repeat the entire conversation, as if the one the night before had never occurred. You had forgotten it. Every word."

Oh shit. "No! I just wanted to clear up—"

"On January twentieth, you had lunch with Nat Brower and agreed on an advance for a book. Two weeks later, his agent called Accounting and asked where the papers were. You had never submitted them, had never cleared the advance with me."

"Oh. Well. It must've—"

"What was the figure, Scott? How much did you agree to pay?"

Preston's shorts were soaked. A searing spasm shot through his lower bowel. "Offhand? I can't—"

"Would you like me to go on?" Warren pulled a sheet of paper from his pocket.

Preston looked at his shoes. They were nice shoes. From Brooks Brothers. Old and comfortable, made supple by a thousand applications of Meltonian Cream. *Good-bye, shoes.*

Dolores Stark held up a hand to Warren. She said softly, "Margaret?"

Preston looked at Margaret. She was clutching her purse in a death grip, as if trying valiantly to transfer all her bilious fury to that leather sack.

When she spoke, her voice was flat, dead. "When was the last time Kimmie had friends home, Scott?"

The question struck Preston as petty, inane. "When was the last time you had your legs waxed? How the hell should I know?"

"It was months ago, Scott, months and months ago. And do you know why? Because she doesn't dare bring her friends home anymore because she never knows what kind of shape you're going to be in and it's no fun to be humiliated by your own father."

Resentment bred with anger spawned recklessness. "That's nonsense! I never—"

"No, you never vomited on the living-room floor or fell down the stairs. But do you remember the night you were in the kitchen having a little Stoly from the freezer and Kimmie and Wendy Porter came in and you said with a cute little leer on your face that you thought Mary Benson had a really nice pair of hooters?"

"I . . ." He did not remember.

"I didn't think so. How about her birthday last year when she had a slumber party and you decided it would be jolly to put on some 'good' music and dance—just you and your friend Johnnie Walker and SIX FIFTEEN-YEAR-OLD GIRLS!"

Preston saw the veins on Margaret's temples pulsing, and he imagined rivulets of poison dripping from her lips.

Kimberly put her head in her hands and sobbed. Preston said, "Kimmie . . ." He wanted to go to her, to hold her, but he felt dirty, as if his touch would contaminate her. So he lashed out at Margaret. "Why did you bring her here? Why are you so cruel?"

"Because she's part of you, Scott," said Dolores Stark. "Everyone here is part of you. Everyone your life touches becomes a co-alcoholic with you."

"Whoa! Just whoa!" The four syllables of the forbidden word had pushed Preston's reflexive trigger. "Don't you steamroll me, lady. I may be a bad guy now and then, but I am not an alcoholic."

"I see." A nauseatingly beatific smile played on her face.

How serene she was, how imperturbable, how . . . superior. She seemed to anticipate his every response. Was he so boringly predictable?

"No *fucking* way," he said, using the proscribed F-word to demonstrate conviction and determination. And to rattle Dolores Stark.

She smiled again. "So what do you propose to do about being a bad guy, Scott?"

"I'll quit."

Margaret snorted.

"No, I mean it. Seriously. I know I've quit before, but that was just to prove I could. I didn't have any motive to really quit. But now I do." Preston warmed to his own argument. He saw an escape. "This has been really helpful for me. I didn't see that I was affecting other people. But now that I have, now that you've made me see it, I'll quit. Once and for all."

He smiled at them all, imploring them to believe this façade of gratitude, hoping that none of them could see behind it to the scenario rolling before his eyes: a beaker of iced Stolichnaya floating on a bar, reflections of mahogany dancing in the diamond liquid.

"When, Scott?" Dolores Stark asked.

"When what?"

"When are you going to quit?"

The answer was in his mouth. He intended to say, "Right now," or "This minute." There was no percentage in telling them the truth because they wouldn't understand that it takes a couple of days to taper off properly.

But before a word could be shaped by his thick tongue, Dolores Stark said, "Monday, right?"

He stared at her. *The bitch is psychic.*

"You don't want to quit on a weekend. You can't do it. Nobody can. It's unreasonable to try. There are just too many pressures. You're bound to fail. And then you feel even worse." She paused. And then that accursed smile again. "Right, Scott?"

Preston's mouth must have been hanging open, for he felt a breeze on his teeth. He whispered, "Right."

"You're not going to quit, Scott."

He was hypnotized. "I'm not?"

"No, because you can't. We think we can, and we try, we really do try, and we do quit. For a week or ten days or two weeks or, some of us, for a month or two. But we always go back." She wasn't smiling now. "No, Scott, there's only one way, and that's the way you have to take."

"What's that?"

Dolores Stark looked at Margaret and Kimberly and Warren—a final confirmation of unanimity—and then said to Preston, "We want you to go into treatment."

"Huh?" It took a beat for the euphemism to register and then to shed its nicety and reappear as the monster it was. "A loony bin? Me? Forget it." Preston didn't realize he was shouting until he heard Warren's stern voice in soft contrast to his own shrill protests.

"We didn't come here to vote on it, Scott. The only choice you have is: You can go into treatment, or you can get fired."

"And divorced," Margaret added.

Preston swallowed acid. "Nice, Warren, really nice. Judge and jury . . . Look, I can't just hop on a plane and—"

Warren reached inside his jacket and withdrew an airline-ticket folder. "One o'clock, JFK to Santa Fe."

"Santa Fe? What's in Santa Fe?"

"The Banner Clinic."

"Banner! That's a lush bin!"

Dolores Stark leaned forward and smiled. "And . . . ?"

He ignored her. "Who's gonna pay for it? These places have to cost—"

"Insurance," said Warren. "Every dime."

"But . . . but . . ." Doors were slamming in Preston's head, shutting off avenues of escape. "I don't have any clothes. I don't even have a toothbrush!"

Preston saw that, unwittingly, he had given Margaret a cue. Sucking in her cheeks and cocking an eyebrow to show smarmy righteousness (one of her more annoying personal habits), she stood and went behind his desk and returned with a packed suitcase, which she deposited on the floor before him.

Preston sensed that he was falling through a slick dark cylinder with no bottom. He put out a hand to Warren. "What about the Benson book? It needs a lot of work. And the Gregory. The Gregory is in big—"

"I'll take the Benson. And I thought I'd give Debbie a crack at the Gregory . . . show what she can do on her own."

"Debbie?" Preston said, gagging. "Debbie Browning?"

"She's talented, Scott. You've said so yourself."

I'm being gang-banged from every quarter. "Jesus, Warren, it's great to be indispensable."

"It's because we *do* need you that we're doing this, Scott. If we didn't care, I'd give you your walking papers right now."

Dolores Stark nodded to Kimberly.

With quavering voice barely audible, Kimberly said, "We don't want to lose you, Daddy."

Preston slumped in his chair and squeezed his eyes. *These people have no decency. They will stop at nothing.*

Dolores Stark rose and went to Preston and put a hand on his shoulder. He loathed being touched by strangers. He recoiled, but she did not remove her hand. She smiled. Of course. Nothing surprised this woman.

"Bet you wish you had a drink right now."

Impulsively, ludicrously, Preston began to deny it, but then he saw in her eyes a wisdom born of pain and exuding sympathy. He believed for the first time that she truly knew things about him that he didn't. Wordlessly, he nodded.

"I did, too." She grinned. "When they came for *me* five years ago, I raced into the john and drank a quart of Scope."

Preston was appalled at the effect her words had on him. Even as he reacted, he didn't believe it. He felt that she had just kissed him—not sexually but spiritually—and that the kiss had somehow shrunk the tumor of loneliness that had been blooming in his guts. He gaped at her.

Still smiling, she said, "Let's have a shooter, then."

Margaret jerked in her chair. Kimberly bounced as if hers were on fire. Warren frowned and smoothed his hair and said, "Actually, I'm not entirely sure that's . . ." He trailed off. But none of them *did* anything.

Dolores Stark circled the room, gazing at the bookcases, reciting titles to herself. She stopped and stood on tiptoe and pulled a book off a top shelf. She read the title aloud: *"A la Recherche du Temps Perdu."*

If Preston had not already concluded that Dolores Stark was the Uri Geller of the booze business, he would have been surprised. As it was, he was almost amused as he watched her open the hollow book and pull out the half-full pint of 100-proof vodka.

"Proust is a safe stash. Nobody ever *reads* Proust." She uncapped the bottle and started toward Preston, for some reason taking the long route around behind the desk. She stopped six feet from him and held out the bottle.

What was she doing? *Just give me the bottle!* She wanted him to fetch it, to grovel for it. But why? *I thought you were my friend!*

He lunged for the bottle. His hand was six inches from it when she upended it, and eight ounces of salvation drooled into the wastebasket. He stopped, his hand still extended, a clot of bile rising in his throat.

"Whoops!" said the heartless, vindictive harpy. She picked up the wastebasket and sloshed the vodka around the scummy bottom. Then she took a step toward him. "One last social drink before we go?" A nasty grin crinkled her stony face. "Sorry I don't have a twist."

He hesitated for a second, no more, but long enough for Kimberly to see that he was tempted. Her look of ashen horror engraved itself on the tablets of his mind.

He slumped back in his chair, his face contorted by a racking sob.

Dolores Stark set the wastebasket on the floor and said cheerily, "Welcome to the rest of your life."

3

H_{E WOULD HAVE} skipped from Kennedy Airport—would have found a motel with a cool, dark bar and spent a couple of days thinking things over—if Dolores Stark hadn't latched on to him like a Velcro suit and stuck with him from the office to the plane.

He would have dodged into the men's room and knocked back six ounces of Dr. Smirnoff's finest from the pewter flask in his briefcase, if she hadn't searched him like a zealous nanny and confiscated the flask, as well as the foil-wrapped packet of Valium that he always carried in his watch pocket, just in case.

He would have at least managed a few quick seethroughs on the plane if the virago hadn't had the appalling bad taste to summon a supervisor and instruct him to tell the chief stewardess that Preston was not under any circumstances to be permitted to consume anything—including not only beverages but also sauces, condiments, garnishes and flavorings—that contained ethyl alcohol. She even warned him that Preston might feign cardiac arrest in a desperate attempt to con a beaker of brandy from a naïve flight attendant. Preston saw the supervisor sneak glances at him over Dolores Stark's shoulder. He hated being noticed, cherished privacy and anonymity and the freedom they gave him to keep his little secrets. Now he had been publicly branded as a loon.

For two thousand miles he sat in his seat and felt the stewardesses eyeball him as if he were a Palestinian terrorist. When he went to the john, two of them hustled the liquor cart out of his way and guarded it like wrens protecting their eggs.

As the plane touched down in Santa Fe, Preston had to admit that he felt virtuous: This was the first time in his adult life he had flown sober. He had always believed that flying in an airplane was unnatural if not downright impossible, a patent violation of reality. The unanesthetized mind analyzes the experience and must conclude that *it cannot be happening*. The only way a rational man can endure flying, therefore, is to distance himself from the fact that it *is* happening. To Preston, there were but two groups of people who could fly sober: those whose critical faculties had been permanently damaged, and pilots, who had been conditioned to worship machines beyond all reason.

So virtuous did he feel that he decided to reward himself with a drink or two. He deserved them, of course—after a day like this, he deserved a jeroboam—but he also needed them, if he was to suffer through an afternoon and evening of Mickey Mouse bullshit, slogans ("Welcome to the rest of your life," she had said to him. *Jesus!*) and facile and phony protestations of love and hope. He had edited enough self-help books to know that in the universe of therapies, everybody always loves everybody. He did not love everybody. And as for hope, he had found it to be a one-way ticket to disappointment.

He had had four hours to think, and he had decided a few things. His wife, daughter and employer believed that he had a drinking problem. So, *ipso facto*, a problem existed. But to Preston, the problem was largely one of perspective. None of them drank at all—oh, a glass of wine now and then, but that wasn't drinking. If he had married the girl he squired around the watering holes of New Haven back in the sixties, a giddy tippler who could bend an elbow with the best of them, the perceptions of him would have been entirely different. He wondered where she was. She had been brought up, as he had (and as Margaret and Warren definitely had not), to recognize booze as a fine tool to be used judiciously for the relief of anxiety and stress. She would have understood that the only way Preston could shuffle along from day to day was to take periodic chemical holidays from himself. She wouldn't have called that a problem, not when he had never missed a day's work, never had a drunk-driving conviction, never brawled or made a public display of himself. She would have known that the memory lapses Warren trotted out as ammunition were just . . . memory lapses. Everybody has them.

Warren and Margaret didn't understand, because they couldn't.

If in the land of the blind the one-eyed man is king, then in the land of the teetotaler the social drinker is a rummy.

Dolores Stark was convinced he was an alcoholic.

But on what did she base her conviction? On what she had heard from Margaret and Warren (and from Kimberly, though she wasn't a reliable witness, having been primed by Margaret). Dolores Stark didn't know him, couldn't appreciate what it was like to live inside his head.

Exactly what was an alcoholic, anyway? He bet that if you put a hundred people into a room, you couldn't get three of them to agree on a definition. Legend had it that Ulysses Grant was an alcoholic, but then Lincoln was supposed to have said something like: "If liquor fueled the job Grant did for this nation, then I'll have a case of whatever he's drinking." Winston Churchill kick-started every morning with brandy and kept pouring it on all day long. The stereotype was the bum who slept in a doorway and drank Thunderbird from a bag, but maybe he was the same guy who used to sleep on a couch in Pound Ridge and drink Cutty Sark.

It was all a question of perceptions.

He didn't blame Dolores Stark for her perceptions. She was in the salvage business. She *had* to believe he was a wreck wallowing in despair. She had to label him and try to convince him that the label fit. After all, she could hardly coax somebody into treatment—which was, remember, the way she made her living; more than a little element of self-interest there—by hinting that now and then he overserved himself with margaritas. She'd be out of work in a week.

And Preston wasn't knocking treatment. There were people who needed it. No question. Especially for drugs. When drugs got their claws into you, they didn't let go. You had to be cleaned out, then broken down and built up again. And there were probably people for whom booze was like that. They couldn't give it up. They were hooked. Treatment was the only way out.

For him, though, it was overkill, like treating sniffles with penicillin. He could have quit on his own. It would have taken him a few more false starts, but he could have done it. Sure, sure, he knew the old joke: "I have no trouble quitting; I do it all the time." But what had been missing was motivation, and now he had that. What distinguished him from the true alcoholic who could never quit on his own was the fact that (except on certain days like today), Preston didn't *need* alcohol. He *liked* alcohol. There was a difference.

But he would humor them, at least for a while. He'd join the roster of movie stars and country singers, rock drummers and middle linebackers, who had put The Banner Clinic on the map. A stint at Banner was almost a required credential for the Beautiful People these days.

Mostly, he was going in because no matter what he thought, Margaret's threats and Warren's were real. Maybe they were overreacting, maybe they were misguided, but they had the power to cause him a lot of pain, and he had quite enough pain these days, thank you very much. How long he would stay was another matter.

Besides, who could say that he wouldn't get anything out of it? He might learn something. The worst that could happen was that he'd dry out for a while. On full salary. That couldn't hurt. Everybody could use a good flushing. He might even meet some celebrity lush who would write about his or her experience.

Sign 'em up. Celebrity confessions were selling like Big Macs.

Everybody benefits. Virtue plus twenty percent.

Meanwhile, he had to concentrate on how to wrap his fingers around a couple of quick pops before he met the driver from Banner. He had been told that the driver would meet the plane, which he assumed meant—what with airport security precautions—that he'd be waiting at the baggage carousel.

He stood up before the plane stopped—incurring from a stewardess a baleful glare but no reprimand because, he figured, she was still afraid that if she said anything aggressive he might go into apeshit DTs—and worked his way to the front. It had to take fifteen or twenty minutes to unload everyone from an L-1011, so if he was first off, he'd have plenty of time to down a brace of white ones. Hell, four or five. Skate into the clinic on a nice comfortable cloud.

The plane stopped, the door hissed open, he stepped out onto the ramp—and immediately a hand the size of a spare tire grabbed him by the arm.

"Scott Preston?" said a voice as resonant as the voice of James Earl Jones.

He looked up into the face of Lawrence Taylor—or his big brother—the most gargantuan man he had ever stood face-to-face with. At least six feet six, an easy three hundred pounds. He was wearing white trousers, white running shoes, a starched white short-sleeved shirt and a black necktie.

He lowered his nose to Preston's mouth, sniffed and said, "You clean?"

Preston gasped. "I beg your—"

"You sober?"

Preston tried to summon outrage, but his "Of course!" came out as a squeak.

"Good. Makes life easier for both of us." He steered

Preston down the ramp. As they stepped into the terminal, he said to an airline agent, "Thanks, Harold."

"Anytime, Chuck. Pilot said this one was a pussy-cat."

This one? What was he, a chimpanzee? The pilot had been talking about him? Over the radio? Screw this, he'd had enough. He tried to pull away. Not a chance. His arm would separate from his body before it would escape from the vise at the end of Chuck's arm.

With gentle upward pressure, Chuck had him scuttling along on tiptoe.

"Okay, I give," Preston said. "Time out."

Chuck set him down and looked at him and seemed to decide that Preston would not flee the jurisdiction. He nudged Preston forward and shortened his step to synchronize their paces.

They passed a bar. The bottles standing against the mirrored wall were illuminated from above, and they glowed with a magical light. Half a dozen men were crouched on stools, their hands cuddling cold glasses filled with warmth. Preston felt an ache, of envy, of nostalgia. He imagined that he was a sailor setting off on a voyage of unknown duration into unknown seas, looking back at his loved ones waving from the shore.

His pace slowed. Chuck looked at him, saw what he was looking at, and said, "Don't even think about it. You show up at Banner blasted, they'll lock you up and put you through the whole de-tox number."

They stepped onto an escalator leading down to the baggage area. "So," Chuck said pleasantly. "You're a juicer."

"A what?"

"Makes sense. Fella dressed like you, it's either juice or blow, and you don't have blow in your eyes."

Preston stared at him.

"Me, I was into blow. Forty grand a year." He shook his head. "Can't believe it, looking back."

They collected Preston's suitcase. Chuck's hand wouldn't fit inside the handle, so he hung it from one finger. On him the suitcase looked like a purse.

"Where did you play football?" Preston asked as he followed Chuck out of the terminal and into the parking lot. The question was not a guess: A man Chuck's size had been either a football player or a backhoe.

"TCU, then the Steelers for three seasons. I was just getting good when some dude showed me how much fun it was to shove shit up my nose."

"Oh. I'm . . . sorry."

"Yeah. Like they say, life's a bitch, then you die."

The car was a black Cadillac limousine with the letters *B. C.* stenciled in gold italics on the driver's door. Chuck dropped the suitcase in the trunk and opened one of the back doors. "There's fruit juice and sodas and stuff," he said. "And a TV if you want to watch fuzz and squiggly lines."

"You mind if I sit up front? I don't feel like riding in a hearse."

"Suit yourself." Chuck reached to open the front door. "I'm supposed to tell you: If you feel the need to regurgitate or defecate, please give me enough notice so I can pull over to the side of the road."

"What?"

"Don't blame me. They make me use those words."

Preston got in. Chuck shut the door and went around to the driver's side and squeezed behind the wheel.

"Do people *do* that?" Preston asked.

"Oh yeah. I had a guy—a priest, for crissakes—take a dump on the floor. Another time, I had this poet who said I was like that guy Charon, you know, the one who guards the River Styx? 'Chuck,' he says, 'they all pass your way.' Then he puked."

"Well, you don't have to worry about me. I'm fine."

"Right." Chuck's lip curled in what may have been a smile. "*Now* you're fine. Tell me how you feel when we get closer." He pulled out of the parking lot and headed north.

For a while, the landscape was all taco stands and gas stations and curio shops and by-the-hour motels. Then the sleaze thinned out, and Chuck turned off the highway and aimed the bow of the ebony ship into what struck Preston as perfect Hunter Thompson country—a ribbon of shimmering pavement that led directly to hell. On all sides, nothing but sand and cactus; ahead, nothing at all.

Preston's stomach growled as a bubble of gas caromed around a cavity. He swallowed bile and said, just to hear the sound of a human voice, "Everybody spends a month here?"

"If you shape up. Stormy Weathers was here six months. They decide for you. If you got any brains, you do what they say."

"They're that good?" He craved comfort.

"The best. The story is, when Stone Banner dried himself out and decided to start his own joint, he stole the best people and the best gimmicks from all over the country. Smart. Specially for some dude who made his name sitting on a horse, hollering 'Let's get 'em, boys!'"

"What's he like? Banner."

Chuck reached into his shirt pocket for a pack of cigarettes. He said only, "He's helped a pile of people." He offered Preston a cigarette.

Preston shook his head. "I don't."

"You will." Chuck lit up.

"I haven't smoked in fifteen years."

"Uh-huh." His face was expressionless.

Smug, Preston decided. That was the word for these people, for Chuck and Dolores Stark. They thought they knew everything. Everyone was predictable, followed a pattern. Surprises were against the law.

Preston said, "Are you a Calvinist?"

"You mean like a Moonie? No way."

A tiny town rose in the heat haze and hung like a mirage over the desert and then soundlessly flashed by and vanished behind them.

Hills began to emerge on the eastern horizon. At first they were black lumps, then gray, then—as the Cadillac closed on them at one hundred miles an hour—purple, their contours sharpening against the sapphire sky.

Chuck pointed at what now loomed as mountains, and he said simply, "In there."

"Where? What?" There was no "there" there. The road seemed to plunge straight into the mountains. The Banner Clinic was underground? Preston was damned if he'd spend a month in a cave.

But at the base of the nearest mountain the road swooped to the right and snaked through a narrow pass between shoulders of rust-red dirt.

Chuck flicked a finger toward a plateau atop one of the hills. "See up there?"

Preston saw a sprawling white edifice of stone and

glass, on which rays of the afternoon sun played like a thousand restless fingers.

"That's Stone Banner's very own place. Got a swimming pool, tennis court, three-hole golf course, the works. He calls it Xanadu, like in *Citizen Kane*."

The road spilled them into an oasis of green surrounded by the pastel hills. An automatic sprinkler system bathed sections of Bermuda rye grass at programmed intervals. Stands of palm trees offered shade to ducks floating on man-made ponds. A complex of adobe buildings—beige with red tile roofs—hunkered in the middle of the oasis. The road looped in toward the buildings, then out again, then made another loop by an airstrip and continued on, to nowhere.

There were four adobe buildings, arranged in a square. The largest fronted on the paved roundabout. Chuck stopped the limo at the curb before a huge black-glass door, beside which, embedded in the adobe, was a discreet brass plaque that said THE BANNER CLINIC. He did not turn off the motor but popped the trunk and got out.

Preston followed. It was like stepping from a refrigerator into a sauna. The first breath of hot air hurt his chilled lungs.

Chuck handed him his suitcase and said, "I'd take you in, but I gotta hump back and collect a lady lawyer coming in from Pasadena. 'Sides, you look like you can make it on your own."

Preston managed a smile. "I hope you make it back to the NFL."

"Not this pickaninny. I stray too far from here, for sure I'll find me a snowdrift and stick my nose in it."

"For*ever*?"

"There's no such thing as forever, friend. All I know for now is, I got to serve a life sentence saving my life."

Preston suddenly felt ill. He let Chuck take his hand and shake it.

"Kick back and let it happen," Chuck said as he ducked into the car. "You feel like a sack of wet turtle turds now, but believe me, when you get out of here, you'll feel like the prince of fuckin' peace."

Don't leave! Preston wanted to shout. *Take me with you!* But all he did was wave feebly as, at the helm of his great black clipper, Chuck receded toward the distant pass.

He stood, suitcase in hand, as frightened and forlorn as a thirteen-year-old on the threshold of boarding school—alone, lonely, abandoned. His head ached. His stomach ached. And as he raised a hand to wipe sweat from his brow, his fingers trembled before his eyes.

He turned and looked at the building. There was nothing overtly menacing about it, no bars on the windows, no guards at the door. But, he supposed, there had been nothing overtly menacing about Treblinka, either.

He took a deep breath and a step toward the door, then stopped at the sound of an engine approaching fast. Maybe it was bringing another victim. Maybe they could pass together into the nether world. He squinted into the lowering sun and saw a light-colored sedan roaring by the airstrip. The heat rising off the macadam made the car appear to be a hovercraft.

An emergency admission, he decided: a child with a drug overdose, or a husband in critical withdrawal, or a wife with a hemorrhaging ulcer.

The car was a big BMW, probably going 120, and at the last moment before it would shoot by the entrance to the roundabout, its brakes squealed, it careened to the left and almost lifted up onto two wheels and shrieked to a jolting stop a few feet from Preston.

Preston wished he wanted to help the panicked parents carry the stricken child into the clinic, to offer a supporting shoulder and soothing words to the disoriented husband or the exsanguinating wife. But he didn't. All he wanted to do was dematerialize into the ether. So he stood aside.

Through the tinted glass of the BMW's windshield, he saw what looked to be a woman beating a giant animal.

The passenger's-side door opened, and out tumbled a flurry of gray fur with a fluffy white tail—and a human head.

Preston's mind tried to deny the reality, strove to discern it as a hallucination. Delirium tremens.

But reality would not be denied. It was a man dressed up to resemble a rabbit.

The man rolled on the ground and struggled to his knees. Immediately the driver's-side door opened and disgorged a frenzied woman—a little sprig of a thing but mad as a hornet and with fists flying like a cyclone.

"Son of a *bitch*!" she shouted. "Worthless bastard . . . stupid shit!"

"But baby . . ." the man moaned.

"Don't 'baby' me, scuzzball!" She kicked the man in the stomach. He rolled into a ball, furry fingerless mittens covering his head. She was wearing low, pointed-toe boots, like jodhpurs, and now she stepped back and aimed for an opening through which she could kick him in the head.

From the moment Preston had been old enough to accept the existence of hostility (somewhere around three or four years old), he had made it a rule never to get involved in other people's unpleasantness. He wished he didn't have to be involved in the unpleasantnesses of his own life. Scenes were tacky, confrontations to be avoided. If you had something nasty to say, put it in a letter.

But here he saw the very real prospect of a man being murdered by a lunatic. He declined to be responsible for another Kitty Genovese. He had no choice.

He stepped forward and grabbed the little woman by the arm, unbalancing her, and he said, "Let's take it easy."

He was almost a foot taller than she, so she had to look up at him, and yet when she spoke, he had the sense that she was speaking down to him.

"Who're you?" she snarled.

He smiled, to show her that he meant no harm, and said, "You don't want to cripple him."

"I don't?" She looked at Preston as if he were a gravy stain on her blouse. Then, without another word, she spun away and—fast as a mongoose—turned back and kicked him in the balls.

He made a noise like a punctured tire and sat down, hard, beside the rabbit man. Nausea welled up into his throat, his eyes lost their focus, and waves of agony pulsed through his groin. Shamelessly, he covered and comforted his aggrieved balls.

The woman strode back to the BMW and climbed aboard.

"Hey, Bugs!" she called through the open window.

The rabbit man looked up warily as the head to his costume—erectile ears, plastic nose, mischievous eyes with viewing slits cut through the pupils—flew out the window and landed in his lap.

"Count on it," the woman shouted over the sound of her revving engine, "that's the last head you'll ever get from me." She snapped the car into gear and peeled away.

I am marooned with a man who thinks he is a rabbit. Preston looked at the man and then at the sky and the mountains and the pristine adobe buildings and the curb on which they squatted like aimless derelicts. *I would kill for a drink.*

The rabbit man raised one of his paws and, in poor imitation of Mel Blanc, chattered, "Aaaaah . . . what's up, Doc?"

"Sweet Jesus," Preston murmured, holding his head.

"She's a pisser, isn't she?"

"That midget?"

"Good thing you didn't call her a midget. She'd've *really* kicked ass. She can't stand size-ists."

"You're *married* to that?"

The rabbit man nodded and grinned and leaned back on his fuzzy elbows. He was taller than Preston, skinny as a pickerel, with the sharp beak of an osprey. His eyes were deep-set and shadowed by a shelf of bone and bushy brows. Wherever he lived, whatever he did for a living, he seldom saw the sun, for his skin was pasty white, splotched here and there with islands of gray.

"Look at it from her point of view. I'm at this office party, celebrating our best year ever, sales up like four hundred percent over last year thanks to AIDS and whatnot—I make condoms, the whole line, ribbed, pimpled, speckled, French ticklers, reservoir tips, you name it—and we're all s'posed to dress on a business theme. So I get up like a rabbit—you know, people are doing it like rabbits, which is why we're doing so well, like that. Well, she won't go to the party 'cause she says, and who can blame her, 'What the hell am I s'posed to dress up like, a blow job?' So I'm driving home and I'm having a little trouble with the old yellow line—I guess I probably had about a hundred tequila sunrises—so I do the old, you know, one-eye gambit''— he covered one eye with one hand and mimicked driving with the other hand—''and it helps, but I guess not enough, 'cause this smokey pulls me over, and he does a double take when he sees this rabbit driving a BMW. Well, I tell you, these things''—he raised one of his rabbit feet—''they sure suck when it comes to walking a straight line, so we go downtown and I fail the breath test—*fail* it! I think I *killed* it!—and they see on the computer that I've got a couple of other DWIs pending, so they haul me right up there before the night-court judge, and he asks me why am I dressed like a rabbit. So I tell him the whole story—I mean, why not? The tequila's got me nice and mellow—only he's not so amused, and he pitches me in the drunk tank along with all these other dingbats and fags and weirdos, when all I am is dressed like Bugs Bunny, not exactly a felony. Like they say, it was a night to remember. Come the dawn, they give me two choices: ninety to one-twenty in the slam or a rehab center—which is like *no* choices, right?—and then they call Clarisse. She has to take time off from her job to come fetch me—she does Swedish

massage over to the Emerald City spa for the rich and
lamebrained, the woman's got hands like bear traps—
which already sets her teeth on edge, but when she ar-
rives I'm gone because they gave me my wallet back,
so she has to search the whole strip till she finds me in
a gin mill where I'm downing a few eye-openers.''

He shrugged and smiled. "See? She's got a right to
be a little . . . miffed.''

Preston was enraptured by the tale, awed by the man's
insouciance. How could he be so cavalier? If Preston
had ever done anything remotely comparable to what
this rabbit had just recounted, he would have . . . would
have what? Seen a shrink? Joined a monastery? He
didn't know, but he certainly would have known that he
couldn't handle alcohol. He would have quit drinking.
For sure.

*I am on an alien planet. I do not belong here. Where
is Chuck? If I wait long enough, he will return and take
me . . . where? Anywhere.*

"Ever been in a joint before?'' asked the rabbit.

"Me?"

"Me neither.'' He studied the adobe building. "Gotta
beat jail, though. Gotta be a cruise. Do what they tell
you, say what they tell you. And when you get out, just
be careful where you go boozing.''

"You mean you don't want to stop?''

"Drinking? What for? Drinking's not a problem for
me. I'm just unlucky. I get caught a lot.'' He cocked
an eyebrow at Preston. "You *do* have a problem?''

"People seem to think so.''

"Fuck 'em if they can't take a joke. What do they
know?'' He rolled up onto his paws, stood and re-

garded himself critically. "She could've left me a pair of pants."

Preston rose and grabbed his suitcase and straightened his tie. He joined the rabbit before the big black-glass door.

"By the way, I'm Scott Preston."

"Duke. Duke Bailey."

Preston shook his paw.

"What was it Hamlet said?" Duke asked. " 'Once more onto the beach, we happy few, we band of brothers.' "

"Something like that."

"You scared?"

Preston swallowed and nodded. "Shitless."

"No sweat. They don't torture you. They can't find out anything you don't want 'em to."

"I guess."

It's what I'll *find out that worries me.*

4

H̶E SAT ON a couch in the main lobby of the clinic, feeling ill. He had been violated.

First, they had taken him into a gray room furnished with nothing but a gray metal table, and there the executive director of the clinic—a cheesy polyester gladhander who wore a button that said, "Hi! My name is GUY! Have a GREAT day!"—tore up Preston's suitcase. Literally. He prized up the lining and removed mouthwash, after-shave lotion, two rolls of mints ("Sorry, Scott, but some people press cocaine into mint molds") and, worst of all, the collected stories of John Cheever, the collected stories of Irwin Shaw and Boswell's *Life of Johnson*. For consolation Preston was given—given? They were bestowed upon him as if they were the Dead Sea Scrolls—the only two books he would be permitted to read in the next four weeks: a dippy little prayer book called *Twentyfour Hours a Day* and the A.A. bible, which, Hi!-My-name-is-GUY! told him, "everybody calls The Big Book." ("The Big Book!" What was this,

Dick and Jane go to A.A.? "Look, Dick, look at Spot! Spot is falling on his ass! I bet Spot has a *problem*!")

"Focus, Scott," Guy explained when Preston protested the confiscation of his books. "Books are an escape. They take you away, let you forget. We don't want you to forget, Scott. We want you to focus, focus, focus . . . on your disease."

And at the word "disease"—like some Pavlovian cue—Guy (whose last name, according to the plaque on his desk, was Larkin, though evidently nobody ever used last names around here) embarked on the whole alcoholism litany again. When Preston declined to fall to his knees and kiss Guy's hem and confess to being a hopeless lush, Guy said, "Oh no, I wasn't an alcoholic either, Scott," and proceeded to recite his whole tale of woe, some blather about nobody knowing he had a problem because the only drinking he ever did was at night in his garage, where he'd filled the windshield-washer container in his car with vodka. One night he didn't show up for bed, and his wife found him passed out on the air filter.

Why was it that all these people felt they had to spill their guts to you right away? Preston didn't feel like spilling his guts to anybody, ever.

When Guy didn't find any contraband in Preston's suitcase or in his clothes, he said, "I'm real proud of you, Scott. That's a very positive sign," and he directed Preston to the infirmary. The fun had just begun.

The infirmary was another office off the lobby, run by a manatee of a woman named Nurse Bridget, who took Preston's height and weight and blood pressure and samples of his several fluids and (of course) had to tell him about her husband, who was a fireman until the time he climbed a ladder and rescued a woman from the fourth floor of a burning building but then, because he was smashed out of his mind, dropped her off the ladder from three and a half stories up, and about how she and Sean spent his enforced retirement watching game shows and drinking Reunite until he died of cirrhosis and she was committed to an institution by her daughter, Bridey.

All the while Nurse Bridget was inflicting her life story and her sphygmomanometer on Preston, he heard grunts and protests through a closed door behind her, and at about the time she was launching into the details of her progress through the twelve steps of Alcoholics Anonymous, the door sprang open and out staggered Duke, looking like a man who had just been a plaything for the KGB.

He saw Preston and said curtly, "You gay?"

"Me? Hardly."

"Too bad. This place is paradise for fruits." He looked back into the room from which he had emerged, and he shouted furiously, "Have a nice day!" and then, clutching a terry-cloth robe around his middle, he lurched out of the infirmary.

A second later, a short, porcine male nurse appeared in the doorway of the back room. He was forcing his chubby fingers into a pair of rubber gloves. He reached to the side, then brought his hand back into view and beckoned to Preston—with a rubber-covered index finger slathered with a clot of Vaseline.

Nurse Bridget was fiddling with the blood-pressure bulb, and the needle must have jumped off the dial because she took a step back and exclaimed, "My stars!"

As Nature is kind to human beings and erases all specific memory of pain, so Preston was spared any physical recollection of the discomfort of having his fundament probed, not for malignant polyps but for suppositories filled with controlled substances. He could not, however, expunge the memory of the indignity of lying face-down on a steel table while the creature took a leisurely journey up what he called Chocolate Avenue and regaled Preston the while with the saga of his descent into the black hole of Valium addiction.

Now he sat in the lobby, beside Duke in a robe and slippers. They did not speak, did not look at each other. It was as if they were both ashamed.

There was nothing medical about the atmosphere in the clinic, no signs pointing to EMERGENCY or admonishing SILENCE, no crepe-soled attendants rushing about on missions of mercy, no uniforms of any kind. The passersby, and there were many, could have been secretaries or bureaucrats or doctors or patients, for they all wore casual street clothes.

The decor was simple and understated. A visitor might have discerned only two hints about the purpose of the place. There were ashtrays everywhere—on stands, screwed into walls and on practically every flat surface. Smoking was not merely tolerated, it was encouraged as an acceptable replacement crutch while the afflicted learned to maneuver without the braces of booze. And there were two semiabstract posters, which, after long study, appeared to contain the messages "One Day at a Time" and "Easy Does It."

Duke crossed his legs, uncrossed them, crossed them the other way, uncrossed them. Preston couldn't tell whether he sought comfort or modesty, and he didn't much care, for he had locked his mind on to a vision of a hand opening a freezer door and withdrawing a bottle of Stolichnaya and pouring the gelid syrup into a tulip wineglass and swirling it around and raising it to his lips and—

A commotion approached across the lobby. There was no reason for Preston to assume that it would home in on him and Duke, but he did. And it did.

It was a Hispanic behemoth, wearing sandals hewn from truck tires, jeans so often washed in such virulent detergents that they were flayed and gray, a black T-shirt whose mesh fabric strained against a cylinder of suet and each of whose sleeves was rolled up around a package of cigarettes, and enough tattoos to recount the entire history of the discovery of the New World. All Preston could see of its head was a drooping Zapata mustache, for the rest was enveloped in a haze of cigarette smoke.

It greeted everyone it passed: "Hey, man!" "What's goin' down?" "How they hangin'?"

It stopped before the couch and proffered its hand to Duke. On the extended arm Preston made out the legends "Born To Hang," "Fuck Death—I'll Take Dishonor" and "The Only Living Abortion."

"Hey, man," it said, a cigarette crushed between its front teeth. "Hector . . . junkie . . . lulu."

To Preston's amazement, Duke brightened. He held

out his hand and allowed himself to be yanked to his feet. "Duke," he said. "DWI . . . lulu."

Hector pumped Duke's hand, discarded it and took Preston's. His teak-colored eyes waited for Preston to speak, but Preston didn't know what to say. It was a foreign language.

Duke rescued him. "His name's Hector. He's a junkie. And he's like me, a lulu: He's here in lieu of going to jail."

"I see."

"You?" Hector said to Preston.

"Scott," Preston began. Then he stopped. He refused to say the word "alcoholic." Or "rummy." Or "lush." He was not these things. But what could he say? Social drinker? Hardly. Then a word occurred to him, a word from his last connection to the real world.

"Juicer," he said.

Hector nodded. "Kinda name's Scott? First or last?"

"First. Scott Preston."

"Poor WASP bastard. Parents who give their kids two last names oughta have their balls cut off." Hector squashed his cigarette in an ashtray, unrolled a sleeve and let a pack drop into his hand.

He offered a cigarette to Duke, who snatched it and said, "I'm s'posed to quit."

Hector lit it for him with a denim-burnished Zippo. "We're all s'posed to quit everything alla time. Piss on 'em. *Some*thing's gonna kill us. Might's well be something fun."

He offered one to Preston, who declined, then lit one for himself, sucking so hard on the weed as the flame touched it that by the time he closed the lighter, a third of the cigarette was ash.

Duke was smiling at the cigarette in his hand. Color suffused his face, wiping away the wan and pasty look. "All *right*," he said.

"Okay, man," said Hector. "Let's boogie."

Hector led the way down the corridor. Duke shuffled behind in his paper slippers. Preston brought up the rear, carrying his suitcase. The procession looked like a cartoon: the Pillsbury Doughboy leading a demented invalid who was followed by a worried porter.

"Happened to your clothes?" Hector asked Duke. "Lice?"

Lice! What kind of world do these people live in?

"Long story. The old lady'll send me some." Duke paused. "Maybe."

"I'll lend you some," Preston said.

Duke shook his head. "They won't let me. They say I gotta wear this thing, and everybody I meet I gotta explain why I don't have any clothes."

"They won't let you *wear pants*?"

Duke smiled weakly. "Therapy."

"Keeps the memory green," Hector said with a glance back over his shoulder. "Never let you forget what kinda asshole you been. They made me wear a bag over my head for two days. . . . Said I was too worried about my image. No big thing."

Preston felt his pulse thundering in his temples. *I will not let them make a public display of me.* His fingertips tingled. He recognized the onset of hyperventilation. He stopped and breathed deeply. A fuzziness was creeping up his neck.

Hector arrived at a glass door. As he held it open for them, he noticed Preston's complexion, which had turned the color of goat cheese. "Samatter with you?"

Preston pointed to the tube of ash dangling from Hector's lips. "Can I change my mind?"

Hector grinned and flipped a pack of cigarettes from his T-shirt sleeve and shook one loose for Preston. A Camel regular. The nitroglycerine of smokes. "Survival," he said as he gave Preston a light. "What it's all about."

Preston inhaled deeply, and his outraged alveoli immediately rebelled. He coughed and sputtered.

"First one's always a bear," Hector said. "Give it two or three, then it'll grip you good."

The taste was foul, dirty. Preston took another drag. This time he coughed but once, sharply, and he could feel a soft warmth spreading across his chest. A third drag. There. Not so bad. "Fifteen years," he said.

"In ten minutes it'll be your buddy again. You'll need it. Muthafuckas done stole your *best* friend."

That tone of voice. Dolores Stark, then Chuck, now Hector. Certitude. No doubts, no questions. In less than three minutes, Hector had learned all there was to know about him. Or thought he had. And Hector was just an inmate.

No! We are not all alike. If Faulkner declined to accept the end of man, I decline to accept the sameness of all men. We are each blessed with our uniqueness.

Aren't we?

Hector slipped two more Camels into Preston's pocket and ushered him and Duke through the door,

out into a quadrangle enclosed by the four adobe buildings. It was large, probably a square acre, and contained a swimming pool; an exercise area featuring a
jungle gym, a set of parallel bars and some free weights;
and three small copses of palm trees that gave shade to
painted wooden benches.

As they walked toward one of the other buildings,
Preston asked Hector, "How long've you been here?"

"Here? Forty-one days."

"But I thought—"

"Yeah, but I always fuck up so they have to keep me
longer."

"Always? You've been in other . . . places?"

"A couple. Hazelden, St. Mary's, Smithers, Betty
Ford . . . lessee . . . oh yeah, and Fair Oaks. I've seen
the U.S. of A."

"Why?" The word had barely slipped from Preston's
lips when he realized that it sounded nosy, critical. *Do
not piss this man off!* "I'm sorry. I—"

"What's to be sorry?" Hector shrugged. "They say
I can't function without structure. I get out, I take
dope. I don't hurt nobody. I just take dope."

"These places . . . they don't help you?"

"Sure they help me. I don't take dope in here, do
I?" Hector pointed to a wooden sign over the door of
the building they were approaching. "Here we are."

"Chaparral," Preston read. "Quaint."

"Yeah. They's all named after Stone's flicks. That
there's Bandito. Over there's Geronimo. Twenty freaks
in each, boys and girls together. Main building's Peacemaker."

They entered Chaparral, passed in the entryway a pay

phone and the door to a lavatory, and came to the common room. It was an unadorned rectangle, half of which was taken up by what an interior designer would call a conversation pit—a sunken floor filled with low squooshy couches and chairs. The other half contained four round tables (each with six chairs), a refrigerator, a sink (piled high with ashtrays) and a coffee machine.

"Not bad," Duke said. "Where is everybody?"

"Lecture. Today's Dr. Lapidus on"—Hector recited from memory—"'chemical triggers and the alcoholic reflex.'"

"You don't go to lectures?"

"Oh yeah, but I heard that sucker 'bout a thousand times and I never did drink anyway, so when there's people to pick up they send me." Hector started down a hallway.

Duke said to Preston, "You want to room together?"

Before Preston could reply, Hector burst into raucous laughter and said, "You slay me, man."

In the hallway, Hector passed two or three doors, then stopped at one. He pointed at Duke, rapped once on the door and pushed it open. "Lewis!" he called.

"I thought everybody was—" Duke began.

"He had a tummyache." Hector smiled, the way a child does as he waits for you to discover the spider in your stew.

From inside the room came the sound of a hair dryer whirring to a stop. Duke hovered at the door, Preston behind him. Just inside the room was the open door to a bathroom, and from this angle they could see in the bathroom mirror.

They saw the reflection of a man of indeterminate age—possibly mid-forties, possibly mid-fifties. The skin of his face was shiny, as if it had been mechanically tightened. His hair was lush and full and champagne blond. It was styled into a pompadour into which he had wrapped three plastic curlers.

The man saw them in the mirror too, and he beamed and said, "Well, hel*lo*!"

Duke took a step backward, and for a moment Preston thought he would either faint or flee. But then Duke gathered strength from some inner well. He cleared his throat and said to Hector, "You are not a nice person."

Hector touched Preston's shoulder and guided him farther down the hall.

I am a character in an Edgar Allan Poe story. What will be behind my door? A minotaur? A satyr?

His room was empty. Not just empty but vacant, containing no sign of another occupant—no clothing, no mess, no spoor. Never had Preston been so grateful for nothingness. He would have solitude, precious solitude, from which he could suck the sustenance necessary for survival on this hostile planet.

Marcia Breck stood in the hallway and reviewed the patient-admission sheet on her clipboard.

A Yalie, with a master's from Berkeley. Big hitter with a New York publisher. Kid in private school. Wife who can probably trace her family back to William the Conqueror. Country club. Volvo station wagon. Plays squash and tennis.

A programmed life. Success foreordained. Acceptance inevitable and assumed from birth. A sense of entitlement. Polite, considerate, amiable. Illness an inconvenience. Alcoholism inconceivable, simply not done.

Tight as a sphincter.

She detested the type. They made her life miserable. They were smart, slick, superior, good with words and facile at parrying direct assaults and making them ricochet off into a mist of maybes. How do you cure someone you can't reach? How do you get him to deal with a problem he's convinced doesn't exist?

Give her a street junkie any day, or a homeless wino or a brawling drunk or a truck driver who had jumped the median divider and wiped out a whole family. They had reached bottom; they knew they didn't just have a problem, their lives were on the line. She could talk to them in simple English, and they'd listen. They could identify with her story, could appreciate her as a Lazarus that they too might become. They recognized authority.

Not like Yalies with Volvos, who regarded treatment as a reunion where we all get together and iron out a few petty differences. Man to man. Good show.

Okay, Mr. Scott Adams Preston, take your best shot. Make me earn my money.

She rapped once on the door and pushed it open.

He was hanging clothes in the closet. He was tall and slim, his hair close-cut and combed. His complexion looked good. He wore a tailored narrow-lapel suit, a button-down shirt and a rep tie. The polish on his shoes glowed in the sunlight that streamed in the western window.

A living relic of the sixties.

"Scott? I'm Marcia."

Preston smiled and held out his hand. "How do you—"

"I'll be your counselor."

"Oh?" The smile stuck. "Oh."

"You were expecting Spencer Tracy."

"I wasn't expecting a—"

"A woman."

"No."

"A black woman."

"That hardly has anything to do with it."

"No. Hardly." *Stop it! Don't pick at him till you have to. You'll have plenty of chances.* She let herself smile. "How do you feel?"

"Nervous."

"That's all?"

"What am I supposed to feel?"

"There's no 'supposed to.' " She paused. "Are you an alcoholic, Scott?"

"No. At least I don't . . . well, people say I have a problem."

"But you're not an alcoholic."

"Define an alcoholic. I've stopped for weeks at a time, months even."

"Let's not worry about definitions, not yet. What I see so far is a lot of denial."

"So far? Fifteen seconds?" *Jesus! Everybody knows everything around here!*

"Let me warn you about one thing you're going to feel, because you won't recognize it at first: loneliness."

"I'll be all right. I'm pretty self-reliant."

"Sure you are. You don't need people. Family,

friends. You've got it together, right? Who's your best friend?"

Preston looked away, as if searching for a name. What was this woman driving at? Was she going to call all his friends, involve them in this charade? Not bloody likely. "I don't see what this is . . . Forget it. You wouldn't know him."

"Oh, I'd know him, all right. He's so close to you that you've turned to him every day. He's been with you in all the good times and all the bad. He's so close he's gotten inside you and consumed you. And now he's gone, Scott, and you're going to miss him. Your old buddy Jim Beam or Jack Daniel's, or maybe you've hung out with the exotics, like Comrade Stolichnaya."

Preston's head jerked. He felt himself blushing.

Marcia laughed. "It's that Russian, right? I knew it. Can't trust a Commie, Scott. Just when you're getting to be buddies, he up and deserts you." She reached out in a friendly gesture and touched his arm. He flinched. She left her hand there, forcing him to accept her touch. "You'll make new friends in here, friends who want to help you. 'Cause Jim and Jack and the Commie, they were going to do only one thing for you, Scott, and that's kill you." She removed her hand. "You've already made one friend. Duke asked if he could bunk with you. But he's already been assigned with Lewis."

"Frankly, I think this is best for me." Preston gestured at the empty room. "I'm comfortable by myself. I don't mind solitude."

"Uh-huh. If we do have to give you a roommate, do you have any preferences?"

"Not really. Someone who reads, I suppose. Maybe

likes the Mets, listens to . . . I don't know . . . James Taylor . . . Beethoven."

"What you'd call a peer."

"I guess." Preston saw her nod and make a note on her clipboard. Perhaps she did understand him, did realize that he, his type of person, responded better to civility than brutality. They'd get along. "What about you? Did you have a . . . problem?"

"Sure. We all did here."

"And who . . . what . . . was your best friend?"

"I loved 'em all . . . separately, together, one after the other, on top of each other. If it could be drunk, swallowed, smoked or poked, it was my friend. What finally got me, though, was elephant tranquilizers. We called them Dumbos."

Preston felt his mouth tangle around a mess of "What?," "How?" and "Why?"

"Because somebody had some. It was a new sensation. I was on the Jersey Turnpike between Camden and New Brunswick. I guess I was going a hundred and twenty, a hundred and thirty. Everything was a blur—lights, other cars, the road. This trooper stops me, and I say, 'I know I'm speeding, officer, but my mother's had a stroke and I got to get to Helene Fuld Hospital before she . . . blah, blah, blah . . .' He says, 'Speeding, huh? Whyn't you get out of the car, lady?' So I say, 'Sure thing,' only I can't. I try, but nothing works: arms, legs, nothing. He looks at me and this big grin cuts his face and he says, 'Lady, I don't know what you're on, but it's got some kick to it. You've been parked in the center lane of this road for the last twenty minutes.' "

Marcia laughed and touched his arm again. This time

he forced himself not to flinch. "That's when they convinced me I could use some help."

"What did you do for a living?"

"Back then? I was a hooker." She saw his eyes bug. The Mets, huh? Beethoven? *How do you like them apples, Mr. Boola Boola?* "How else could I support all my little habits?" She looked at her watch. "Group's in ten minutes. Don't be late."

5

THEY HAD FORMED a circle in the middle of Marcia's office, the five of them sitting in steel-framed folding chairs, heads down, gazing at the floor, forearms on their knees, hands clasped loosely.

Marcia spoke first.

"I'm Marcia. I'm an alcoholic and an addict. I feel pretty good today, because I think Lewis had a real breakthrough yesterday telling us about his feelings for Kevin. I think Hector learned something from that, too, but it may be up to us to help him see what it was. And I feel good about Cheryl. She's been letting that bastard guilt ride her pretty hard, but maybe now she's ready to throw him in the dirt. I feel good that Scott's with us. . . ."

Gimme a break! Preston grimaced and clenched his fists. *Don't talk about me. Make believe I don't exist.* He let his eyes wander around the circle, expecting to see someone nudge someone else, expecting to hear a derisive snigger. But all heads were bowed.

"These twenty-eight days will be just the beginning

for Scott. He's got a long, long road ahead, and it's up to us to be his guides.''

Marcia stopped and nodded to Hector, who sat to her right.

Smoking wasn't permitted in therapy, but Hector, in whom nicotine withdrawal provoked panic that had once led to threats of violence against the clinic's Methodist chaplain, had been granted dispensation to pack his gums with snuff. He sucked his cud and thought of something to say.

''I'm Hector. I'm a junkie. I guess I feel okay today, no problems. . . . But I got to say, I don't know what Lewis and what's-his-name . . . Kevin . . . got to do with me. Like, the last thing in the world I want to do—I mean, it comes after cutting my tongue out and maybe kissing goats—is—''

Lewis sat up straight and opened his mouth, but Marcia pointed a finger, silencing him, and said to Hector, ''It's not about mechanics, Hector, it's about relationships. We'll go into it later.'' She nodded at the fragile little bird who sat to Hector's right. Cheryl.

''I'm Cheryl. . . .'' She sounded like a frightened kitten, as if worried that any sound above a whisper would give offense. Though Preston kept his head down, his eyes refused to look away from her. She was tiny and so thin that her head looked oversized and her bones seemed to be held together by her clothes. A cap of ebony hair surrounded a face made up only of lips and cheekbones, for the eyes lived in dark caves deep in her skull.

''I'm still sad that Karen graduated yesterday. I mean, I'm glad she made it through, but I'm really going to miss her. I see her starting out on a new life, and it scares me, 'cause I don't know how much of a life I can have and . . . well, I guess you could say I've got mixed feelings about it all.''

When, after a beat, Cheryl said nothing more, Lewis smiled at Preston and declared, ''My name is Lewis, and I have the gift of alcoholism.''

''What?'' Preston realized he had spoken out of turn, and he added quickly, ''Excuse me.''

Marcia said, ''Lewis, that's not fair to Scott.''

''Oh, all right.'' Lewis shrugged. ''I'm Lewis and I'm an alcoholic. I'm a bit upset today because I have a new roommate whom I *do* not like. He treats me like I've got leprosy. Not that I'm not used to dealing with homophobes, but this one is particularly conceited in im*ag*ining that I'd ever *want* to put a move on him, and . . . well, it's just so tiresome having to justify yourself to every new bigot that comes along. Anyway . . .'' Lewis dismissed the thought with an imperious wave.

Silence. Preston's time had come. He had nothing to say. What could he say that would mean anything to these people—a hooker, a junkie, a fruit and an anorexic? He had nothing in common with them. Their problems were theirs. If they wanted to blab about them, that was their business. His problems were his, and he'd deal with them. They couldn't understand.

A drop of sweat fell from the tip of his nose.

''Scott . . . ?'' Marcia said softly.

No way out. ''I'm Scott, and . . . ah . . . I guess I wouldn't be here if I didn't have a problem, but . . . I don't know . . . I'm nervous as hell.''

"Nervous isn't a feeling; it's a condition. How do you feel?"

"Scared, then."

"What are you scared of?"

"I'm not sure, really. It's kind of like . . ." Blessedly, the quotation came to him. ". . . that 'undiscovered country from whose bourn no traveler returns.' "

Preston saw Hector and Cheryl exchange a mystified glance. They thought he was speaking Chinese. Good. Now maybe they'd believe him when he said he didn't belong here. His whole frame of reference was different from theirs. *He* was different.

He did not see Lewis look at Marcia and then turn away with a barely contained grin of delicious anticipation.

Marcia didn't raise her voice. It was as flat and matter-of-fact as a razor cutting through an artery.

"Listen to me, you arrogant prick: I don't want to hear you quote anybody—living or dead, famous or not—in this group ever again. You got that?"

Cheryl gasped. Hector and Lewis smiled.

Preston stuttered. "I b-beg your p-pardon. . . ."

"Quotes are a cheap way out, a way to avoid your own feelings. You've been shutting off your feelings for years, drowning them in booze, anesthetizing yourself from life. Remember I told you you'd feel lonely but wouldn't recognize it? Your best friend isn't there anymore to give you distance from your feelings, so instinctively you go to the next best thing: You use somebody else's words about feelings. Understand?"

It took Preston a second to say, "I never thought of that."

"No, you sure didn't." Marcia smiled at him. "Besides, the parallel isn't right. Hamlet's 'undiscovered country' was death. Yours is life."

Preston gaped at her. *This woman is dangerous.*

"Now," Marcia said, resuming her hands-on-knees position, looking once again at the floor, "I want us to help Cheryl deal with her feelings about losing Karen. But I want Scott to help too, and he can't help till he knows us a little better. So let's everybody remember one thing we didn't want to deal with or we didn't know about ourselves before we got here. I told him about my trip with the Dumbos." She laughed. "I'm not sure he believed me, but it's the truth. . . . Hector?"

"No sweat, man," said Hector. "The thing I'd blocked most was that when I stabbed myself it wasn't no accident." He looked at Preston. "I tell you, man, when you take a handful of reds in the morning and a handful of yellows at night, and in between you're sniffin' and snortin' whatever the dude's got, there comes a time when you're out of fuckin' balance. I stared at that knife for musta been five minutes before I stuck it in my guts, and I still swore up and down it was an accident." He laughed. "You believe that?"

"No." Preston shook his head. "I can't. I really can't."

"Sure you can, Scott," Marcia said with a crooked smile. "You can relate to that. All he was trying to do was make his quietus with a bare bodkin." She turned to Hector. "Which is how some douchebags say 'off yourself.' " She pointed at Cheryl.

"It's all about blindness," Cheryl began. "That's what the disease does, it blinds you. I never drank liquor, so I couldn't be in trouble, right? I never once missed work. 'Course, that might have been because I didn't have a job. I never drank in the morning. Why should I? I slept all morning so I could drink all the rest of the day. You're supposed to eat a balanced diet, so I found something with malt and hops and grain in it. A hundred and eighty calories a can, twenty-four cans a day, I *had* to be eating enough." She shook her head. "Christ, what a jerk!"

Immediately, Hector leaned over and wrapped her in one of his huge tattooed arms. "C'mon, tell guilt to take a hike."

Lewis patted her knee. "It's all in the past, hon. What's done is done." He looked up at Marcia and said, "This isn't helpful."

"Yes, it is, Lewis. Your turn."

Lewis sighed. "Well, if we're talking about blindness, how about convincing yourself that a vodka enema is a perfectly normal way to have a social drink?" Lewis paused dramatically, pleased to see all eyes locked on him.

He hasn't told this one before, Preston thought. He must've been saving it for some special moment.

"I'd just had an ulcer," Lewis continued, "and I couldn't drink. But that just meant that I shouldn't take alcohol into my poor abused stomach, right? So one night when Kevin was sitting there getting sweetly smashed on one of our thirty-dollar bottles of Margaux, I got angrier and angrier till it occurred to me that my

House of Heavenly Highs had a front door *and* a back door.''

''Mutha . . .'' Hector said.

''Don't knock it till you've tried it. Fastest high I ever had in my life. Up the gee-gee, in the bloodstream . . . *liftoff!*''

Lewis laughed, which must have given tacit permission to the others to laugh too, for Hector suddenly guffawed and Cheryl tittered and Marcia chuckled. Preston put his hand over his mouth and tried to swallow his laughter—he did not feel entitled to assume membership in this fraternity—but a staccato ''unh-unh-unh'' escaped between his fingers.

Marcia let the laughter subside and then said, ''How does this make you feel, Scott?''

''Like an alien. This isn't me. I've never done these things. I can't conceive of doing them.''

''Well, what *have* you done? There must be *some* reason you're here.''

''Actually *done*? Nothing. That's my point. If this . . . these stories, these experiences . . . if this is alcoholism, or addiction, or whatever you want to call it, that's not me.''

''Right. You know, Scott, the fun thing about this disease is, it grabs everybody in a different way. Cheryl's friend Karen, she didn't *do* anything either. She just drank half a bottle of wine a day, every day, couldn't stop. And because she couldn't stop she got to hate herself, couldn't stand how weak and worthless she was, couldn't see the point of going on.''

Marcia paused, and she looked at Preston and wondered if the time had come. Was he strong enough?

Should she wait a day or two, let him get his bearings before she . . .

Piss on it. It's Miller time, Scott. Here we go.

"Let me paint a picture for you, Scott. Let me paint a picture of a nice, sophisticated, college-educated, upper-middle-class New York guy who doesn't know it but is drinking himself to death . . . a real hard-core, dyed-in-the-wool rummy. Okay?"

"If you must." Preston sighed theatrically. "Go ahead: Take two from column A, two from column B, and create your stereotype. But that's not me."

"No, no. I know. This'll just be a rough portrait, a lot of guesswork. But let's say, if any of the things I describe don't apply to you, raise your hand. Okay?"

"Sure." Preston hoped he looked bored, hoped no one else could hear the locomotive sounds his heart was making.

"Let's see . . ." Marcia gazed at the ceiling. "He grew up in a family where booze was part of the diet: drinks with lunch, drinks before dinner, drinks at the country club. The rule was, when you're happy you have a drink to celebrate, when you're sad you have a drink to console yourself. In college he was proud of his capacity. He could hold his liquor. That was the deal: A gentleman drank as much as he could hold, no more.

"He got married, had a kid or two, kept drinking. No problem. Then, in the past couple of years, a change: Once in a while he'd say something or do something that the next day he'd feel like apologizing for. Even worse, some days he couldn't remember that he'd said it or done it. Maybe a friend would call up and say, 'Boy, you really tied one on last night,' and they'd have a good laugh till he'd have to face that rough moment and ask—with another awkward little laugh—if the friend knew how the car had come to be parked sideways in the driveway, or maybe how the car had gotten home at all.''

Preston stared at the floor. He felt sweat running down the crack in his ass. His ears popped as the muscles in his jaw ground his molars together. He longed for oblivion.

"Don't forget, Scott," Marcia said, a sunny smile on her face, "stop me whenever I miss the mark. By the way, does the name Richard Speck mean anything to you?"

"Speck? No."

"Richard Speck woke up one morning a lot of years ago, and he couldn't remember the night before either. Maybe he had a good laugh about it, I don't know, but it didn't last long because what he'd done the night before was knife eight nurses to death in Chicago. They say he still doesn't remember doing it. He swore he didn't know he had a problem. Anyway, that's not you. So: Our nice New York college guy, he and his wife don't go out much anymore. Maybe it's because they're not asked much anymore, or maybe it's because he thinks dinner parties are a bore, and the real reason is he can't drink as much as he wants to at somebody else's house or at a restaurant because, naturally, it'll be a little embarrassing when he falls asleep at the table or shouts at the waiter—both of which he can do at home and who cares. Oh, maybe the wife cares, but she's used to it, and if his kids care, well . . . kids are taught not to criticize grown-ups, they just keep it all bottled up inside themselves, and he doesn't have time to notice that the kids aren't bringing friends home the way they used to. Maybe he has some vague memory of the last time his kids' friends came over and he was standing there waving a drink at the TV set and calling Dan Rather a jerk-off. Maybe not.

"Now, throughout all this, he has a feeling—just a feeling—that this isn't exactly normal, and all he wants these days is to feel normal. It used to be that booze made him feel good, really *good*, but now the best he can hope for is normal. So he has a couple of pops every hour or two, all day long, and most times he gets away with it fine, but now and then he raises his voice when he shouldn't or challenges his boss over some stupid thing or sleeps past his stop on the train. It's gotten to be more than *now and then*, though. It's to the point where the people who love him have decided to call him on it. But he thinks: What do they know? They don't have to get through my day. They—"

"You know what this is?" Preston interrupted. "This is every cliché in the book."

"I see, Scott. And clichés don't apply to you."

"Not . . . not *all* of them. I'm not just a catalogue of textbook behaviors."

"You're special."

"I'm *me*, that's all. Everybody doesn't *have* to fit your cookie mold."

"Okay, Scott. How about you buy this one thing: The deal's gone bad. The gentleman isn't holding the liquor anymore. The liquor's got the gentleman. Cheryl, remind Scott. Give him the word."

"Blindness," said Cheryl.

"Uh-huh. The disease has blinded you, Scott. It *isn't* normal to have to take a sedative drug just to ignite the day. It *isn't* normal to swallow so much of a chemical that it kills your memory. It *isn't* normal to shut down two-thirds of your sensory system every day of your life." She leaned forward, forcing him to look at her. "How's your sex life, Scott?"

"None of your business."

"Sure." Marcia laughed. "I've been there."

Hector said, "One time it got so bad for me that I warned God I'd sell my soul to the devil if He didn't give me one more hard-on."

Lewis said, "I hope He said no, for all our sakes."

Marcia raised a hand and stopped Hector before he could threaten Lewis. She said to Preston, "Forget the portrait. Can you tell us *why* you drink, Scott?"

"Sure. A combination of conditioning and a high-pressure life. Publishing doesn't pay well, but it demands a lot. You feel you—"

"Stop! No more 'you.' No more 'one.' No more impersonal third-person singular. You can't skate away with generalizations. I want to hear 'I.' "

He nodded. "I feel I have to maintain . . ." He stopped. "Man, that feels awkward."

"Doesn't it though? You're learning."

"Anyway, I—we—wanted a house and a car and a kid who goes to good schools. At work there's a lot of pressure to find the best-seller. I try to write magazine articles on the side, do movie reviews. You know what it costs to keep a child in private school, pay a mortgage? Before the first of January is over,

I'm looking at out-of-pocket after-tax expenses of about fifty thousand dollars. I—''

"Wait a sec. Let's make a list here. The reasons you drink the way you do are, one, a high-pressure job; two, a lot of financial demands; three, it's just a habit. Is there a number four?''

"Opportunity, I guess. Every day there are business lunches, cocktail parties. It's a boozing business.''

"So we'll call number four peer pressure or environment.'' One at a time, like a child counting for its mother, she raised four fingers.

Preston sensed a new danger, another knife being unsheathed.

"I'll grant you, Scott, that's heavy stuff. I don't know how you've survived this long.''

Here it comes. He said, "You don't have to patronize me.''

"Yes, I do,'' she said. "I really do. Because for a college boy with a brain, you are without a doubt the stupidest *fuck* I ever did meet.''

Preston had been prepared, so he was able to be angry. "What's this good cop/bad cop routine?'' he said. "One minute you're my friend, the next you're sticking it to me.''

"I'm your friend, Scott. But friends don't like friends to lie to them. Don't take my word for it. Hector, what did you think of Scott's explanation?''

Hector said, "Horseshit.''

Cheryl, unprompted, said, "Right on.''

Lewis looked at Preston and said, "Why isn't *every*-body in publishing with kids in private school a falling-down drunk?''

"What we're trying to tell you, Scott, is you don't

drink because you have problems. You have problems
because you drink. And you drink the way you do because you *can't not*. It's got you, Scott, and it ain't
gonna let you go. You gotta shake the fuckin' monkey
off your back and *kill* the sucker.''

You don't drink because you have problems, he repeated to himself. *You have problems because you drink*.
Wait a second. That is a revolutionary thought. He
didn't have anything to say, but his mouth must have
been open because Marcia raised a hand.

"Don't argue, don't question, don't fight," she said.
"Just think for a while. You got enough to chew on." She
slapped his knee. "And listen. And if you have something
to contribute, *then* speak, because we're going to try to
help Cheryl deal with her loss of Karen." She took Cheryl's
hand. "It feels like a little bit of you died, doesn't it?"

"Yeah," Cheryl said, "and I only knew her three
weeks."

"You know why it hurts so much?"

"We had a lot in common?"

"That too, but more: It was the first intense relationship you ever allowed yourself to have, the first one you
didn't shut off with—"

Suddenly a shriek erupted in a room nearby—a pained
and painful, ear-piercing, genuine goosebumper of a
human cry of agony.

Preston started out of his chair, wide-eyed, frightened. Marcia grabbed him by his belt and slammed him
back into his chair. No one else had stirred.

"Don't worry about it," Marcia said.

"What was *that*?"

"Self-expression." Before she could reassemble her
words to Cheryl, another shriek exploded and dissolved

into a wail of despair, punctuated by a crash and some muted rhythmic thumps.

Marcia smiled at Preston and said, "See? Therapy can be a real blast."

6

DUKE FLATTENED HIMSELF against the wall and covered his ears to blunt the blades of pain that the tumult before him was inflicting on his tequila-ravaged brain. Maybe he'd picked wrong; maybe he should've gone to jail. Treatment was supposed to be mellow, soothing. Nobody'd told him therapy was war.

He wished he could be absorbed by the paint. Yet he wouldn't have wanted to miss this. It was better than *Animal House*, something to regale his children with (children, that is, if Clarisse would ever again give him access to her pearly gates). It was just that he wanted to be a spectator, not a player, and he knew that as long as he was visible, somebody was going to insist that he join the group grope. These people were like the Red Chinese: We all work together or we don't work at all. You say you want to march to your own tune, they grab you by the flute and stick it up your ass till you agree to play the national anthem along with everybody else.

He couldn't remember exactly how it had happened, but somehow this tedious therapy session—everybody mumbling about how they were prisoners of alcohol or how the demon cocaine still visited them in their dreams; he thought he'd go off his tree listening to all the whining—had suddenly exploded like a skyrocket. Somebody had said something about somebody else being uptight and superior. Then some other person had said you can't go out into the world thinking you're better or even different because that leads to isolation, which is a prescription for failure. Then the object of all this said she was sick of being picked on and she felt like kicking the shit out of all of them, and then Dan, the counselor, said something like "Why don't you, then?" and WHAM!—like when a fist hits a mirror, the place was a shambles.

The folding chairs had been kicked back and cast aside. Six people were bunched on the floor, as if praying to the God of Weird. One of them—Dan, the escapee from Woodstock, with his scruffy beard and granny glasses—was holding a chair and encouraging a fiftyish woman who looked like a rejected bratwurst (overstuffed in all the wrong places) to beat the crap out of it with a stuffed cloth baseball bat. And not just *any* fiftyish woman. This was NATASHA GRANT (or her remains, anyway), one of the great movie stars of the past forty years, who had defined glamour for two generations, who had had too much too soon and too often, and who had always believed that she *was* the fantasy creature described in press releases, a belief difficult to sustain when the press releases started describing how she had been fired from this picture and that TV show for being smashed, stoned or simply bloated.

Now this raving beauty over whose image Duke and countless millions of other ambitious lads had pulled their puds was nothing more than raving—a frowzy, frazzled fishwife gone berserk, howling, weeping and cursing. At a chair.

The four other votaries—including a man whom Duke recognized as a former Padres shortstop named Clarence Crosby—were all clustered around Natasha, shouting, "We love you, Nat!" and "Feel the love, Natasha!" and trying to pat and hug her, which was a dangerous game, since Natasha was flailing like a dervish, waving that club, which, if it caught you right, could do damage, no question, especially to the face or the balls.

Dan ducked behind the back of the chair to keep from having his nose pulped, and when he peeked out from a new angle he spied Duke.

"Duke! Get in here!"

"Me?" Duke didn't move.

"Get in here! Now!"

"But what am I—"

"Tell Natasha how much you love her!" Dan ducked as the club skinned the top of his head and Natasha shrilled like a stepped-on dog.

"Oh . . . right." Duke took a couple of steps forward. *I haven't even been introduced to the woman. Why should she believe I love her? Maybe I should offer to show her my sheets.* He kneeled down and tried to nudge his way into the mass of thrashing arms and legs, but a little butterball of a woman—all Duke knew about her from this one session was that she was a hairstylist who still had nightmares about how she had permed an entire glorious head of hair off her best customer while ripped on Gallo chablis—hip-checked him and blocked his way.

"You're new," Butterball sniffed. "You *can't* love her as much as I do."

"Right you are," Duke said, and he backed off.

Dan poked his head up. "Duke!" WHOP! Natasha swung the club and clipped just enough of him to knock his granny glasses across the room and into the leaves of a rubber-tree plant. He ducked down again and shouted from his refuge behind the chair. "Duke! I'm warning you! *Participate!*"

"You're the boss." Duke dropped to his knees again and pushed forward.

Butterball wasn't having a bit of it. "You don't even know what love *is*!" She hit Duke with her hip.

"Sister, I'll be brutally frank with you," Duke said. "I don't *give* a shit." Then he feinted with a little dipsy-do and whacked Butterball with his own hip.

Because he was taller than she, and stronger, and because Butterball was off balance, she pitched face forward directly on top of the box-office queen, who, with an enraged yelp, was driven forward into the chair and knocked it up on two legs so that it, in turn, collapsed onto Dan. Two other worshipers, evidently assuming that this was all part of the script, piled on, shrieking, "Natasha! Natasha! We love you!" and "I feel the love all over!"

From somewhere far away, muffled by upholstery and flesh, Dan could be heard crying, "I think that's enough for today!"

Duke rolled to his feet and surveyed the wreckage.

Clarence Crosby crawled free and joined him. "Man! What you make of that? That's *love*!"

"I think it's time to break for a gin-and-tonic and a shrimp salad," Duke said.

And then the voice that had cooed to a billion ears in half a hundred films over two-score years called out, "Get the fuck offa me! I think you broke my goddam leg!"

Marcia knelt before Cheryl's chair and held Cheryl's hands and looked up into her face as if hoping to lure her eyes out from their hiding places. "Don't grieve for it," Marcia said. "Cherish it. It was a sober friendship and it was wonderful. There'll be others."

"Maybe." Cheryl wouldn't free her eyes to look at Marcia. "Maybe not for me."

Marcia sighed. Without turning around she said, "What do you think, Scott?"

What did he think? What would anybody think? *This is a sad, sick little girl.* But he couldn't say that. "I think . . . I think maybe it's wrong . . . no, I don't mean wrong, but . . . maybe it doesn't do any good to worry about what's going to happen . . . maybe it's better to be happy for what *has* happened, and to have hope." *Oh shit. I've probably said something asinine. Now Marcia'll whip around and kick me in the teeth.*

Marcia didn't react to him at all. She stroked Cheryl's hands and said, "Do you hear what Scott's saying? He may not know it, but what he's saying is, One day at a time. That's the only way we can make it, any of us. By being grateful for every day we've had and living today the best we can. One day at a time."

Cheryl nodded.

Lewis wrapped an arm around her again and said, "It's higher-power time, hon."

Marcia looked at her watch, stood up and extended her arms out to the sides.

Immediately the others stood too. Hector took one of Marcia's hands and held his other out to Cheryl, who took it and held her other out to Lewis, who took it and held his other out to Preston.

What now, O Lord? Ring-around-a-rosy? Preston let Lewis take his hand, felt him squeeze it, conquered an impulse to snatch it back and wipe it on his trousers and jam it into his pocket. Marcia took his other hand.

They bowed their heads and (with Preston humming in incoherent harmony) together prayed, "God, grant me the serenity to accept the things I cannot change, the courage to change the things I can, and the wisdom to know the difference. . . . Amen."

Nice, Preston thought, and he was about to ask Marcia who had written the prayer when Lewis suddenly spun on him and embraced him and said, "Welcome, welcome. . . . You'll find love here."

Help! Preston panicked. *The guy's flipped his wig. Holding hands was too much for him.* Preston's arms stuck out like branches, his hands flopped helplessly. He thought of tripping Lewis, throwing him to the floor, subduing him till medical help could be summoned.

Then he saw, over Lewis's shoulder, that Hector was embracing Marcia, that Marcia then embraced Cheryl, that Cheryl then embraced Hector.

I guess it's hug time. Tentatively, he let his hands pat Lewis on the back. Abruptly Lewis pulled away and was replaced by Hector, who obviously didn't like hugging men any more than Preston did and squeezed him quickly and violently—like crushing a fly—and pulled away, to be replaced by Cheryl, who flitted in and out of his arms like a hummingbird.

Marcia hugged him last. He did his best to respond,

but it wasn't much—about as convincing as social kissy-face in the Grill Room at The Four Seasons.

Marcia knew. She winked at him and said, "You are one hard-ass nut to crack. But I'm gonna do it."

The doors to the two therapy rooms opened simultaneously, and as the patients poured out there was the instantaneous combustion of a dozen cigarettes.

"You look like shit," Duke said to Preston.

"Thanks." He glanced over Duke's shoulder. "Hey! Did that used to be Natasha Grant?"

"Don't get in her way," Duke said. "She makes Clarisse look like Mary Poppins."

"I was going to marry her, live in her mansion and cover her with unguents." Preston couldn't take his eyes off her. "She could be somebody's maid."

"She was never true to you. All the time you thought you were her one and only, I was boffing her brains out."

The crowd was ambling toward the front door, and they followed.

Preston said, "It sounded like you were playing rugby in there."

"This is dangerous stuff, man. I never knew treatment was a contact sport."

A cigarette machine stood against the wall by the front door. "A buck and a half!" Preston said. "When I was smoking, cigarettes were fifty cents." He fished in his pocket and found four quarters.

"Welcome to the wonderful world of addiction." Duke dropped two quarters into Preston's hand.

Preston studied the machine. "What's a good brand?"

"That's not the point."

Preston looked at him, nodded. "Right." He pumped the coins into the machine, closed his eyes, ran his fingers along the levers and pulled one.

As they followed the crowd toward the main building, Preston said to Duke that if he believed in such things, he'd place bets that Marcia had ESP: She knew more about him than he knew about himself. At least, that's what it seemed like.

"Go on," Duke said. "They got *you* believing it now?"

"I don't know about believing. But she's sure got me wondering."

The dining hall reminded Preston of prep school: a white, brightly lighted, antiseptic room bisected by steam tables. One side was reserved for counselors and staff, the other for patients.

They collected plastic trays and sets of flatware wrapped in paper napkins, and joined the line.

"I figured out the trick to survival here," Duke said as he reached a bony arm under the plastic "sneeze bar" and grabbed a Jell-O salad. "Keep 'em focused on other people. Then they can't zero in on you."

Preston took cottage cheese with a cherry on top. "You'll never learn anything that way. You're here. You might's well get something from it. Besides, you've got an ego like everyone else. You want *some* attention."

Duke took a plate of meat that looked orange under the heat lamps. "Listen: After today, I don't even want old hippie Dan to *think* about me. I was lucky to get out alive. You shoulda seen that loopy Natasha. If that chair'd been one of her eight husbands, man, he'd be nothing but a smear on the rug."

Preston took a bowl of stew full of mocha things and a glass of iced tea, and he and Duke turned to find a table. Most of the tables were occupied, and though the atmosphere in here was congenial, if not merry, and everybody seemed to be chatting and nobody was looking mopey or hostile, he didn't feel like sitting with strangers. He and Duke found an empty table for four.

"They've got you coming and going," Preston said as he sat down. "They say you're only here to ask questions about yourself; then they say if you have to ask questions that means you've got the problem. Bang! Gotcha!"

"I'll admit anything," Duke said. "For twenty-eight days, I'll admit I'm a Chinaman if they want."

A voice behind them said, "An idiot, yes, but a Chinaman . . . that's a reach."

It was Lewis, and with him was Hector, and without being invited they unloaded their plates on the table.

Lewis said, "Hector told me to tell you we'd only join you if you promise not to make a pass at us."

"Like hell!" Hector protested. He did not appreciate being teased. "I never said that."

Duke waited until they had settled, and then he said, "Lewis, you can worry about earthquakes, you can worry about terrorists, you can worry about being buggered by guys from the planet Mercury, but *me* you do not have to worry about."

Lewis smiled. "I'll count my blessings."

Preston had his fork poised over his stew when he noticed that Hector was muttering some Spanish words and had his eyes closed and his hands folded before him. He put his fork down.

Hector finished his prayer and pulled a medallion

from under his T-shirt and kissed it. "Amen," he said. "Fuckin' *starvin'* . . ." He grabbed a slab of white bread and scooped a glutinous brown mash of beans and wiener sections onto it and folded it over and packed it into his mouth.

Preston took a couple of bites of stew. He looked at Lewis. "You said . . ." He hesitated. "Is it all right to talk about what went on in—?"

"Of course!" Lewis laughed. "Nobody has any secrets here. Nobody *can*. I've already heard about Natasha's Tennessee Williams act, and that Mr. Wonderful here"—he pointed at Duke with his fork—"tried to start an orgy."

"Hey—"

Preston cut Duke off. "Lewis, you said, before she stopped you, you said you have the *gift* of alcoholism."

"Indeed I did," Lewis said. "I like to think of it as a gift, like Mozart's, only malignant. Not everybody has it, and having the gift alone isn't enough. To be a *real* alcoholic you have to practice. The trouble is, they insist it's a disease, and they don't welcome theories that muddy the waters."

Hector spoke through a shoal of franks and beans. "Bein' a junkie ain't special. Anybody can do it."

"*I* couldn't," Lewis said. "I tried heroin once. It made me deathly ill." He turned to Preston. "I don't bother to fight the powers that be. I just clutch at every straw of dignity in life that I can."

"Why are you limping?" Marcia asked Dan Farina as they walked to the dining hall. As always, he tended to walk closer to her than was smart; as always, she edged sideways and kept a full yard of daylight between them.

Dan told her he had been crushed by half a ton of drunks. "But it was great! I finally got Natasha in touch with her anger. After four weeks of holding out on me, I think today she killed all her husbands and her mother and her sister who's always resented her."

"How do you know she wasn't acting?"

"Just to please me? She doesn't give a hoot about me. She's the most perfectly self-absorbed person I've ever seen. I don't think anybody else exists in her world, except as a foil for her. You know: 'Enough about me. Tell me what *you* thought of my performance.' There's a word for it."

"Solipsism."

"Solipsism. Right."

"But that's what I mean. You have power over her. If you don't give the okay, she doesn't leave here. Or at least doesn't get her medallion and the kiss on the cheek. Maybe she thought: This guy wants to see me bust loose. Okay, I'll bust loose. Here we go. Busting Loose, Take One."

"No, she was genuine. I can tell genuine anger."

"She's an *actress*."

"Would she do that?" Dan frowned as he held the door to the dining hall for her.

"I'm probably wrong." Why spoil his day? she thought. "Your glasses are still cockeyed."

As they joined the food line, Marcia looked around the patients' section and saw Preston sitting with Lewis and Hector and someone she didn't know.

She said to Dan, "What's your new one like? The beanpole over there."

"Duke? A lulu. He's still locked up in his bad space.

But I'll reach him. I'm pretty sure he felt the love today."

"I wish mine was a lulu. They're down in black and white. They try to deny they've got a problem, you show them the court order. I've got myself William F. Buckley, Jr."

"No kidding?" Dan looked over his shoulder.

"You know what I mean. Ivy League. Smart. Articulate. This whole unpleasant business is all a *ghastly* mistake."

"They're protected."

"Genetically and socially. They don't *do* the real colorful stuff, don't get arrested, don't stab somebody, almost never end up in the gutter. They don't bottom out. Denial's real easy."

Dan took some pears on a bed of wilted lettuce. "Even when they die of it, the obit says 'congestive heart failure' or 'a long illness.' " He picked up a bowl of chopped apples and nuts and put it on her tray.

"Don't *do* that!" she hissed.

"You like fruit. You put fruit on your cereal every morning."

"That's at home. This is here. Here we're *colleagues*, nothing more. You don't know squat about me except for lunch."

Dan grinned and shook his head. "You're paranoid."

"Bet your honky ass I'm paranoid. I like my job. I'd like to keep it."

"Lecture time," Lewis said as he piled his plates on his tray.

Preston had been smoking a cigarette with his coffee, watching Marcia and the other counselor go through the

line. He saw the guy put something on her tray, saw
she didn't like that. *Interesting. Is there something going on there?* He wanted to ask Lewis, but Lewis was
already walking to the line of people waiting to pass
their dirty dishes through the window into the kitchen.
He stacked his dishes and got up.

He stood in line behind Lewis, who was behind
Cheryl.

When Cheryl passed her tray through the window,
the matronly scullion looked at the untouched food and
leaned down and said to Cheryl, "You gotta *eat*, child.
Else, you never get well."

Cheryl said, "I didn't feel so good," and she turned
away.

Lewis waited for Preston to dispose of his tray, and
they walked together toward the door.

"Everybody seems 'up' here," Preston said. "Everybody but her." He pointed ahead to Cheryl.

Lewis nodded. "Poor baby. She's twenty-two. She's
got cirrhosis. They've already done two liver biopsies,
and the tissue they got was dead both times. They want
to do another one, but she's terrified that if they pull
another dead plug it'll be her death sentence. You can
live with half your liver gone, even two thirds, but if
three quarters is nothing but scar tissue, then it's just a
question of when."

"How do you get cirrhosis at twenty-two?"

"Well, one fabulous way is to start at fourteen putting nothing—*nothing*—in your mouth but beer." He
opened the door and held it for Preston, and they walked
down the corridor toward the lecture room. "She knows
what it'll be like. Both her parents went that way: confusion, disorientation, hallucinations—they come from

ammonia the liver won't process—then maybe coma, maybe not, then probably esophageal varices.''

"A what?"

"The liver can't handle anything more, so it shunts it all by. All the blood goes up through the esophagus. Basically, you puke away your life blood. All of it.''

Jesus Christ! Preston felt *his* blood draining into his shoes. They reached the door to the lecture room, and Preston leaned against the jamb and took a deep breath. He saw Lewis looking at him, concerned, and he tried to smile. "It's been a long day."

Lewis nodded. "Sensory overload. You've heard about taking life one day at a time? Cheryl's a little girl who has no choice. All the shrinks can do is help her appreciate every day as a gift. Not so easy when you hate yourself so much for trying to kill yourself that you feel like . . . killing yourself." Lewis paused and looked at Preston—gray, weak, clutching the doorjamb. He winked and said, "Isn't it beautiful? I told you: It makes Mozart's gift seem almost . . . well, pedestrian.''

7

THE BLACK DAIMLER circled the roundabout with the silent grace of a crocodile and stopped before the front door of the clinic. The chauffeur got out, tugged at his jacket to erase the wrinkles from the shoulders, and opened one of the back doors.

A young woman stepped out of the car and, while the chauffeur went to the trunk to fetch her suitcase, stared at the simple adobe building. She wore sunglasses, though night was well on its way and stars could already be seen in the violet sky. Her long blond hair gleamed against her navy blue cashmere sweater. She had not known how to dress for the occasion, so she had taken her mother's advice—"Make believe it's a regular hospital, darling. Wear something simple and understated, something that won't say too much"—and had worn a white silk blouse, a pleated linen skirt and medium-heel navy pumps to match the sweater. She had left her jewelry at home, all except her signet pinkie ring and her gold Rolex.

"It's cold," she said.

"Only at night." The chauffeur shut the trunk. "I don't imagine you'll have much call to be outside at night."

"No."

Carrying the suitcase, the chauffeur started toward the building, but the young woman took a couple of quick steps and caught up with him and put a hand on his arm.

"I'll take it," she said. "I'd rather."

"Of course." He handed her the suitcase and tipped his hat and said, "Good luck, Miss 'Cilla."

"Thank you, Simpson. For everything."

The lobby was empty; the two offices on the left were dark. A light shone in an office to the right, so she set her suitcase down and walked to the office door. A large woman in a white uniform sat at a desk, making notes on a file in a manila folder. She sensed a presence at the door and looked up.

"Hello, dearie." She grinned. "Checking in?"

The young woman nodded, and the nurse gestured to a chair beside her desk.

"I'm Nurse Bridget. And you're . . . ?"

"Godfrey . . . Priscilla Godfrey?"

"Oh yes." She opened a drawer and searched for an admission form.

Priscilla noticed an ashtray on the nurse's desk. She opened her purse, took a cigarette from a silver case and lit it with a gold butane lighter.

Nurse Bridget waited until Priscilla had returned the lighter to her purse. Then she took Priscilla's free hand in hers and looked at it. The fingernails had been bitten to the nubs, the skin around them ravaged and scarred.

"I'm sure glad you're here, dearie," she said.

Priscilla snatched her hand back and buried it in the pleats of her skirt.

Nurse Bridget stood, reached across the desk and, gently, removed Priscilla's sunglasses. "You won't be needing these," she said. "You won't have to hide anything, ever again."

"Hi, Guy!" fifty voices shouted in ragged unison.

Preston, Lewis, Duke and Hector sat in the back row of the lecture room. The director of the clinic, Guy Larkin, stood before a podium at the front. Behind him was a blackboard on which someone had chalked "Korsakoff's Syndrome."

Preston looked at the backs of the people in front of him. There were T-shirts and sport shirts, heads of long shaggy hair and heads of close-cropped gray. An elderly woman was knitting.

Preston heard a subdued belch to his right. He turned his head and saw Hector nibbling at a cigarette.

Larkin smiled broadly and said, "Dr. Lapidus was scheduled to speak tonight about the effects of ethyl alcohol on the encoding of memory engrams—Korsakoff's Syndrome. But there's been a last-minute change."

"Oh, damn!" someone said.

Someone else said, "My friggin' favorite, too."

Larkin held up a hand for silence. Then, with a flourish reminiscent of a carney barker introducing a two-headed woman, he rolled his wrist and extended his arm to a side door and proclaimed, "Ladies and gentlemen . . . Stone Banner!"

The side door sprang open and in ran—*ran*—the man

who had done more than any other (with the possible exception of John Wayne) to cement the modern myths about the American West.

As Stone Banner took the podium and Larkin descended to a seat in the front row and most of the audience applauded reflexively, Lewis bent to Preston and whispered, "Isn't he *gorgeous*?"

It wasn't the word Preston would have chosen, but he guessed it was appropriate. Officially sixty years old, Banner could have made a credible case for being anywhere from forty-five to seventy. He was deeply tanned, glamorously craggy, flat-bellied and fit. His mane of silver hair played nicely against the trove of gold that decorated him: a gold chain with gold crucifix around his neck, on one wrist a gold elephant-hair bracelet and on the other a gold chain-link bracelet, and gold rings on each pinky. He wore a silk shirt open to his sternum, tailored jeans and high-gloss cowboy boots.

"Please, please." Banner held up his hands to quell the applause. "There are no stars here. We're all brothers and sisters in recovery." He closed his arms and raised his arms like Jimmy Swaggart and began, in his resonant baritone, "God, grant me the serenity . . ."

While the congregation chanted, Lewis bowed his head and whispered to Preston, "You know he's a miracle of modern surgery."

"How so?"

"He's had so many lifts, they're worried if they try one more, the strain'll be too much and his nose'll fall off."

When the prayer was done, Banner hooked one thumb in a belt loop, rested his other hand on the podium and turned his head slowly from side to side, making brief eye contact with everyone in the room. Preston noticed that Banner knew instinctively how to stand so that the overhead light highlighted his features and made him look like a Remington sculpture.

"It's a high," Banner began, "a really great natural high to see all the new faces here, all the new lives about to begin. You may be scared, but let me tell you: Stone Banner was scared, believe it or not. You may be lonely, but Stone Banner remembers the loneliness . . . the shakes and the horrors."

What about the third-person rule? Does he remember that? Where's the compulsory 'I'? Or, because it's our candy store, are we allowed to indulge ourselves in regal syntax? Preston watched Banner as he recited the litany of his addiction—Preston didn't have to listen, for the words were predictable, the circumstances and situations only slightly more colorful than those experienced by ordinary mortals, the end inevitable (the retired cowboy riding into the sunset on a cloud of cocaine and vodka)—and he sensed that he was being treated not to a confession but to a performance: gestures melodramatic, choked pauses perfectly timed, shy smiles pleading for understanding.

"So there I was, in my private black hole, and suddenly I realized: I can't do it alone. And I looked up into the sky"—Banner looked up at the acoustic-tiled ceiling—"and I said, 'I can't do it, God, can you?' And He did."

Banner smiled, and Guy Larkin applauded, which was the signal for everyone else to applaud.

"But I didn't come here tonight to bore you with my drunkography," Banner said. "I came here on a special mission. Normally, our graduations are done in the privacy of our own units, but tonight we're going to have a love-in. We're going to celebrate the graduation of a truly great lady. Ladies and gentlemen . . . brothers and sisters . . . please join me in . . . in *appreciating* my friend . . . *your* friend . . . Natasha G.!''

Banner stepped back, gestured at the side door and clapped his hands.

The side door flew open, and with a wave and a grin, Natasha Grant wafted into the room.

Preston said, ''My God!''

Lewis said, ''Oh my!''

Duke said, ''And to think: I could've fallen on her . . . right on top of her. It would've been easy.''

What they saw now was the Natasha Grant not of fact but of fantasy, transformed, it seemed, by a legion of magicians. The bulges of suet were gone, the pasty complexion was now rosy, the frazzled Brillo hair was now a pillow of shining waves and curls. Her lips were a glistening magenta invitation. She pointed them at the audience and silently mouthed the words ''I love you.''

Banner hugged Natasha, and she offered him her cheek and permitted his lips to pass within a millimeter of it. Then they parted and turned to the audience, and Banner held her hand and said, ''The journey isn't easy for any of us, but for some of us it's doubly hard. Some people, the public, see a silver spoon in our mouths, but they don't know that that spoon can choke us.'' He flashed a smile at Natasha. ''Natasha G. was literally born in a trunk. . . .''

Natasha G. How cute. Pseudoanonymity. And as Banner started down Natasha's memory lane, Preston fancied a therapy session among public figures: *Ronald R., meet Ayatollah K., who overdosed on God. Ron had a reality problem, fried his brain with sweet dreams . . .*

The door behind Preston opened and quickly closed, and a woman sat in the empty chair across the aisle. He would not have bothered to look up if he hadn't smelled her. He recognized her perfume, a rich and spicy fragrance that, for reasons he had never questioned, had always triggered his erotic reflexes. It was called Opium. So he did look up, and for probably the twentieth time that day he vowed to apologize to the young author he had defamed as pretentious. Once again he felt he had been punched in the soul.

She was beautiful. No, that wasn't enough. She was his ideal. She was all the passions of his youth in one manifestation: Donna Reed and Lizabeth Scott and Lauren Bacall, Scarlett O'Hara and Puccini's Mimi, Emma Bovary and Anna Karenina. She was purity and perfection, recklessness and vulnerability.

She was sniveling, seized by sobs she couldn't stop and wanted to conceal. She rooted in her purse for a tissue and, when she couldn't find one, dabbed delicately at the tip of her nose with the sleeve of her sweater.

She's wiping her nose with cashmere! Preston was captivated. The gesture was grotesque. His left brain decreed it disgusting. His right decided it was . . . sweet. He plucked a handkerchief from his hip pocket and leaned across the aisle and pressed it into her hand. Her eyes flicked up at him, shiny and blue, grateful and supplicating, meek and aware.

Banner droned on in his paean to Natasha G.:

". . . and when she couldn't handle the pressure, why, someone was always there with pills or a glass of sherry or, later on, a little potato juice in her orange juice—just for an eye-opener."

Preston had to speak to her, had to imprint himself in her mind as more than a mere handkerchief. But what could he say? All his gambits were twenty years out of date. He bent down and reached over and touched her arm and whispered, "What unit are you in?"

She looked at a white card in her purse and whispered back, "Chaparral."

"Great! That's a great unit. You'll love that unit."

"How long have you been here?"

English! My God, she's English! You heard it: She said "bean," not "bin." "How long have you bean heah?" A blond Vivien Leigh. Be still, my heart!
"Oh . . ." Preston faltered. He needed authority. Seniority. He couldn't tell the truth, couldn't say "eight hours." ". . . a while."

The door behind them opened. Marcia stepped into the room and tapped the woman on the shoulder and beckoned her to follow. She rose and, without looking at Preston, went out into the hall. The door closed behind her.

No! Preston was frantic. *Not before you know how much we have in common. I went to Yale!*

"Today Natasha begins a new life," Banner proclaimed, "and she'll make it because she has new strengths. She has a higher power."

Natasha interrupted on cue. "And my higher power, my friends, my dear, dear friends"—she opened her arms to embrace the universe—"is *you!*"

There was a burst of applause, and someone shouted, "We love you, Natasha!"

"Oh yes," Natasha responded. "The love is flowing between us like a roaring river."

Preston lost control. While everyone applauded again and a few whistled and a couple shouted declarations of love, he slid off his seat and crawled the few feet to the back wall and pushed open the door and squeezed through the opening out into the hall—and found himself staring at a khaki skirt and a pair of coffee-colored knees.

"Hello, Scott," said Marcia.

"Oh. I . . ." He saw the blonde standing beside Marcia. She looked frightened.

She held out his handkerchief and said, "Here. I'm terribly sorry. I didn't mean—"

"No, no." He scrambled to his feet. "I just . . . I mean, I thought you might need some help with your bags."

Marcia said, "I think we can manage."

Code. What she was really saying was: *Never try to shit a shitter.*

"Right," he said. "Well . . ." He held out a hand to the woman. "I'm Scott."

She didn't shake his hand, just gave him his handkerchief. "Priscilla."

"Right. . . . Nice to meet you."

The sounds of applause and cheers came from inside the lecture room.

"You're missing the good part, Scott." Marcia picked up Priscilla's suitcase.

"Right. Well . . ." He turned back toward the door, but he didn't go in. He stood and watched the white linen skirt and the navy blue cashmere sweater and the fall of golden hair follow Marcia down the hall and out into the night. Then he leaned against the wall and pressed his head to the cool plaster. *What are you doing? You are coming apart! You are a married man!*

The door to the lecture room sprang open, and Hector barged out, the flame from his lighter already igniting the cigarette in his mouth and singeing his Zapata mustache. He saw Preston and said, "I know what you mean, man. All that love shit makes me sick too."

Duke came out and grabbed Preston's arm and led him down the hall. "Hey," he said, smiling, "you don't waste time."

"I wasn't—"

"I been trying to figure why a smart guy like you comes to a joint like this. Now I know."

"You do?"

"Damn right. You've found yourself a nookie farm."

At ten o'clock that night, someone—Preston didn't recognize the voice—walked down the corridor and rapped lightly on each door and announced, "Ten o'clock." Whoever it was was this week's Town Crier. Announcing the time twice a day, at bedtime and reveille, was a "therapeutic duty." Each patient was assigned one, to add even more order and discipline to his or her tightly structured day. A list on the bulletin board in the common room had told Preston that this week he was "Hazel"—his duty was to vacuum the hallway outside the bedrooms.

He sat on the edge of the bed, smoking a cigarette. He didn't want the cigarette, it didn't taste good, it burned his throat and fuzzed his tongue. But it was something to do. Smoking passed the time.

He had no radio, no television. They had confiscated his books. His head felt like a crowded subway car, packed with irritable, impatient, uncomfortable people longing to breathe free. Since this morning—this morning! It felt more like a week ago—his brain had been besieged, barraged, battered and overdosed with turmoil, terror and emotion.

He wished he could remove his head and put it in a drawer till morning. *Tell yourself a story. Make up something about a princess with golden hair, trapped in a castle of sorrow.* But he wasn't a storyteller. He was a midwife for other people's stories. He tried to summon from memory parables or sonnets, couplets or limericks—anything to give him remove from his thoughts. All that came to him was a fragment of Yeats:

> *"Never shall a young man,*
> *Thrown into despair*
> *By those honey-colored*
> *Ramparts at your ear,*
> *Love you for yourself alone*
> *And not your yellow hair."*

Useless. Counterproductive. All it did was redirect his brain back to the sorceress who had suddenly . . . what? *Punched me in the soul.*

What must it have been like for her to grow up so lovely? Was there a brain beneath all that beauty? There was pain, certainly, for why else was she here?

He went into the bathroom and flossed and brushed

his teeth. That killed two minutes. He took a leak. Thirty seconds. He returned to the bedroom and had another cigarette. He debated going to sleep. No. If he went to sleep now, he'd be up at four. Two hours to stare at the wall.

Then he remembered the two books Larkin had given him. He had stuffed them into the bureau, behind his shirts. He knew they weren't stories, didn't tell diverting tales of derring-do. But they were words, at least, and maybe they held an anecdote or two. He opened a drawer and shoved aside his shirts.

He left "The Big Book" where it was—he wasn't ready for a lot of A.A. cant—and retrieved the little black *Twenty-four Hours a Day*. He propped up his pillow and leaned against the bedstead and opened the book at random.

January 2: MEDITATION FOR THE DAY

You are so made that you can only carry the weight of twenty-four hours, no more. If you weigh yourself down with the years behind and the days ahead, your back breaks. God has promised to help you with the burdens of the day only. If you are foolish enough to gather again that burden of the past and carry it, then indeed you cannot expect God to help you bear it. So forget that which lies behind you and breathe in the blessing of each new day.

What about accountability? What about promise? What kind of philosophy was this? "Don't blame me; don't expect anything of me."

He turned a bunch of pages.

JULY 27—A.A. THOUGHT FOR THE DAY

To paraphrase the psalm: "We alcoholics declare the power of liquor and drunkenness showeth its handiwork. Day unto day uttereth hangovers and night unto night showeth suffering. The law of A.A. is perfect, converting the drunk. The testimony of A.A. is sure, making wise the simple. The statutes of A.A. are right, rejoicing the heart. The program of A.A. is pure, enlightening the eyes. The fear of the first drink is clean, enduring forever." Have I any doubt about the power of liquor?

" 'Uttereth hangovers?' " Preston said aloud. "Bull-shit, Billy Graham!" He slammed the book and flung it across the room.

Listen to the words: "sure," "perfect," "right." And all stated with the sublime confidence that they had been handed down by A.A.'s number one draft choice, God.

He had been shanghaied into the God Squad.

How could he deal with this? He wasn't even sure there *was* a God. And if there was a God, what was it? Why should it necessarily be some uppercase He? And no matter what it (He, She) was, Preston found it inconceivable that it (He, She) would have the time or the inclination to focus on the petty problems of an aging editor who could no longer drink like a gentleman. As a child, Preston had wept at the unfathomability of infinity because it struck him that if things had no beginning and no end, then the present (meaning his life) had no significance whatsoever in the scheme of things, since in all probability no scheme of things existed. Now he was being com-

manded to communicate with some incredible per-
sonification of the infinite.

Forget it. He had twenty-seven days to go. If people
could endure months of having their toenails torn out
and their balls hot-wired in Argentine jails, he could
survive twenty-seven days of self-righteous blather.

Duke was right: Shut up, hunker down, and when
you get out, just watch where you drink.

The crier passed by his door again, saying, "Ten-
thirty . . . lights out."

Preston stripped to his boxer shorts, climbed into bed
and turned out the light. He had no hope of falling
asleep in this strange bed in this strange place, surrounded by these strange people, and without any
chemical cradle.

He sought a vision that would accompany him into
unconsciousness, something warm and comforting.
Home? No: the scene of the crime. Office? No: a nest
of vipers.

Priscilla. Ah, yes. He pulled the sheet up under his
chin and closed his eyes and smiled.

What room was she in? He decided she was in the
last room on his corridor. He decided that it looked
exactly like his room. He decided that, like him, she
had no roommate, was sleeping alone. And as he was
thinking of her, he decided that she was thinking of
him, wondering who that bizarre, impulsive—but not
unattractive—man was. She had been busy unpacking
and had not had time to undress before the "lights out"
call, so now she was undressing in the moonlight. (Was
there a moon? Who cared? Posit a moon.) The sweater
came off first, then the white silk blouse. The skirt was
unwrapped (Was it a wraparound or a step-in? Never

mind.) and draped over a chair. She kicked off her pumps
and stood in the moonlight in her expensive, sheer, very
brief underwear. White underwear. No. Beige. No. Better still, ivory. Yes, she stood there in her ivory
underwear, just bra and panties, thinking of him. Then
she reached back and unsnapped her bra and let it fall
down her arms, and the moon highlighted her breasts.
(Were they large or small? Sort of medium, between an
orange and a grapefruit, say, artichoke-size, with discreet areolae and dainty nipples which, because she was
thinking of him and sensing that he was thinking of her,
were swelling until now they began to cast their own
shadows.) She hooked her thumbs into the waistband
of her panties and began to peel them down her legs
. . . and suddenly there was a knock on her door and
she hobbled to the door with her panties around her
ankles—why didn't she put something *on*, was she
crazy?—and opened it, and there was Guy Larkin
dressed up like a fireman, complete with slicker and
sloping helmet and fire ax, and he was telling her it was
time for a fire drill and didn't she realize it was dangerous to have her panties down around her ankles,
she'd never be able to run for her life like that, so she
reached for her closet door and presto! Larkin was gone
and she was all dressed again, so she had to start at the
beginning with her sweater . . .

"Yevahsatonanybuddysfuckinhead?"

Preston jerked upright, his hands before him to ward
off a blow. "What? What?"

"I say, yevahsatonanybuddysfuckinhead?"

There was a monster at the door, framed in the dim
light from the corridor.

"What?"

"What the fuck this 'what' shit?" A foot kicked out and slammed the door. A hand brushed a wall switch and turned on an overhead light.

He was six feet tall or more, dark as an old and lovingly tended saddle, perfectly bald. He wore jeans, high-top black sneakers and a white T-shirt. He looked like he was made of whips, for all his sinews stood out in relief against his skin. His eyeballs were the color of rosé wine. Beads of sweat clung to his head like droplets of rain on a waxed car.

"I say one more time, nice and slow: Has you yes or has you no ever sat on anybody's fuckin' *head*?"

"Wha—? No!"

"Well, you gon' have to sit on my fuckin' head lickety-split, 'cause I'm on a *bad* fuckin' jones." He shivered.

"A what?" *Wake up! Lord, let this be Act Two of the dream!*

"Whaffor you keeping whattin' me? You don't know 'bout jones?"

"No!" Preston clutched the sheet to his chest. He wondered if he could make it out the window before this maniac killed him.

"God *damn!*" He kicked the wall. "I *told* them motherfuckers not to put me in with some fuckin' rummy." He kicked the empty bed, jamming it against Preston's. He took a step toward Preston, stabbing a finger at him. His pink eyes were wide, and a rivulet of drool ran down his chin. "Listen up, sumbitch . . ."

Preston dropped the sheet, put a foot onto the floor, guessed that he could make the window in two steps. If he shoved his bed back against the monster's knees . . .

"You get me a junkie in here *now*, else . . ." He stopped and his eyes rolled back and he moaned and grabbed his stomach and began to shake. He tottered, stumbled against the wall, whirled and fell face-forward onto the empty bed.

Preston leaped up, sprinted across the room and yanked open the door. The corridor was empty. He ran into the dark common room. "Help!" he shouted. "Somebody help!"

Somewhere in the building Bruce Springsteen was singing. Preston followed the song to a little office in the back of a dark cul-de-sac he hadn't known was there.

A pudgy young woman with a pockmarked face, wearing a Grateful Dead T-shirt and a name tag and safari shorts with more pockets than a pool table, was sitting at a desk and making notes in the margins of a ratty copy of Erich Fromm's *Beyond the Chains of Illusion*. She looked up as Preston rounded the door.

"I need a junkie!" he gasped.

She smiled. "Are those underpants or a bathing suit?"

Preston looked down, and as he moved, the fly of his boxer shorts opened and the head of his pecker peeked out.

"Underpants," she said.

He covered his crotch. "I need a junkie."

"You've found one." She extended her right arm and pointed to a ladder of scars on the inside of the elbow. "What can I do for you?"

"There's this . . . this *person* . . . who keeps telling me I have to sit on his head because he's got a problem with somebody named Jones."

She laughed and reached across the desk and pulled a clipboard toward her. She ran her finger down a list of names. "You're Scott Preston."

"He's hallucinating!"

"No, he's not. He's just on a bad jones. Let's see . . . Hassan. Khalil Ali Hassan, aka Twist." She pushed the clipboard away. "You don't know about jones?"

"That's what *he* said. Then he kicked the bed. Then he fell down."

"Heroin withdrawal. There's good jones, when you just sort of feel like shit for a while, and bad jones, when you get the shakes and the shivers and the sweats and the pukes and cramps like you can't believe. He won't bother you."

"He wants me to sit on his head!"

"Don't do it. It's a free country."

"He'll kill me!"

"Tell him to fuck off. He gets pushy, smack him in the chops. Shape he's in, one good whack and he'll fold."

Here we go again. The certainty. The cool. The omniscience. He wanted to scream at the woman, to grab her by the throat and force her to dial 911. To *do* something.

But what he did, of course, was lean forward until he could read her name tag and then say, "Miss . . . Sandra . . . I have never hit another human being in my life. I would miss, or I would break my hand, or I would drive him into a homicidal fury."

And what she did, of course, was smile and say, "There's a first time for everything, Scott."

He took a deep breath, not sure that he wouldn't begin to cry, not much caring if he did. "I beg you," he said. "Come with me. Maybe he needs help. I wouldn't know what to do. Maybe he's dead. Come with me."

"Sure, Scott." She stood up. "We aim to please."

As they walked down the corridor, Sandra kept glancing at his shorts. "I've never understood why people wear those underpants," she said. "Doesn't your dick get cold?"

"It isn't outside that much."

"I'd think your rocks'd rattle around, too." They arrived at the door to his room. "Anyway, whatever turns you on. . . ."

Sandra pushed open the door, and Preston followed her inside.

"See?" she said. "Sleeping like a baby."

"He's in my bed."

He was curled up in a fetal ball, the covers pulled over his shoulders. A sweat stain was spreading on the pillow. He was snoring and shaking.

"Tell you what, Scott. You want to move him, move him. But if I were you, I'd sleep in the other bed."

"Yes. Right."

" 'Night, Scott."

"Thank you."

At the door, Sandra turned and said, "Just for safety's sake, put your wallet under your pillow. If he wakes up in the middle of the night and doesn't know where he is, he may get frightened and decide to go over the hill. You never know what he'll want to take with him."

"Right. Good idea. Under the pillow." *That way he'll have to kill me to get my wallet.*

When Sandra had gone, Preston got his wallet from his trousers and tucked it in the waistband of his shorts.

Then he pulled the mattress off the empty bed and dragged it into the bathroom.

It fit, mostly, with one end under the sink and the other curled up against the door.

PART TWO

8

Two on, two out.

Bottom of the third (and last) inning.

Drunks 2, Junkies 1. And hadn't *that* caused an uproar, who'd be a Drunk and who a Junkie. There were barely enough players to make up one team, forget two, and Marcia—chooser of sides and coach of both teams—could hardly put her three star junkies on the same team, not when one, Crosby, had been the National League's MVP two years ago; and another, Twist, had played high-school ball, could bat from either side and had the reflexes of a spider; and the third, Hector, had in batting practice demolished one softball and driven a second so far into the desert that no one could find it. So she had assigned Hector and Twist to the Drunks. Hector hadn't cared ("Long as you don't trade me to the Homos, I don't give a shit"), but Twist had rebelled, claiming that to be called a drunk was damaging to his self-esteem ("A drunk got no self-esteem, he slobbers and falls all over hisself, but a junkie, he got plenty 'cause he just takes hisself to a separate world and leave me be"), and that had led to an argument with Marcia about the nature of chemical dependency and the similarity of different addictions ("It doesn't matter what we call ourselves, our problems are all the same"), with historical references made by Twist to great junkies ("Jimi Hendrix and John Belushi, they died like *men*! They didn't rot away and puke thesselves to death") and Hector countering, "Dead is fuckin' dead and it don't make no difference 'cause either way you don't get no more pussy." Clarence Crosby had offered to give his place on the Junkies to Twist, but Marcia had said no, it was a matter of principle, so Twist had stalked off the field and declared he was "leavin' this fuckin' place 'cause there's discrimination against junkies" and he'd get the court to send him someplace where junkies got a fair shake and didn't have to suck hind tit to a bunch of scumbag drunks. The betting was that Twist would have packed his bag and walked out of the clinic if Preston hadn't come up with the idea that perhaps his roommate might accept the status of "guest star" with the Drunks. Twist had liked the idea, he didn't really want to leave, everybody could see that, but he couldn't give in so easily, so he had said no, he wasn't going to be a star drunk for anybody, so Preston had said how about if he was a "visiting artist" on temporary assignment from the Junkies. That did it. It was probably the "artist" part that appealed to Twist—that and the fact that the compromise had been advanced by Preston, whom Twist had come to revere as the repository of vital and exotic information about things like New York and the stock market and the English language, even though Preston was a weakling and a lush, which didn't matter because Twist had assigned himself the role of Preston's protector and had vowed to rescue him "in case any of these assholes want to make you their girlfriend or something," a circumstance that Preston regarded as about as likely as the Parousia—but, whatever, Twist agreed to pitch for the Drunks. And as Preston took the field—left and center field, to be precise—Marcia had winked at him and patted him on the ass, just like Davey Johnson congratulating Darryl Strawberry.

Preston bent over and socked his glove and shouted, "No batter baby you can do it no batter no batter blow one by him baby no batter . . ."

From his station on the mound Twist turned and glared at Preston. "You off your fuckin' feed, man? *No batter?* This sucker hit thirty-two home runs las' year. He told me hisself. Four a them off Dwight fuckin' Gooden."

Preston hadn't bothered to see who the batter was: Clarence Crosby. He shrugged, waved his glove, socked it again, called back, "Yeah, but he hasn't seen your stuff. Sock it to him, give him the old dipsy-do, no batter baby no batter . . ."

"This sucks," said Twist. He appealed to Dan, who stood ten feet behind the plate as catcher for both teams and umpire. "How 'bout you lemme *pitch* to this man, 'stead of all this underhand sissy stuff?"

"No way," said Dan. "He's already batting left-handed and cross-handed. He's handicapped."

"*You* say," Twist argued. "I seen him bat lefty 'gainst John Tudor one time, blew the man away."

"Ratshit," said Crosby. "I can't hit dick left-handed."

"Yeah, well, dick ain't pitchin' today."

"Play ball," Marcia said from the sidelines. "This is therapy, Twist, not combat."

"For you maybe. It's my self-esteem at risk here."

On second base, Priscilla took a little dancing lead, faking a dash for third. She had closed her eyes and swung at a puffball from Twist and had hit a dribbler down the third-base line. Butterball had charged in from third, tripped on the ball and fallen on it. By the time Twist had rolled her off the ball and thrown it to Duke at first, Priscilla was safe. The next batter, Cheryl, who was so tiny that it would have taken fiber optics to find the strike zone on her, had walked Priscilla to second.

Preston saw the glow of perspiration on Priscilla's calves, and he wanted to run his tongue along the curve of her muscle. He imagined the sweet-and-sour blend of smells beneath her shirt—salt and Opium—and he wanted to climb in there and bask in the scent. *Stop it! Stop torturing yourself!* These thoughts were counterproductive, a waste of time. Worse: They were against the rules. *Thou shalt not covet thy fellow patients. Thou art all brothers and sisters in addiction, and it is a sin to desire to park thy roger in thy sister.* And no matter how clever he thought he was being, no matter how cool and blasé, Marcia—the clinic's one-woman Thought Patrol—always seemed to know what he was thinking. She had warned him twice. Not that anything had happened between him and Priscilla, not that anything was likely to happen—"happen" being the sly euphemism for the commission of the Deed of Darkness—but Marcia had a nose that could sniff out *fleurs du mal* before they bloomed. And of course she was right.

"Yo! Gloria!" Twist glowered at her. "You hie your

little ass back to the base there. Even *think* about stealing on me, I be all over you like drool on a baby.''

Priscilla scurried back to the base and stuck her tongue out at him.

Gloria. Twist had bestowed the name on her after their first hour together in group, after he had returned from a forty-eight-hour de-tox in the medical unit. They had both been assigned to Dan's section, which annoyed Preston because he was convinced that if he hadn't made a fawning, mooning ass of himself over Priscilla on the night of her arrival, Marcia might have brought Priscilla into her section (with Preston), just for the clinical curiosity of seeing how two rich (by her calculations) WASPs would interact in the caldron of the group dynamic.

During a three-week stint as a night watchman at a savings-and-loan (one of twenty-seven jobs he had held over the past three years), Twist had seen a TV miniseries called *Little Gloria, Happy at Last*, about the agonies and travails of Gloria Vanderbilt. For him, it was like watching a story about people from another galaxy.

But as Twist listened to Priscilla tell *her* tale—mother descended from British landed aristocracy whose fortune sprang from a fortuitous backing of the right horse in the seventeenth century (James II), genteelly addicted to sherry and various prescription hypnotics, dazzled by the dashing scion of an American shipping family (not-so-genteelly addicted to sour-mash bourbon), young Priscilla sent to British boarding schools till she was twelve, then, when her parents moved to America, shipped off to a Connecticut prep school with an allowance of one thousand dollars a month (grass,

Quaaludes and Valium available to cope with the pressures of exams), then on to some horseback-riding college with an allowance of five thousand dollars a month (cocaine plentiful to give zip to sex and meaning to the unbearable emptiness of being), charge accounts at every store in the continental United States, a trust fund larger than many municipal budgets, on her own without anybody who gave a damn except to say "How nice, dear," and finally latched onto by a squadron of hippies who gave her a family in return for letting them live on her ranch outside San Francisco and funding their catholic tastes, until one day, in a brief interstice between coke storms, she saw a sheep giving birth and underwent some sort of psychic revelation, as a result of which she drove her Range Rover into town and staggered into her family's law firm (twelve partners and sixteen associates who did nothing but tend to her family's affairs) and announced that unless she was put away somewhere, she was going to hire one of her hippies to shoot her, so here she was, despite her parents' conviction that this was a lot of overreaction (not to mention bad taste) and their publicly stated belief (reiterated and reinforced daily over drinks) that she had gone to a spa to "get it together"—as Twist listened to all this, he realized that *Little Gloria, Happy at Last* wasn't just a load of made-up shit; people from other galaxies *did* exist and here was one right in the room with him, so, naturally enough, this little girl should be called—no, *was*—Gloria.

Priscilla loved the nickname, loved the acceptance it connoted. There was nothing threatening about Twist. He had no carnal ambitions toward her (Hector had once leeringly hinted otherwise and had had to flee for his

life across the quadrangle, shrieking loudly that it was
all a linguistic mix-up, "I no say nothing about licking
her, I say I bet you *like* her, I'm es*pan*ish for crissakes!
Help!"), for it would no more have occurred to Twist
to introduce Priscilla to Lawrence (as in Lawrence of
Arabia, his fond sobriquet for his member) than to try
to fuck a canary. He had no idea how teeny tiny people
from other galaxies reproduced, but for sure it wasn't
by fucking. Twist regarded Priscilla (Gloria) as his pet.
To her, he was a dark angel watching over her.

"Yo baby you're an artist you can do it throw him a
masterpiece." Preston socked his glove again.

"Where did you learn that talk?" Lewis called from
his station in right-center field.

"Made it up. It's easy."

"For you."

"No. It's all bullshit. Try."

"Do I have to say 'baby'?"

"Say anything you want."

Preston saw Lewis blush as he composed the words.

"All right, honey, throw him one," Lewis shouted,
and he grinned at Preston. "Throw him a hot one."

Twist spun and took a step toward the outfield. "Who
you callin' honey?"

"Twist!" Dan yelled from behind the plate. "Pitch
or I'll call a balk."

"This is fun," Lewis said when Twist returned to the
mound, adding, to be sure it was okay to have fun,
"Isn't it?"

"Yeah," Preston said. "It is." Preston paused, startled to realize that in fact he was having fun. It was as
if acknowledging the reality affirmed it. Fun probably
wasn't the point of the game. He was sure there was

some profound therapeutic purpose to it, like establishing community or encouraging the breakdown of inhibitions. But screw all that. It was fun. "It really is."

He *was* enjoying himself, and not only this moment, this afternoon. He felt good, a kind of cleanliness and balance. He had been sober for fourteen days. He was sleeping for seven hours at a stretch—not lying in a coma for four hours and then thrashing around in a sweat for the next three—and was dreaming and now and then actually recalling his dreams. He woke refreshed, confident that he could face the day.

Only once had he found himself longing for a drink, during his session with the clinic's staff psychologist, an enormously fat and insufferably pious young man (early thirties, Preston guessed) whose brass desk plate announced him as "Myron Frost, B.S., M.S., Ph.D."

Granted, Preston hadn't approached the interview with a positive attitude. He disliked psychologists in general, had always thought of them as unctuous and patronizing, like television evangelists. If a man wanted to be called Doctor, Preston thought, let him get an M.D. and a degree in psychiatry.

Granted, too, he had thrown a gauntlet to this particular shrink by introducing himself as "Scott Preston, B.A., M.A.," and by declaring that if the man insisted on being called Dr. Frost, he would prefer to be called Mr. Preston, which precipitated a three-minute exploration of Preston's hostility toward authority. Preston denied harboring any such hostility and explained that he simply saw no reason to accept Frost as an authority on anything just because he appended the entire alphabet to his name, and for all he knew Frost's several degrees were awarded by some diploma mill that advertised on the back of matchbooks.

Frost's job was to analyze the results of the hour-long, 200-question, true-false "psychological-profile test" taken by every patient and, after consultation with the patient, to conclude something definitive about the patient's history of substance abuse, mental stability, susceptibility to extreme emotions like anger, despair and passion, and, finally, the probability of his or her maintaining abstinence in the real world.

Preston had tried to take the test honestly, but some of the questions had taxed his tolerance. In reply to the statement "I believe that cats are stealing my luggage," for example, he had crossed out the true/false options and written, "Only on buses." And to the statement "Water is my enemy" he had answered: "Damn right, and vodka my friend."

Frost opened Preston's file and tapped the answer sheet with his pencil. "Your lack of respect comes through in your answers," he said.

"I don't have much respect for fools," Preston replied, "especially fools with power. Whoever wrote that test is a fool."

"All the questions don't pertain to everybody. They're not meant to. The test has to—"

" 'I believe that grapes are fascist'?" Preston cited from the test.

"Some people believe that."

"Then they don't belong here."

"Who are you to judge?"

"Well, I think it's reasonable to assume that anyone who believes in his heart of hearts that Adolf Hitler was a grape has problems that stopping dope isn't going to solve.''

''So now you're a doctor, are you?''

Preston took a deep breath. ''Look, your worship, let's stop slinging titles and get down to it: What does the test tell you about me?''

''You're arrogant. You think you know it all.''

''Wrong. No, maybe not wrong, but the test doesn't tell you that. You've decided that because I'm being a pain in the ass.''

Frost leaned forward and let his flabby lips part in what passed for a smile. ''I'm used to unhappy patients, Scott. I—''

''Mr. Preston.''

''All right. Mr. Preston. I don't let my personal feelings intrude on my work.''

''Sure. . . . Never mind. Go on.''

''You're a loner. You don't like accepting help and you won't ask for help. You think intelligence is the answer for everything.''

''Nothing new there. Marcia figured all that out in thirty seconds.''

''Do you like Marcia?''

''You bet.''

''Why?''

''She's smart, she's honest, she doesn't make moral judgments. She is one terrific teacher.''

''She's black.''

''No kidding.''

''How do you feel about blacks?'' That same flabby smile again.

''I don't feel about blacks. I feel about people.''

''How does she feel about whites?''

"How the hell should I know?" *What is this man doing?* "Hey listen, Sigmund . . ."

Frost waved his hand and looked down at the test sheet, withdrawing the question, dismissing the issue. "There's one very serious thing I should warn you about," he said, looking up. "I think you're in danger of committing suicide."

"What?" Preston started out of his chair, then sat back. "That's horseshit and you know it. You have to tell me that. You have to tell everybody that."

"I do? Why?"

"Because everybody here has to be convinced that they're terminal. If they drink again, if they use again, if they so much as utter the words 'dry martini on the rocks' or 'cut me a line,' they're gonna die, from cirrhosis or AIDS or catching fire or sucking on the barrel of a gun. It's your franchise, dealing in absolutes."

Frost shook his head. "The pattern is very clear." He tapped the answer sheet again. "You show all the signs of someone in danger of killing himself."

"I see." Preston gripped the seat of his chair, squeezing the rage into his fingertips to keep it out of his voice. "Could you tell me which answers led you to that fine conclusion?"

"None in particular. As I say, it's a pattern. But it's very clear."

"To you."

"Yes."

"Because you're trained."

"Well, yes."

"And you're going to put that in my file."

"I am. I have."

"Dr. Frost," Preston said, and slowly he stood up.

"I'm leaving now, because if I don't I may prove you wrong and commit not suicide but homicide."

Frost gave a little jump. One hand moved to the edge of his desk. "I think we should talk about your anger."

There's a button under there. He pushes it and in comes the SWAT team.

Preston walked to the door. "I didn't have any anger till I came in here, so I know where it comes from and I know what it's directed at. It's very well focused."

"All right. We'll talk again, Scott. Meanwhile, think about what I said. I worry about you. I think you're a potential suicide."

"I worry about you, too, Doctor. I think you're a terminal asshole."

Outside in the corridor, Preston looked at a water cooler and fantasized that its pipes were full of Stolichnaya, and he drank deep.

Otherwise, the desire for the solace of booze hadn't occurred to him. Perhaps it was because in this artificial environment his entire existence was concentrated on the avoidance of alcohol. Perhaps it was because no problem—no tension, no anxiety, no worry—was permitted to fester long enough to require suppression. Everything was talked about immediately and exhaustively. Marcia's perceptions about him were spooky: He could hide nothing from her. She read his face and his voice, his answers and his silences, and she drew conversation from him as a tick draws blood from a dog.

He had called her on it one day, suggesting jocularly that she had implanted herself in his brain like a monitoring device.

All she said was "Say hello to your higher power, Scott."

"What, you mean God?"

"Not necessarily. Communication. Realizing you're not alone in the universe. Taking sustenance from other people. That's all the higher power has to be."

"I don't get it."

"You will."

Perhaps it was the friends he had made, all of whom shared the same basic problem he had, all of whom talked about it constantly and without embarrassment. With glee, even. Duke, who delighted in horror stories—the gorier the better—and who had taken to embellishing his own to keep up with his fellows, while continuing to deny that he had a problem (he was just unlucky). Twist, whose disdain for drunks was beginning to be tempered by amusement—he thought they were like performing seals—though he still declined to acknowledge that they shared his purity of addiction. Priscilla. Priscilla was . . . was what? Despite the technical innocence of their relationship, Preston knew that Priscilla could become—was beginning to be, might already . . . *say it!* . . . damn well *was*—a problem.

He had called home only once, after the mandatory five-day waiting period—they knew that if they allowed you to call in the first day or two all you'd do was bitch and moan and beg the folks at home to get you *out* of here because you were being tortured by a cult of religious fanatics. He hadn't given any thought to the call before he placed it. Why should he? He was the warrior calling home from the front, the loved one locked in durance vile, the adventurer reporting back from unknown shores of spiritual antipodes. Surely they were eager for contact with him.

Kimberly answered the phone and squealed and said,

"Daddy! How you *doing*?" and "That's great!" and "Hey listen, I'd love to chat but I gotta go to study group 'cause we have this *awesome* chemistry test on Friday and if I don't get at least a B-minus we can just for*get* Brown or Penn or Middlebury, so keep it up, Dad, we miss you like mad, kiss-kiss," and she passed the phone to Margaret.

Margaret had been waiting to hear from him. She needed to know where he kept the spare keys for the Volvo, which account she was supposed to deposit his paycheck in, whether she had to file new claim forms every time Kimberly had adjustments done on her braces or could send the bill to the insurance company, what she was supposed to tell Tom Trowbridge about why he would have to miss the next four Sunday doubles games at the club ("It would have helped if you'd called him yourself and told him," she said. He said, "I didn't exactly have time. This was all pretty sudden." She said, "You could have called from the airport." He said, "I wasn't thinking about tennis." She said, "Well, you could call him now and save me the trouble." He said, "Okay, I will. I'll tell him I'm on a business trip." She said, "Fine. If that's not asking too much") and whether it was Tuesday and Friday nights that the garbage cans were put out at the end of the driveway or Monday and Thursday nights.

At last, she said, "How are you?"

And he said, "Fine. How are you?"

And she said, "As well as can be expected."

Whatever that meant.

And they hung up.

Preston was hurt and confused. It had never occurred to him that they would write him off, that they had agreed between themselves (probably without ever exchanging a word about it) that the best way to cope with this unseemly interstice in their lives was to pretend that he did not exist, or at least that he had been removed to some dead zone from which nothing he thought, said or did could touch them. He empathized, sort of: They did not understand his affliction, they could not help him and they were not so masochistic as to want to share his pain even if they could, which they couldn't. Besides, they were, presumably, still angry, still resentful. He wondered how they would respond to the summons to come to Family Week, to the invitation to spend a thousand dollars to travel two thousand miles for the pleasure of regurgitating all their anger before a gathering of strangers. He wondered *if* they would respond. He hoped they wouldn't. He could survive without a replay of the scene in his office, thanks awfully.

Preston turned the phone over to Hector, and the farther he walked away from it, the more his anger ebbed. The Volvo keys and the orthodontist and the tennis game evanesced like smoke rings. He didn't have anything to worry about here but himself—a sick thought, perhaps, but then, that was the point. He was sick. He thought for the first time, *I am glad to be here.*

Priscilla shouted at Twist, "Come on, tall dark and gorgeous, throw the effing ball!"

"Watch you mouth, Gloria," Twist growled at her, "or I hit you upside you effin' head." Then he guffawed. "*Effin' head!* I *love* it!" He turned back to face the batter and said, "Okay, sumbitch, here come Dr. Doom."

Clarence Crosby, who had been sitting on his bat as if it were a shooting stick, yawned with theatrical ennui. "Oh, we playin' ball today?" He stood up and waved the bat over the plate.

Twist glowered at the plate, squinted as if receiving a sign from Dan, shook it off contemptuously, nodded at its imagined substitute, straightened up, shot minatory glances at first and second bases, windmilled his arm—once, twice, thrice—and fired a sidearm bullet at Crosby.

To a man accustomed to seeing smaller, lighter missiles thrown at him at speeds of up to ninety-five miles an hour—balls that danced and jiggled, rose, fell and yawed—Twist's pitch was a floating white marshmallow. Crosby reared back on his left leg, pushed off and swung. He'd drive this sucker all the way to Santa Fe.

But because he was batting cross-handed, his reflexive impulse to pull with his right hand and push with his left caused the bat to drop a few centimeters, so it made contact not dead-center but on the lower quadrant of the ball, and instead of disappearing at a forty-five-degree angle into the distant cactus and tumbleweed, the ball arced upward toward the stratosphere.

"Shit!" Crosby said, forgetting where he was and assuming that anyone sober enough to draw breath could catch the ball and end the game. He tossed his bat and trotted toward first base.

Preston saw the ball soar into the sky over right field. He saw that Lewis saw it too, saw Lewis's head loll back and his mouth drop open as he watched the ball climb toward the sun.

"Lewis!" he called. "Yours!"

But Lewis had taken root in the ryegrass.

Preston started to run. The ball was still climbing,

so maybe he could make it from left field to right before it fell.

The ball reached its apogee and seemed to hang for an instant before it began to plummet.

And then Lewis ran. His arms flapped like the wings of a startled egret. His feet were splayed like a duck's. He cried out, "Oh my! Oh my!" When he reached the general area where the ball would surely fall, he scuttled in tight circles, his arms stretched heavenward as if he were praying for rain.

Preston saw that he could not reach Lewis before the ball or the ball before Lewis, so he stopped, and in one of those rare moments of comprehensive clarity his brain registered a framed scene and saw in it both the immediate future and the distant past. Lewis stood like an orant; the ball descended upon him, still accelerating, and Lewis made no adjustment to catch it, for never in his life had he had to catch a fly ball. He had never thrown a ball with his father, never had friends to play catch with. He had the hand-eye coordination of an infant.

"Lewis!" Preston called. "No!"

The ball passed between Lewis's hands and struck him on the top of the head and bounced off onto the grass.

For a second Lewis stood, and his head swiveled toward Preston and there was a look of bewilderment in his eyes.

Then, like a poleaxed buffalo, he fell face down and lay still.

Priscilla ran from second base, Cheryl and Duke from first, Marcia from beside home plate.

Preston reached him first. He knelt beside him and

saw that he was breathing. But there was dirt in his mouth and on his nose, so Preston rolled him over and sat down and rested Lewis's head in his lap.

"Don't move him!" someone shouted.

Someone else yelled, "Call the doctor!"

By the time Preston had wiped away the dirt, he and Lewis were surrounded by a circle of mourners.

"He dead yet?" asked Hector.

"Nah," said Crosby. "It was a lousy pop fly."

"Don't die, Lewis," Cheryl said. "I couldn't stand it."

Preston stroked Lewis's forehead. "He's not gonna die. Are you, Lewis?"

Lewis moaned. His eyelids fluttered and opened, and he saw the faces staring down at him. He looked up at Preston, and Preston smiled.

"Did I catch it?" Lewis said.

Crosby said, "Yeah. I was out by a mile."

Twist looked quizzically at Crosby, then said, "Fuckin' A . . ."

Lewis lay in Preston's lap, and his eyes traveled from face to face. Then they filled with tears, and the tears spilled over and ran down his cheeks.

"Hurts, huh?" Preston said.

"The fuck you think, man?" said Twist. "Get bopped in the gourd like that."

"No," Lewis said. "No. It's . . ." He sniffled and choked on a sob. He raised a hand and gestured at them all, and through his tears he grinned. "Nobody's ever cared for me before. I'm so . . . happy."

Cheryl laughed and dropped to her knees and hugged Lewis. Lewis took one of Preston's hands and pressed it to his cheek.

As in the stories of dying people who have out-of-body experiences and see themselves at the moment of death, so Preston imagined himself distanced from this tableau. *What am I doing? This can't be me.*

He looked up and saw Marcia. She was smiling at him, and when their eyes met she raised a hand and gave him a thumbs-up sign.

9

"I'VE JUST DECIDED something," Priscilla said.

"Oh?" Preston held his breath as he awaited her latest epiphany. He never knew what would come out of her exquisite mouth. One night it had been "I think I love you a little, but it doesn't mean anything because nothing's real here." Another night she had said, "I'm not sure if God puts people like me on earth as a trial for people like my parents, or if it's the other way around."

They were in the desert, outside the boundaries of the clinic, and the night was so clear that Preston could believe that every star of every description that had ever been—quasars and pulsars, supernovas and giant dwarfs (whatever the hell any of them actually were)—had been convened to shine down upon them.

They were not supposed to be together. They had signed out separately for brief, solitary "meditation walks," permitted between the evening lecture and bedtime, and had left the unit at different times and by different exits. As usual, they had met in the shadows by one of the duck ponds and had begun a languid circuit of the grounds.

And as usual, Priscilla walked holding not Preston's hand but one of his fingers, which now and then she squeezed to punctuate something she said.

The walks had begun with a chance meeting—Preston strolling aimlessly outside as an alternative to the numbing, soporific boredom of reading *Twenty-four Hours a Day* or "The Big Book," or listening to Twist detail the manifold victories to which he had led Lawrence in the vineyards of snatch. He had found Priscilla kneeling alone, letting grains of sand run through her fingers as she wept at some cosmic loneliness she couldn't comprehend. He had said little that first night, had been thrilled to be with her and to let her talk and to murmur empathetic things that had encouraged her to accept a bond between them. For all he knew, she was so vulnerable she would have responded to a friendly lizard. He didn't care.

By now, the walks had become cherished times of discovery. Priscilla's family code had forbidden the expression of feelings, and so, over the years, the unused muscles of her emotional center had atrophied. Those extremes she could not control she suppressed chemically. Now for the first time she was exercising those muscles, and like a paraplegic relearning to walk, each new step was an experience of sublime joy. Nor had she ever been encouraged to have opinions: What possible good could they do her, went the logic, when everything of importance in her life was decided for her by parents and lawyers and accountants? Suddenly in Preston she had found someone who asked what she thought about things, who listened, who commented, who cared. In the beginning, of course, she hadn't thought much about anything, so Preston had urged her to analyze and appraise and come to conclusions, and now as she developed opinions she collected them and prized them, as if each were a child to which she had given miraculous birth.

Preston was utterly smitten with her. That was the word he had lit upon: "smitten." He had never contemplated the word "love." Love was out of the ken of aging farts like him, something (like acne) reserved for the young and callow. Besides, what was there to be in love with? His role as Pygmalion to her Galatea? No, he didn't have that kind of ego. Her sweetness and innocence? If that was all you wanted, you might as well buy a puppy. Sure, he loved her beauty, but how do you actually *love* beauty? Hang it on the wall and adore the bejesus out of it? What had smitten him, he thought, what had captivated and transfixed and obsessed him, was an amorphous quality Priscilla represented, a resurrection of his dreams, a tantalizing echo of what might have been.

He refused to consider the possibility that what might have been could yet one day be, for this was an infatuation like that experienced by teenagers on spring-break cruises. She was right: Nothing was real here. Reality was Volvo keys and dental bills, commuter trains and cranky parents. An emotion born in a fantasy land had no future except as a fantasy.

Right?

Maybe.

So what? One day at a time, they said, and that's how he was living it.

"Yes." She squeezed his finger. "I've decided that happiness isn't having more. It's wanting less."

"That's nice."

"I may have read it, but I think I just made it up. Anyway, it's true." She smiled at her own decisiveness. "All my life, the people who've wanted me to be happy—and my parents really do want me to be happy, I know they do, even though I'm beginning to think that maybe it's because if I'm happy that proves they're good parents and they can chalk it off like it's another chit they've earned at the club, they've passed Parenting— they've always begged me, 'Just tell us what you *want*.' I never knew how to ask for what I wanted, 'cause I never knew what it was, so I'd think up things and convince myself I wanted them, like cars or horses or who cares, and everybody, myself included, would be disappointed when I didn't bubble over like Shirley Temple—one of my doctors made me watch all her movies to learn what happy was—and now here I am without anything, I mean without any *thing*, and I think I'm happy."

"It can't only be not having something that makes you happy," he said. "You must have found *some*thing you didn't have before."

"A friend." She squeezed his finger again. "My truest friend ever."

This woman is ten years old! Preston hated his thoughts. They were making him feel like a child-abuser. He wanted to say, Doesn't that confuse the female in you? Doesn't it make your guts rumble? It sure confuses *me*. My own pitiful version of Twist's mighty Lawrence feels like he's being whipsawed between heaven and hell.

But he was ready to say none of those things. He was searching for a less dangerous response when she rescued him.

"You know what made me think all that stuff?" She pointed up at the mountaintop on which Stone Banner's white redoubt glowed in the starlight like a fairy-tale castle. "Do you think Mr. Banner is happy, up there alone with everything anybody could ever want?"

"Who knows what makes him happy? He's helped a lot of people. Maybe there's comfort in that."

"I wonder if he has a friend."

"What makes you think he's alone? I'll bet he—"

"He told me."

"He . . . *when?*"

"The other day. He stopped me in the hall. He sure is handsome."

A sack of ball-bearings dropped into the pit of Preston's stomach—dense, incredibly heavy pellets of jealousy. "What did he say?"

"Not much. Just that he sometimes holds A.A. meetings up at his house on Sundays to—the way he said it—ward off the lonelies. He said maybe I'd come up sometime."

"Don't go." The flat command in Preston's voice surprised him.

"Why not?"

Because I don't want you to! "Because . . . because . . . You don't really believe he's alone, do you? He's probably got a flock of bimbos up there catering to his every whim."

Priscilla was silent for a moment as they reached the apex of their walk and turned back toward the clinic.

Then she said, "Sex is a bummer."

"It is?"

"It's just a way for people to show who's boss."

"You've decided that."

"That's how it's always been for me. People've always wanted to . . . to do it . . . to me just to show they can."

"It doesn't have to be that way."

"That's what Barbara Cartland says, but she isn't real either."

By the time they reached the point where they would part to reenter the building by the doors through which they had left, Priscilla was not holding his finger, was barely grazing it with the tips of her own. She seemed subdued, either confused or depressed.

They stopped, and Preston said, "See you."

She gripped his finger again. "Would you kiss me?"

"Wh—? . . . I mean, sure. But why?"

She smiled at him. "What a silly question. Because I'd like you to."

"To prove it doesn't have to be that way?"

"This isn't sex, dopey. It's friendship."

Oh yeah? I put my mouth on yours, and feel your lips, and taste you, and this isn't sex? What is it, cribbage?

"Okay."

He bent down to her and put a hand gently on her cheek and the other index finger under her chin and tilted her head up to him. His lips, open, touched hers, closed, and he smelled Opium and dared his tongue to caress the softest—

A light exploded in his face, and a voice shouted, "Hold it right there, Jack!"

They jerked apart and turned and blinked into the beam of a flashlight.

"Who the fuck are you?" said Preston, opting for aggression over submission.

"The nightmare in your wet dream," said the voice, which sounded young but bloated with a cockiness that came (Preston guessed) from the armor of a badge and a gun.

The light swung around and passed quickly over a tubby figure in a security guard's uniform. From its hip was slung a revolver that would have made Clint Eastwood walk with a list. Then the light swung back again to Preston and Priscilla.

"What do you want?" Preston asked.

"It ain't what I want, bub. It's what you want, and it looks like you ain't gettin' any. Not tonight. What's your name?"

Priscilla said, "That's disgusting."

"May be, honey, but you were the one kissing it."

Preston said, "This is absurd. I was kissing my friend good night."

"I don't blame you. What's your name?"

Preston paused. "Harry Reems."

The guard thought for a beat, then said, "Bullshit. Harry Reems ain't here. I'da noticed."

"Scott Preston," Priscilla said imperiously. "My name is Priscilla Godfrey. And I find this whole business in very bad taste."

"That's your problem."

Preston heard the scratch of a pencil on notepaper.

Priscilla said, "What's *your* name?"

"What's my name got to do with it?"

"I intend to report this incident."

"That's *my* job!"

"Then we'll both report it, and we'll see whom the district attorney believes."

"The *what*?"

Priscilla held out her hand to Preston. "Good night, Scott," she said. "Thank you for the walk." She turned and marched toward the clinic.

The light followed her, and Preston in his darkness heard the guard mutter, "Holy shit!"

Marcia awoke, wrenched from her sexy dream by the rush of water and clunk of plumbing from the toilet in the apartment next door. She didn't bother to look at the clock on the bedside table. It was 5:45 A.M. It was *always* 5:45 A.M. exactly when the short-order cook in the apartment next door exploded in a carnival of excretions.

Marcia had long ago concluded that the man's peristalsis was run by a quartz movement, and that his toilet functioned on a Jeep transmission.

She looked over at Dan, debating whether or not to wake him and use him to finish off her dream with a dash of the real thing. He slept on his back, his mouth open, his eyes never completely closed. A sliver of white eyeball showed between the lids. He looked dead.

One appetite soured, others clamored for attention. Her bladder suddenly felt full. Her mouth yearned for the bitter balm of coffee. And though the prospect of running made her knees and ankles ache, she had been clean long enough not to doubt the tonic that exercise would give her. Get the beta endorphins pumping early on, and she could deal with whatever the day threw at her. Miss them, and every minor glitch would summon forth an imp to taunt her from the alleys of her mind, begging her to ease the pain with just one drink, just one pill.

As she sat on the john, she tried to remember what time last night she had had her last pee. It seemed that the intervals between urgent pees were growing shorter, that she couldn't hold her water the way she used to. Not surprising. Her kidneys probably looked like used Brillo pads, after twenty years of fighting toxic chemicals. Damage done is damage done. What would it be like in five years? Would she be peeing every five minutes? Have to wear a bag?

Probably.

Stupid bitch.

Stop it!

Destructive thinking. Which leads to despair. Which leads to hopelessness. Which leads to . . . Hell, why not have a couple of short ones, take your mind off it awhile?

She laughed aloud, amused and amazed at the relentlessness of the demon that would live forever within her, pleased and grateful that she recognized all its cues and could parry every thrust.

No. Not every thrust. Never say "every." Never get cocky, or one day you'll wake up on the floor of some gin mill and say to yourself, How did *that* happen?

"Good morning to you too, you devious bastard," she said to the demon, and she stood up and flushed the toilet and pulled on her running shorts.

She didn't bother to lock the door as she left the apartment. She hadn't seen the key in months, assumed she had lost it, and besides, keys were a sour little joke to the residents of the Montevista condominium units.

The locks were about as secure as Sesame Street lunch-boxes, and every door in the place could be opened with a harsh word. (Those who had gone to the trouble of installing dead-bolt locks had found them neatly and completely removed, a procedure that required no surgical skills since the doors in every unit were made of two layers of pressed fiberboard with hollow space between.) Security in Montevista was maintained by a simple principle: If you don't own anything worth stealing, nobody will steal it. When Marcia had first moved in, she had owned a Sony Worldband radio, a JVC VCR and a Panasonic color television, as well as various items of jewelry of some intrinsic (but mostly sentimental) value. All had vanished within a week, and she had then had to endure the initiation rite of visits by several cluck-clucking neighbors who recited the facts of life in Montevista. Now she owned a ten-dollar radio and an old black-and-white TV, and when she and Dan wanted to watch a videotape, they rented a VCR with the tape.

It was not only abject surrender that had made the neighborhood quite safe. There was also a pervasive attitude of Enough Is Enough, as if the community had concluded that it had done its part to accommodate the Dark Side, and now it deserved to be left alone. One night a pair of drunken thugs had mugged a couple in front of their building. The couple's cries awakened some neighbors, and before the muggers could reach the end of the block they had been bludgeoned senseless with baseball bats.

Marcia walked out onto the stoop in the chill blue morning, careful as always to avoid the crumbling sandstone of the second and fourth steps and to check for rats breakfasting on the uncollected garbage beneath the stoop. She took a couple of deep breaths and began to lope along the sidewalk.

Trained though she was to ward off black thoughts, to search for the tiniest thread of gold in every cloak of dross, her day inevitably began in a mist of gloom. She didn't know why. Perhaps it was the nature of addictive personalities to look on the down side of everything, to regard the proverbial glass as always half empty, not half full. Perhaps that was why they turned to chemicals, to bring them up to a healthy level of optimism. Or perhaps it was the old cliché that the trouble with being sober was that when you woke up in the morning, you knew that this was as good as you were going to feel all day long. Whatever, it always took her several minutes to slip into the rhythm of running, to get her mind to drift, and those moments were assaulted by the nasty reality of the 140 units of the Montevista condominiums, followed by the rest of the dusty, dirty little town of Tesoro, New Mexico.

It wasn't that this was a poverty pocket, far from it. It wasn't Appalachia or Harlem or some Cleveland ghetto. There was no unemployment here. People made a living: eighteen, twenty-two, maybe even thirty thousand a year. A used car in every garage. They were teachers and mechanics, waitresses and truckdrivers, bartenders and nurses and shoe clerks and . . . substance-abuse counselors. The rocks on which the society was built. And the society, in its wisdom, didn't value them much. Nobody was *going* anywhere. This was all there was, this was as good as it got. Live for today, because tomorrow's going to be just the same. No future to hope for.

What the society seemed to value—from what you read, anyway—was stockbrokers and bond traders and lawyers and movie stars and hockey players, people who generated money without producing anything of substance, people who sat back East and got rich by being limited partners in tax-shelter scams like the Montevista condominiums in Tesoro.

Stop feeling sorry for yourself!

She turned the corner by the lumberyard and ran past Manny's Hermosa Cafe, whose *huevos rancheros* did a better job than Drāno in cleaning out your plumbing. She was beginning to feel suffused with the crisp, clean air, and the grimy cloud was dissipating.

Nobody had forced her to ingest every chemical combination known to science, or to drink every liquid fermented from malt, rye, barley, wheat and potatoes. Nobody had whipped her into being a counselor. Being a counselor was her life insurance.

She was doing okay: twenty-four thousand, plus full medical and dental, plus retirement at half pay after twenty-five years. Dan did about the same. Of course, they'd do better if—as Dan kept suggesting—they actually moved in together. Save about a thousand a month, what with cutting one rent and one set of utilities. But— as she kept responding and he refused to believe—they'd do better for about fifteen minutes, until Stone Banner (or, just as bad, anyone on his board of directors, a roster of worthies that included two retired studio executives, two defeated senators and three professional-team owners, one each from the AFC, the NFC and the NBA) found out about the arrangement, and then they'd both be on the street and scavenging for food stamps.

Dan was sweet, but he was an unregenerate flower child. He didn't realize that peace and love had been nailed into their coffins by James Earl Ray and Lee Harvey Oswald.

She was cruising easily as she passed the Señorita Linda Beauty Salon. She had gone a mile. By her training schedule—two hundred yards for every cigarette she smoked the day before—she had about a mile and a half to go.

The formula was idiotic, self-deceptive, self-destructive.

But then, that's what being a junkie was all about.

When she returned, Dan was in the shower. Marcia poured herself a cup of coffee and turned on *Good Morning America*. A reporter was interviewing a prostitute at a hookers' convention in Las Vegas. The topic: techniques of safe sex in the age of AIDS. All very decorous, the reporter red-faced and squirming as he tried to construct clinical questions out of euphemisms.

Another thing to be grateful for. When Marcia was hooking, AIDS didn't exist in humans. Patient number one hadn't yet screwed the monkey, if that was really how it had jumped from apes to people. If AIDS had been around, by now she'd be one more Jane Doe rotting in a potter's field somewhere.

Speaking of sex . . . maybe she'd go join Dan in the shower. Always a good way to start the day. Better than a Bloody Mary.

The phone rang. She thought of not answering it. She hated the telephone. It was a bearer of bad tidings, especially at seven in the morning. The best she could hope for was a wrong number, or maybe a computer offering free dance lessons.

As she listened to the caller from the clinic, all her lubricious thoughts seeped away. Her work day had begun.

"Who was that?" Dan came out of the bathroom, buck-naked and scrubbing his hair dry.

"Your princess and my Yalie have been at it again."

"What happened?"

"Security guard caught them necking in the desert last night."

Dan draped the towel over his shoulder and filled a coffee cup. "I thought you talked to him."

"Twice! I leaned all over him, told him he was victimizing her, told him no matter what she looks like she's really about twelve, gave him the whole arrested-development number, told him what he's doing is hitting on his daughter."

"You think it's true?"

She shrugged. "I'm not a shrink. I just wanted to disgust him. WASPs disgust real easy."

"And he said . . . ?"

"Denied everything. Fucker's a master of denial. Reminds me he's married, Priscilla's just a friend, what's wrong with having a girl as a friend, they haven't *done* anything, not going to *do* anything . . . He won't admit his marriage has already hit the iceberg and it's probably too late to keep it from going to the bottom."

"He can mess her up something fierce . . ."

"You think I don't know that?"

". . . playing his sophisticated games with her. They don't mean anything to him, but she's like a Vietnam boat person landing in San Francisco. New rules, new world. You tell her black's white, she'll kiss your hand

and follow you anywhere. She's probably already made him her father and her brother. It's no big step to—"

"I know. And they leave here and he goes back East and there it is again: The world has fucked her over."

"You got to throw him out."

She paused. "Not yet."

"Then *when*?" Dan shouted. "After he's humped her in the bushes? He's got no right to wreck her head. That's the rule and you know it: Kill yourself if you want, but you're not taking anybody with you."

"First I want to make sure what really happened. Some of those security guards shouldn't be allowed to play with anything more complicated than a coconut. Then I'll have one last talk with Joe Ivy."

"Talking to him's a waste of time. You just said so."

Marcia shook her head. "Trying to embarrass him's a waste of time. Now I'm gonna scare him."

"What, threaten to throw him out?"

"Worse." She kicked off her running shoes and walked into the bathroom.

She was at the front door, on her way out to her car, when she noticed the package on the floor. "What's this?" she called to Dan, who was in the living room reading the paper and having a last cup of coffee. She always left the building ten minutes before he did—a precaution lest someone from the clinic, a janitor or a cook or another counselor, should drive by and see them leaving together. Dan's own apartment was two buildings down the road in the Montevista complex, but the buildings were identical and only a dedicated sleuth would have remarked that he seemed to be coming out of the wrong one.

"What?"

"This package."

"It came while you were in the shower."

"He came to the door?"

"He rang from downstairs. I buzzed him up."

"What did he say?"

"Nothing. He just wanted to be sure this was your apartment."

"You signed for it?"

"Of course."

"With your name?"

"What did you want me to sign?" He chuckled. "George Bush?"

Marcia picked up the package and looked at it. Anger and fear rose together inside her like a bilious stew. She carried the package into the living room, dropped it on the coffee table and sat beside Dan on the couch. She wanted to slap him, to shriek at him, to grab him by the throat and terrify him. But he was trained to dismiss hysterical theatrics, so she swallowed her anger and clenched her fists so hard that she drove her fingernails into her palms, and she spoke in a soft, controlled, superficially loving but profoundly condescending voice.

"Daniel . . ."

"Hmmmm?" He was reading the basketball line scores.

"Why is it we play hide-and-seek about living together?"

"For heaven's sake, Marcia. . . ." He glanced up from the paper. "We've been through this—" He stopped, seeing the intensity in her eyes. He sighed. "Okay. I say it's because we're not married. We live in a conservative, blue-collar community, and people who live together are sinners. You say it's because we're . . . we're—''

"An Oreo cookie. You are white, a card-carrying member of the master race, and I am of the Negro persuasion. In the good old days, right-thinking people would have hanged us by the neck until we were dead. Now, in the age of enlightenment, they might settle for burning down our house and riding us out of town on a rail, covered with tar and feathers.''

"And I say you're being paranoid. No one gives a hoot. They're too wrapped up in car payments and overdue rent and how to feed their kids and—''

"Wrong. When things are bad and there's nothing they can do about it and they can't figure out why they're getting shafted, people blame dragons. Jews are dragons. Blacks are dragons. *We're* dragons.''

"You're crazy.''

"Am I?'' Marcia paused. She closed her eyes and squeezed the bridge of her nose, searching for a new tack. "Okay,'' she said after a moment. "Forget our landlord. Forget our neighbors. What about the people at Banner? The board. Remember, these are people who think civil rights means the right to keep slaves.''

"How could they find out?''

"You don't think they'd care enough to do their very best? To find out, I mean.''

"How could they?''

Marcia picked the package off the coffee table and placed it between them on the couch. "The guy who delivered this, what was he, UPS?''

"I don't know.''

"Did he wear a uniform?''

"I didn't notice.''

"Do I order a lot of stuff from the Sharper Image?"

"How should I know? I don't—"

"What do I need from the Sharper fucking Image?" Her anger overflowed. "An electric fork? A nuclear-powered razor? You see me throwing my goddam money down the toilet?"

"What's the *matter* with you?"

"Look at the package, Dan." She held it up and pressed it to his face. "Look at it."

He pushed it away. "I see it."

"We're in the last few years of the twentieth century. Computers run our lives."

"So?"

"When was the last time you saw an address label from a corporation that probably does fifty million dollars a year . . . when was the last time you saw an address label from a company like that *handwritten*?"

Dan looked again at the package. He said nothing, nothing at all.

10

PRESTON WAS LATE, the last to arrive in Chaparral's lounge area, and all the chairs, couches, bean-bag pillows and squooshy cushions were filled. The members of both therapy groups were there, assembled to celebrate Lewis, who sat on the throne of honor: a Windsor chair placed in the center of the room. Lewis wore white espadrilles, no socks, white ducks, a red-and-white candy-cane-striped silk shirt and a red silk neckerchief knotted at the side. He was trying to look serious, but he couldn't stop grinning and touching his hair.

Preston thought Lewis looked like a waiter at a pretentious New Hope restaurant, one of those androgynous types who come to your table and say, "Good evening, my name is Sean, I'll be your waiter tonight. Before I take your beverage order, may I tell you our chef's specials?" and then reels off the entire menu from memory, including the things nobody ever eats, like brains in black butter and squid in its own ink, and then ends with a flourish as if expecting applause for reciting the whole damn Koran without a mistake.

It was an uncharitable thought. Lewis was a nice guy, genuinely and unselfishly nice. He was graduating. Let him have his moment.

But Preston didn't feel charitable. He felt empty, wasted, which wasn't surprising since he had spent the past ten minutes clutching the rim of a toilet bowl and puking up his guts, out of . . . what? Fear? Anger? Resentment? Frustration? He didn't know and at the moment didn't care, but whatever it was had come on him like a stroke or a seizure, had caused him to lurch out of Marcia's office and bolt for the john. He had stopped in his room to wash his face and brush his teeth, which was why he was late.

Marcia hadn't begun to speak, but she was already circling Lewis like an auctioneer at a cattle sale. Preston knew she saw him come in, wouldn't have been surprised if she fired a lethal dart at him, but she ignored him as he looked around for an empty seat, didn't find one and so sagged down onto the carpet and leaned up against a wall at the back of the room. He assumed Priscilla was somewhere in the room, but he didn't look for her. He was curious—*curious?* frantic!—to know if she, too, had been subjected to an inquisition, but not desperate enough to risk eye contact with her. He didn't need another session with Savonarola just yet.

"Dearly beloved," Marcia began solemnly, "we are gathered here because"—here she smiled and stamped her foot and gave herself a high-five—"because, god-*damn*itall, Lewis has made it!" She applauded and everyone applauded with her. Lewis blushed, and one of his hands fluttered over his hair like a hummingbird.

"You may wonder why it's so amazing," Marcia continued. "After all, a lot of people make it through Banner, and some of them actually stay clean. Lemme tell you what we saw, I mean Dan and I, when Lewis got here. Here was a man with two and a half strikes against him. He's a rummy, he's gay and he hates himself for being both. It's all his fault. He's worthless, lower than snail shit, and his Significant Other—not exactly a straight shooter himself—gets his jollies by convincing Lewis that he's right: He *is* worthless."

Significant Other. Preston smiled and stopped listening to Marcia's account of Lewis's ascent from the slough of self-hatred. Of all the in-group terms, all the A.A. bumper-sticker slogans—like "One Day at a Time" and "Easy Does It" and "Keep It Simple, Stupid"—he liked "Significant Other" best. It used to be that drunks had wives and husbands, boyfriends and girlfriends. Not anymore. Nowadays, guys did it to guys, girls did it to girls, nieces shacked up with uncles, deacons socked it to choirboys. Establishment labels became value judgments, value judgments bred guilt in the nonconforming, and here in treatment guilt was a villain. They had to find a neutral term, something that would connote a relationship without judging it, something that would work as well for a man married to the same woman for forty-three years as for a freak who had taken to poking his pet llama.

Significant Other.

Preston's Significant Other was Margaret. Technically. No question, though, in the past three weeks the relationship—in Preston's mind, anyway, and he had no idea what was going on in Margaret's—had become much more Other than Significant. Probably because of the isolation, the lack of contact. Possibly because of Priscilla.

Forget it. Forget Priscilla. Or if you can't forget her, stay away from her. Or if you can't stay away from her altogether (and that's downright impossible around here), at least ignore her.

Sure.

You better.

Or else.

He had been almost finished with his therapeutic duty (this week, as "Mr. Clean," his task was to tidy up the common-room kitchenette) when Marcia had snapped at him that she wanted to see him in her office *now*. He had been expecting it, had prepared a reasoned response that contrasted appearance with reality and cited *Rashomon* (he thought he could get away with this, in private) as a paradigm. The security guard had seen one thing; that was his reality. But interpreted reality was not necessarily truth.

Preston would tell Marcia the truth.

Simple.

He never had a chance.

Marcia sat at her desk. Preston stood before her. He had to. There were no other chairs in the room. Where the hell had they gone? He towered over her, had the advantage of height, but by sitting down she dominated him.

On purpose?

Probably.

For sure.

She had a manila folder open on the desk. Inside was a piece of paper with a lot of typing on it. The arresting officer's report. She scanned the paper, then shut the folder and looked up at him. He saw that her eyelids drooped, giving her a look that was less angry than carnivorous. Like a reptile. She was going to eat him.

"Last night, at nine forty-five P.M., you were seen—"

Preston put one hand in his pocket and raised the other, trying to look casual, in command. "The guy's a jerk. He wanted to see something, so he saw something. Nothing hap—"

"You were kissing her."

"No. I mean, not exactly. If anybody was kissing anybody, she was kissing me. We were talking, about friendship, if you want to know, and she—"

"Don't pull your glib pop-psych bullshit on me, Scott. The two of you were kissing, right?"

Preston sighed the sigh of a martyr. "If you say so."

"I say so. Jorge Velasquez says so. The 'jerk.' He makes seven-fifty an hour, Scott. He supports three kids, a wife with a club foot and a mother-in-law dying of Lou Gehrig's Disease. In the daytime he pumps gas. He hasn't had a drink or any weed in six years. How long has it been since your last drink, Scott?"

Uh-oh. "I apologize. But he came on like—"

"How long, Scott?"

"Seventeen days."

"How many steps are there in A.A., Scott?"

Preston bit his lip, forcing the rising anger back into its pit. "Can we skip the seminar? You want me to grovel, I'll grovel. But just—"

"Answer the question!"

"Twelve."

"How many have you dealt with?"

"Two, maybe three."

"Which ones?"

Preston began to relax. Her attitude was becoming clinical. He could answer questions. "Well, number one: I know I'm powerless over alcohol. My life had become unmanageable. Two and three are tough, fuzzy—the higher-power and turning-it-over-to-God stuff."

"What about number four?—'We made a searching and fearless moral inventory of ourselves.' "

"It's not something you do all at once. You do it—"

" 'You?' Who's 'you'?"

"I. All right. I. I do it a little bit every day. I chip away at it."

"And what have you turned up?"

It was getting easier. A chat. He wished there were a chair so he could sit down, not stand there as if this were a court-martial. "A lot of my problem's self-esteem. I have a really crappy opinion of myself, deep down. It's something I suppose I'll have to work on all my life."

She didn't say anything, just looked at him with those hooded eyes and tapped an eraser on the desk. Then she bit.

"I wouldn't bother," she said.

"What?" He must have misheard her.

"Why fish in an empty lake, Scott? Your self-esteem can't be as low as it should be. 'Cause deep down, where it counts, in the core where the truth lives, you're a shit."

All Preston could manage was "Hey . . ." before his throat closed.

"Who wants to take inventory of a warehouse piled to the ceiling with cases and cases of shit?"

Preston didn't know he had spoken, thought he had

only thought the words "What are you *doing*?," until he saw her start out of her chair and slam her hand on the desk.

"What am *I* doing? It's what *you're* doing, Scott, and what you're doing is taking. Take, take, take. You're like a hyena or a buzzard or something that sucks the eyes out of the weak and weary."

"Can I say something?" He had no idea what he wanted to say. He wanted to stop the assault.

"Go ahead."

"Yeah . . . well . . . you know, it takes two to tango."

She blinked and hesitated, looking for the meat beneath the banality. There wasn't any. "Oh, very good, Scott. Very aware. Very profound. And the Holocaust was really the Jews' fault for not standing up to Hitler, and the kids in the ghettos could make something of themselves if they'd only for God's sake get a *job*. There're no victims in life, right, Scott?"

"You think I'm victimizing her?"

"What would you call it? You may be a *re*tard, all addicts are *re*tards, maybe you stopped growing at nineteen or twenty or twenty-five. But you're a grown-up. Relatively. That girl is a *baby*."

"But I haven't *done* anything!"

"You're doing it. You're getting her to lean on you, confide in you, count on you, maybe even fall in love with you. She has no foundation in her life, and you're letting her build one on you." She paused. "And all you're interested in is a cheap piece of ass."

"You're nuts! You don't know anything. Worse than that security guard what's-his-name who you think is the Second Coming because he doesn't take dope anymore. You want to see something, so you see it. Everybody fits a pattern. Life is a Jell-O mold.''

"So it's more than that. Not just jumping her bones.''

"That has nothing to do with it.''

"You care about her. . . .''

What was this? Suddenly Marcia's voice had gone soft, conversational. He said, "Damn right.''

Watch out! He must have said too much, or the wrong thing, put his foot in it. Somehow. *Keep your mouth shut.*

". . . 'cause I'd hate to think your brains were all in your pants, smart guy like you.'' She smiled. "So tell me: What happens when you get out of here? You tell . . . Margaret, is it? . . . you tell Margaret so long, you've got your act together now, you're taking off, and you and Priscilla head for Barbados or someplace? I mean, we both know she's loaded.''

"I don't—''

"Or maybe you hang in there with the marriage for a while, see how things go, let Priscilla get an apartment and you see her when you can, and every time Margaret looks at you sideways or says something that ticks you off, like 'Why can't you pick up your socks?,' you make a little mark on your mental blackboard, until finally you've got so many marks against her that she says one more thing and *blammo!* you split, feeling like a goddam saint for having put up with her so long.''

"You have a nasty mind. Christ! I haven't thought half that far ahead.''

"That's my point, Scott.'' Again she smiled, and now there was no irony in her voice. "You haven't thought ten seconds from now. You've taken 'One Day at a Time' and twisted it to mean there's no yesterday, there's no tomorrow, there's nothing but right now. No guilt, no responsibility. If it feels good, do it. If somebody gets hurt, too bad. Look out for number one.'' She bent down and pulled open a bottom drawer in her desk. ''But that's not the way it works, Scott. Priscilla's already wounded. I'm not gonna let you cripple her.''

He wanted to shout, to hit her, to rail against the wrong she was doing him, but his mind was like a wasps' nest sprayed with poison—full of creatures dying, furious, perplexed and frightened. Words tried to form themselves and escape, but they merely buzzed around and dropped.

Marcia reached into the drawer and pulled out a pint of vodka. Popov. She put it on the desk and pushed it toward him. ''Have a drink, Scott. Not your brand, but what the hell, right?''

He stopped breathing and, without realizing it, took a step backward.

''Go ahead. You're never gonna make it through here, so why put off the inevitable?''

''Yes, I am,'' he whispered.

She shook her head. ''Not a chance. Oh, I don't think you'll sneak out and get wrecked, or smuggle something in, or steal something—any of the stuff the real high-wire artists do that gets them booted—but if I get one more word that you and Priscilla have been doing anything more than saying 'Howdjado' in the hallway, I'll have your sorry ass out of here so fast you'll think you had a blackout. And I *will* get another word, Scott, because you *will* do something more with Priscilla. You know why? Because you don't have the guts not to.'' She stood up and lifted the bottle and unscrewed the top and pressed the bottle on him. "Go on, Scott. Save me the trouble."

It was at that moment that Preston had felt the sour taste in the back of his mouth and had rushed for the door.

Marcia was concluding her chronicle of Lewis's recovery, saying that the key in his case was *acceptance*: He had to accept the hand that life had dealt him, had to play those cards for all they were worth, not waste a lot of time lamenting that he wasn't holding a pat straight flush, because many a determined player had made a winning game from a busted flush or a four-card straight, since so much of life is a bluffer's paradise.

Then, noticing that Lewis looked utterly baffled, realizing that she had wasted a terrific extended metaphor, she said, "Do you play poker, Lewis?"

Lewis shook his head. "Whist," he said. "And crazy eights when I was a kid."

"Well"—she smiled—"take my word for it. Play the cards you've got, accept yourself for what you are, and you'll do fine."

Now it was time for everybody else to say something about Lewis. Nobody had to, and a handful of people, mostly from Dan's group, who didn't know Lewis very well, didn't volunteer.

Priscilla's hand was the first to shoot up, from behind a couch across the room from Preston. Marcia pointed to her, and she stood.

"You're one of the nicest, sweetest men I've ever known," Priscilla said to Lewis, "and I wish you all the best in your life ahead. I *know* you'll make it." She blew him a kiss. "I love you a lot."

Wait a second here! Where does she get all this love she's scattering around like grass seed?

Hector, the veteran of dozens of graduations from coast to coast, stood next. "When you come in here, you're one a the scaredest muthafuckas"—he looked at Marcia—"sorry . . . mofos . . . I ever seen. But now you really shaped up, got your shit together. You showed everybody you got a real pair of *cojones* . . . parn the 'spression." He shot Lewis a thumbs-up sign. "Sock it to 'em, amigo."

Marcia then recognized Clarence Crosby, who said, "I don't know you real well, Lewis, but I'm not a bad scout, and I tell you this: You can play outfield on my team anytime."

There was applause, and a lot of laughter and a few whistles. Lewis turned even redder, and he busied one of his fingers in the curl of his pompadour.

Duke didn't intend to speak, but Marcia pointed to him anyway and said, "Duke, you were Lewis's roommate."

"I guess Lewis taught me a bunch of things," Duke said, vamping as he got to his feet. "Like, don't judge a book by its cover. I mean, I didn't know what I was getting in for, but then I thought: Jesus, what did *he* think, 'cause when we met they wouldn't even let me wear pants 'cause I'd been dressed like a damn rabbit. But you've been a great roommate, Lewis." He smirked as the laugh line came to him. "And any time you need any condoms, you know who to call."

Duke grinned expectantly, but nobody laughed. Lewis looked at the floor. Duke said, "I make them, that's my business. I wasn't kidding." He sat down.

Twist sat in a chair in front of Preston, and Preston

heard him muttering to himself, as if composing a statement. Preston leaned forward and touched Twist's arm and whispered, ''It's okay, man, say it. You can't screw up worse than Duke did.''

Twist nodded and started to speak as he unfolded himself from the chair. ''Everybody feels sorry for himself, I s'pose,'' he said, looking at the floor, ''and I did too. Hell, it's not *my* fault if I'm a junkie. You would be too, if you was black and dumb and everybody puts you down alla time and all that other bullshit. But Lewis, he got more to feel sorry for than most folks, and he don't ever seem to show it much.'' He raised his eyes and looked into Lewis's. ''What I mean is, you may be one weird dude, but I guess you're 'bout one a the best rummies I ever did meet. So good luck, man.''

Preston patted Twist on the back, and Lewis smiled at him, and a few people applauded.

Preston was beginning to feel good. These were people who had probably never expressed a feeling for another person except perhaps a girlfriend or a mother, had certainly never articulated such a feeling before an audience. He was witnessing a kind of dawn, a birth of honesty and self-awareness, a reaching out by people whose lives had been tight little knots of isolation. Fascinating. More than that. It was . . .

''Scott?''

Preston started. Why was Marcia calling his name? He looked at her.

''I'm sure you have something to say.''

''What?'' He didn't have anything to say. Why was she dragging him onto the stage?

"Words are your living, Scott. Come on. We can't all be spectators."

She read my mind. It's like I've got a neon sign hanging over my head. He looked at Lewis, who was smiling at him, expecting a pearl of eloquence and insight. If she hadn't called on him, he could have kept his mouth shut and nobody would have cared. But he couldn't decline now. Don't rain on Lewis's parade.

"I don't know what I can add," he said as he pushed off from the floor. He reached for nice words. "You're a man of courage, Lewis," he said, "a man of grace and compassion. And if those three things can't help you make it, then we're all doomed."

Lewis grinned. But Marcia just gave her head a little disappointed shake and said, "Nice, Scott. Right from the heart."

Preston didn't know why, wasn't sure how, but he knew he had been slapped in the face.

Marcia took a slip of paper from her shirt pocket. "I have a note here from Cheryl, Lewis. You know she's over at the hospital having another biopsy. The note reads: 'I love you, Lewis. I'll miss you. I don't know if there's a God, but I know you're a big part of my higher power, so wherever you go for the rest of your life, I want you to know that I'll be praying for you.' " As she handed the note to Lewis, as she said, "This is yours to keep," she glanced at Preston.

Lewis used the end of his neckerchief to wipe his eyes, and he said, "Is she okay?"

"She hasn't had a drink today," Marcia said, and she touched Lewis's shoulder. "That's all any of us can ask for. The rest of it's out of our hands."

She had something else in her hand now. "This is

yours too, Lewis,'' she said, and she held it up for all to see. "God knows you've earned it. And God will help you *keep* earning it.''

It was a Banner medallion, a gold-plated coin about the size of a fifty-cent piece. From this distance Preston couldn't see any of the details on the medallion, but he had seen one in a Lucite block in the shrink's office. On one side was the entire Serenity Prayer, on the other a horse rampant, with rider. You were supposed to carry it with you always, in your pocket or on a chain around your neck, were supposed to touch it whenever you had the urge to have a drink or swallow a pill. Preston wondered whether he'd bother to carry his.

After this morning, he wondered if he'd ever get one.

It was Lewis's turn to speak. He looked at the medallion for a long moment, then clutched it in both hands. He sniffled noisily, and when he looked up his eyes were full of tears.

"Faggot,'' he said, and what few ambient room noises there were—rustles and coughs and wheezes and squirms—ceased as if a plug had been pulled. "Fruit . . . flit . . . fairy . . . sissy . . . homo . . . queer . . . gay . . . poofter . . .'' He looked from face to face around the room, and though tears ran down his cheeks, he smiled. "Rummy . . . lush . . . drunk . . . wino . . . alky . . . Aren't those nice words?'' He paused.

"Who are we, all of us? How do we define ourselves? Are we what we do for a living? Are we what we believe? When I came in here, I thought all I was was some combination of those two things: a faggot wino, a rummy fruit, a gay lush. Not smart or kindly or thoughtful or interesting. Other people may have thought of me as a creative designer who worked twelve-hour days. Other people appreciated that I gave to every charity in the state of Florida. Not me. All that mattered to me, all I could see when I looked in the mirror was a drunk fairy. Period. But after four weeks with you all, I know different." He looked at Marcia. "Especially you." He held out one of his hands, and she took it. "You taught me that I am *me*! I am a good person! And anybody who doesn't like it can go . . . can go . . ." He laughed as he spoke. ". . . piss up a tree."

He stood up and said to Marcia, "Thank you for my life," and he wrapped her in his arms.

Some people were crying. Several others were trying not to. Even Preston felt a burning behind his eyes.

They lined up then in single file, and one by one they hugged Lewis. When Preston reached the front of the line, he opened his arms and prepared for the awkward embrace, but Lewis stepped backward and held out his hand instead.

"It's okay," Lewis said, smiling. He took Preston's hand and shook it and leaned forward and whispered, "Don't hate Marcia. All she's trying to do is force you to find the love. It's in there. You just have to find it." He released Preston's hand and turned to the next person in line.

Preston moved away, baffled that everyone seemed to be able to see so clearly inside him, and yet when he looked, all he saw was fog.

"Duke," Marcia called from the door to her office, "you and Scott take Lewis to his ride."

While he waited for Duke and Lewis to collect Lewis's bags, Preston went to the cigarette machine and counted out a dollar and a half in change. He was considering a switch to a menthol brand when the door to the lavatory beside the machine opened and Priscilla emerged.

Two criminals who had been interrogated separately, and now each was wondering what the other had said.

Priscilla's eyes shifted to the background behind Preston, to see if they were being watched.

"Did they read you the riot act?" she asked.

"I'll say. I tried to explain, but she wasn't interested."

Priscilla nodded. "Dan too."

"What did you tell him?"

"I told him to fuck off." She smiled sweetly. "Is that how you say it? I wasn't sure." She touched his arm and walked away.

Duke and Preston each carried one of Lewis's suitcases, and as they walked through the corridors of the main building they flanked him, and he walked a step ahead, like a prime minister or a pooh-bah, and he said good-bye to people he passed, shook hands and hugged and shed a tear with Nurse Bridget. They stood by as he checked out and signed the release forms for Larkin and was given back the things confiscated when he had arrived: two books, a bottle of cologne and a prescription bottle of Seconal.

"I'm proud of you, Lewis," Larkin said as he watched Lewis toss the sleeping pills into a wastebasket.

"Not half as proud as I am, Guy," Lewis said, shaking hands.

There was no car in the roundabout when they got outside.

"Did you call a cab or what?" Duke asked Lewis,

squinting into the distance, which shimmered in the heat waves rising off the road.

"What time is it?"

Preston looked at his watch. "Ten fifty-eight."

"I told him eleven o'clock," Lewis said. "He'll be here. Or else."

Duke said, "Or else what?"

"I'll make his life a misery."

Thirty seconds later a car appeared in the pass, and a moment after that the rented Oldsmobile turned into the roundabout. A young man got out of the car, warily eyeing Preston and Duke.

Young? On second look, Preston wasn't so sure. He seemed young, obviously wanted to be young, but it was hard to tell. He was sleek as a mink, tan, unblemished. His black hair—too black, impossibly black—was slicked back like one of those models for Calvin Klein underwear. He wore a gold Cartier watch on one wrist, a gold braided-wire bracelet on the other, no shirt, just a cotton sweater and (they saw as he walked around behind the car and popped the trunk) heavily pleated trousers and Italian loafers with no socks.

"Kevin," Lewis said as he hefted his suitcases and carried them to the car, "this is my friend Duke and my friend Scott."

Preston said, "Hi."

Duke said, "How y'doin'?"

Kevin acknowledged them with a little nod. He picked up one of the suitcases and put it in the trunk and said to Lewis, "I hope *you've* had a good month. Mine has been vile."

"Poor you."

"Poor me is right." He put the second suitcase in

the trunk and closed it. "Joy quit. On a Friday, if you please."

"That must've made it hard for you."

"You don't *know*." Kevin returned to the front of the car and opened the door.

Lewis walked to Duke and, like a French general bestowing a Légion d'honneur, kissed him on both cheeks and said, "I'll write you. You don't have to write back, but I'll write you." He smiled. "Maybe I'll take you up on your offer."

Lewis didn't kiss Preston. He just said, "May I ask a favor? Let me know how Cheryl is?"

"Sure," Preston said.

Lewis turned to the car and opened the passenger's-side door. Kevin was still standing there.

"Be nice, Kevin," Lewis said. "Say good-bye."

Kevin didn't say good-bye. He said to Lewis, "You know you look terrible."

"No, I don't," Lewis said. "I look wonderful. And don't you forget it." As he climbed into the car, Lewis turned his head to Preston and Duke and gave them a wink.

They waited until the car turned out of the round-about and onto the road. They waved and saw Lewis wave back.

"Marriage made in heaven," Duke said.

Preston had reached for the handle of the front door to the clinic when they heard someone say, "Hey!"

They looked around. They even looked up, overhead, as if the voice had come from the roof. No one.

"You heard it," said Duke.

"I heard it." Preston shrugged and reached again for the door handle.

"Hey!" It was a dark voice, gruff, accustomed to being obeyed. "You wanna make a hunnert bucks?"

There were enough words this time to give them a directional fix. The side of the building. So they stepped back away from the door and looked that way.

A hand was sticking around the corner, holding a hundred-dollar bill.

"The hell are you?" Duke said.

"C'mere."

Duke looked at Preston. "There are two of us."

"Yeah, but . . ." Preston addressed the phantom voice. "Why don't you come out of there?"

"Think I am, gonna rape you?"

"No," Preston said. "That wasn't—"

"C'mon!" The voice was urgent. "Please."

There was something about the delivery—hesitation, maybe—that said that "please" was a foreign word, like *Weltschmerz* or *mal de mer*.

They walked to the corner of the building and, like children playing hide-and-seek, paused and looked at each other before they peeked.

A grotesquely fat man was wedged between the building and the fringing hedge. He was of middling height and appeared to be as wide as he was tall. He wore a sports jacket woven into gaudy checks, a lemon shirt and a silk tie highlighted with multicolored circles, squares and kidney-shaped things and secured with a knot the size of a cantaloupe. His wide, flat feet were encased in enormous slip-ons now half-buried in the dirt beneath the hedge. This was not a man who could tie his own shoes. He was bald, save for a reef of beige fuzz that lapped over his ears and rimmed the back of his shiny skull. Aviator sunglasses hid his eyes. Sweat seemed to squeeze from every pore on his face, as if he were turning on a spit over a fire. He might have been thirty-five. Or fifty.

A hand made of five breakfast sausages springing from a bologna waved the hundred-dollar bill.

The other hand dwelt beneath the man's nose, touching one nostril then the other. He sniffled constantly, and each sniffle ended with a little whistle.

Duke perceived no threat, so he smiled and said, "May I show you to a table?"

"Fuck you," said the man, and he pushed the bill at Duke. "Yes or no?"

"Who are you?" Preston asked.

"Fuck is this?" *Sniff.* *"Jeopardy?"* *Sniff.* "Just get me some toot." *Sniff.*

Duke said to Preston, "He's hallucinating."

Preston said to the man, "Do you know where you *are*?"

"Hey! Read my fuckin' lips!" Very agitated, one hand slapping his nose, the other jerking the bill around as if a fish had hold of it. "Take this and get me some toot! Keep the change."

Duke said, "He doesn't know where he is."

Preston said, "Let's go call security."

They took a step back, started to turn away.

"Hey! No!" Frantic. Both hands dug in the jacket pockets. "Not enough, right? Want more, right? No *prob*lem! Here y'go." Bills flew out of the jacket, crumpled bills and folded bills, bills of all denominations. Some hung up in the hedge, some slipped into the dirt, some wedged between the pudgy fingers.

Duke looked at Preston. "This is one unhappy camper."

Preston said to the man, "I don't know where you think you are, but this is—"

"Make you a deal. Forget the toot. No toot. Toot's *out* of here. Valium. Fifty mills of Valium, you keep the yard. Okay?"

Preston pointed at the clinic. "This is a drugstore?"

"*I* know what the fuck it is! I can't go in there like this. I gotta go up or down, one way or the other. Can't stay in the shithouse. Been in the shithouse a couple hours, maybe more, I don't know, since they pitched me out and left me here."

"Who left you here?"

"They did."

"Who's 'they'?"

"Forget it."

"The point is," Duke said, "you got it backwards. This is the place they take all that shit away from you, not where they give it to you."

"You say."

"I been here three weeks, I oughta know."

"You been here three weeks, you're too fuckin' stupid to learn the ropes?"

"The guy's amazing," Duke said to Preston. "A psychic. He hasn't set foot in the door, already he knows the ropes."

"Believe it," the man said.

"How do you know?" asked Preston.

"Forget it."

Preston said, "This is a waste of time."

Duke said, "He's blowing smoke."

Preston said to the man, "It gets cold at night," and this time he and Duke got almost to the door before the man shouted, "Hey!"

The sound effects were like *Wild Kingdom* when a rhinoceros charges through the underbrush at Jim Fowler. With a gasp and a grunt, the man popped out from the hedge. His aviator glasses hung from one ear. His jacket was sprinkled with tiny leaves.

"How 'bout at least you take me in there with you?" The man was pleading. "I go in there alone, they'll lock me up."

"Say please," Duke said. "I like to hear you say please."

"Fuck—" the man began. Then he deflated. "Please."

Preston said, "Why would they want to lock you up?"

"Everybody always wants to lock me up. It's a curse."

"Come on, then," Preston said, adding as the man walked toward them, "I'm Scott. This is Duke."

"Lupone. Willy Lupone. At work they call me . . . Shit, never mind."

"Unusual name," Duke said. "Your mother's side?"

Lupone pretended he hadn't heard.

Preston asked, "What do you do?"

"This and that."

"In other words," Duke said, "forget it."

"Who got you to come here?" Preston said.

"My family."

"Me, too. An intervention?"

"Huh?"

"They all get together, give you a lot of grief about all the crap you've done, tell you if you don't go in you'll be fired, divorced, the whole routine."

"Right," Lupone snorted. "An intervention."

"The most unpleasant hour of my life."

"Mine took fifteen seconds."

"Jeez . . . efficient."

"They are that."

"What'd they say?"

"Not much. 'Puffguts,' they say, 'you go in the fuckin' joint and clean up your act or we have Li'l Bit—that's my cousin, they call him Li'l Bit—we have Li'l Bit drown you in a puddle and feed you to the lampreys.' " He blew specks of dirt off his glasses and put them on. "Yeah, it's efficient."

Guy Larkin wasn't in his office. Nurse Bridget had gone to the cafeteria for coffee. So they waited in the lobby with Lupone.

Duke offered him a cigarette.

"Shit's poison, man." Lupone shook his head. "I don't mess with that."

"You will," Preston said, with an aware little smirk.

"Pretty cocky, pal."

Preston flushed, but he managed to say, "You'll see."

Duke saw Larkin come out of an office at the end of the corridor.

"Here comes your welcoming committee," he said to Lupone. Then he lowered his voice. "I gotta ask you: What made you think you could get toot in here?"

"I don't think, sonny," Lupone said flatly. "I *know*."

From halfway down the corridor, Larkin called out, in a phony, two-bit theatrical Italian accent that he probably thought was terribly friendly and oh-so-clever, "Aha! Thisa musta be Signore Guglielmo Lupone *[googlyellmo looponay]. Benvenuto, amico mio!*"

Lupone looked from Larkin to Duke to Preston.

"Fuck is this?" he said. "Take-a-guinea-to-lunch week?"

"Say your prayers," Duke said with a grin, and he patted Lupone on the shoulder. "And keep a tight asshole."

‖

THE MOTORIST WHO found Natasha Grant's
body at the base of the mountain told reporters he had
thought at first it was just a pile of old clothes that had
fallen off a truck, and he was all set to drive on by.

"So why'd you stop?"

"There was this coyote eatin' on it."

They liked that. They all scribbled like sixty, and the
two with microphones had to fight to swallow their
smiles.

He was having the time of his life.

He was in his late sixties, a chicken farmer who sold
eggs and parts to local restaurants, and save for a brief
tour with the Navy in Hawaii near the end of the war
he had never been outside New Mexico. He had never
met a reporter, had never even seen one except on TV,
and here he was, suddenly surrounded by them, and all
of them asking him questions, which was doubly exciting since nobody ever asked him questions about anything but chickens.

He could see the sheriff over there beside his car,

about to have a fit and wishing all the reporters would die of a wasting disease. But it was the sheriff's own damn fault: If he hadn't left his radio on while he was getting gas, then the reporter getting gas on the other side of the pumps wouldn't have heard the call on the radio and wouldn't have followed him out here. And the fella at the TV station who always kept his radio tuned to the police frequency wouldn't have heard the back-and-forth between the sheriff and his office. And so forth.

Behind the sheriff was the ambulance. They had given up trying to stuff what was left of the body in a bag and had covered it with a tarp and were shoving it onto a stretcher.

"You always stop when you see a coyote eating rags?"

He took his time. They liked juicy answers, and the juicier his answers the better his chances of actually getting on TV. Hell, maybe even *Entertainment Tonight*. After all, Natasha Grant was a *star*.

"When there's a leg in it," he said.

Score! Scribble, scribble, scribble.

"So you get out of your car and walk over to—"

"Truck."

"Huh?"

"It's an eighty-two Chevy king-cab kinda thing I customized myself, with a—"

"Whatever. You walk over there and see it's not just a pile of rags. What did she look like?"

Pause. Smile. "Kinda like a two-dollar Mexican dinner."

Confusion. "What?"

"You know: red peppers, melted cheese, guaca-mole."

"Jesus Christ!"

Too much. They weren't smiling. The cute one with the microphone looked nauseated. Back off.

"I mean, she was a mess."

"But you could recognize her."

"Oh sure." Just the facts. "See, it was one side messed up, the side hit the road. Other side was real peaceful. No question it was the little girl used to spoon with Dean Stockwell in the picture show."

"Wrap it," said the cute one, and her cameraman slid the big video off his shoulder.

"This be on *Eyewitness News* or what? Me and the wife want to be sure to catch it."

The sheriff declined to make a statement, wouldn't even let them take his picture, and when they tried, he stood with his back to the sun where he knew all they'd get was white burnout and a black blotch on their film or tape or whatever the hell it was. He knew all about reporters, how they bitch up your meaning by using only the words they like, how they can even warp a piece of film with you on it by cutting away to the reporter and showing him—or her, usually her, all the real slimy ones seemed to be women—with the eyebrow raised or the tongue in the cheek, the expression saying, "You don't expect me to *believe* this load of shit." As for "off the record," he knew what it meant: You tell them something and they go ahead and use it and claim somebody else told them too.

Fuck 'em. Them and the vans they rode around in. They'd get nothing from him but bare, undecorated facts, and those not till they'd been established and verified and given the Good Housekeeping Seal of Approval.

At the moment there was only one fact, and it had lain in a heap and drooled out onto the pavement. No problem for the print guys, but he'd been amused at how the TV jockeys had risen to the challenge, shooting by it, over it, around it, putting it in shadow, never shooting directly at it, because you don't want Mom and Pop to spew their TV dinners all over the set during the evening news.

It wasn't an absolute, incontrovertible fact that the corpse was Natasha Grant—there was no I.D. on the body—though anybody who'd ever been to the movies would take an oath. And there was no certainty about how she had died, though unless she had been hit by a bulldozer going eighty miles an hour, it was pretty likely she had fallen the four or five hundred feet from the top of the mountain.

Or been pushed.

Maybe she'd been dead before the fall. Who knew what kind of splash a dead body'd make from that height, compared to a live one? Not him. That was the coroner's job. They'd have to wait for the forensic report, the toxicologist's report.

Maybe she'd been coked-up or freaked-out on LSD or PCP. A long shot, but you had to check out everything. She'd been out of the clinic barely three weeks, had already been on the cover of *People* magazine telling everybody how great it was to be clean, thanking God for giving her another chance at life. All the standard B.S. Okay, maybe not B.S., but it sure was boring. Predictable, that was the word, like there was a hat full of stock phrases and every celebrity lush dipped in and grabbed a few to describe the glories of recovery.

What was she doing around here, anyway? She lived in Beverly Hills, and according to *People* she'd become a demon on the A.A. circuit, telling her story to anyone who cared to hear it, helping stumblebums. The whole nine yards.

Maybe she had come back to speak at the clinic. Maybe she had secretly checked in again—Christ!—had a slip and didn't want to admit it.

No. If she was a patient, she'd be in the clinic, not roaming around the top of the mountain.

He looked up at the mountain. As soon as the ambulance left, as soon as the reporters got bored poking around and packed up their gear and took off, he'd go up there and have a look. He thought he remembered there was a fence around the whole plateau, but maybe it had been taken down or had a gap in it. He hadn't been up there in a couple years.

No chance of them following him up there. They'd be stopped at the gate. 'Course, he would be too, but him they'd let in. He was pretty sure, at least. He couldn't imagine Stone Banner'd make him go back and get a warrant just to have a look around.

But it was hard to tell where you stood with Stone Banner at any given time.

He was a quirky kind of guy.

"I'm Scott. I'm an alcoholic." The word still didn't feel completely natural in Preston's mouth—like a false tooth, there but not really his—but he was used to it. He didn't feel he had to deny it. "I feel okay today." He had nothing more to say, but he knew it wasn't good

enough. He didn't have to look at Marcia; he could feel
her eyes on him. *Think of something.* Like what? Like
how hard it is to parse your whole life, to analyze every
mistake, to assess your progress toward some amorphous serenity—all without appearing to wallow in a
sea of self-pity?

No. Just thinking it sounds whiny.

At last he said, "I feel I'm . . . ah . . . getting there.
Little by little. Sometimes it's like trying to crush one
rock with another, but every day the rocks get a little
bit smaller."

Now he did look at Marcia. One of her eyes was
closed, the other appraised him. Then it, too, closed,
and she sighed. He was positive he could hear her
thinking, Spare us the similes, Scott.

But she let it pass.

She looked over at the new boy, Lupone.

Lupone sat on two chairs, one cheek on each, and
every time he breathed, one of the eight wooden legs
protested. He wore the same checked jacket and the
same bouillabaisse tie, but with a plum-colored shirt.

He was the only person in the clinic who wore a tie,
which, Marcia was sure, was why he wore the tie. To
set himself apart. It was armor worn to warn others to
make no assumptions, take no liberties. He was not one
of them. He probably thought he was being subtle.

He had spent forty-eight hours in de-tox, and this was
his second day in company. She had put up with his
belligerent silence the first day, but today he was going
to get with the program.

She said, "William?"

William? Preston thought. Where does she get William? It's Willy or Guglielmo or Puffguts. But William?

She sounded like a Sunday school teacher asking a kid if he's the one responsible for the god-awful stink in here.

Lupone said nothing.

"William, it's time to cut the shit, stop behaving like a three-year-old."

Color crept up the folds of Lupone's neck, darkening them almost to the color of his shirt.

"Today you speak, or—"

"Or what?" Lupone turned his head and fastened his piglike eyes on her. "Yeah, lady, or what?"

"That's a start. Let's discuss the *or*s. Either you speak, or—"

"Look, lady, let's get a couple things straight here. And this has nothing to do with you being a broad or a *shvartzeh*, okay?"

"Fine." She nodded, and her lips tightened.

That's a smile *she's trying to hold in there!* Preston was amazed, envious, filled with admiration. *If I could ever be that composed, I would rule the world.*

"What it is," Lupone said, "I'm not gonna play the game, see, 'cause I don't have the problem you guys got here. The only problem I got is that I'm here, and the reason I'm here is that if I don't come, my fuckin' cousin's gonna *drown* me, f'crissakes. So I got twenty-seven days to go, and I can do twenty-seven days standing on my head and suckin' my thumb, you better believe it, I done a lot longer than that a couple times, long as you keep off my back. Okay? We got a deal?"

Marcia paused. "We got a deal," she said. She reached into a pocket and pulled out a quarter and flipped it at Lupone. "The deal is, you go make a phone call."

"To who?"

"A taxi. You're outa here."

Lupone held the quarter and looked at it as if it were a scorpion. He said, "Hey . . ."

"'S the matter, William?"

"I *can't*!"

"Sure you can." She smiled. "It's easy. Reach out, reach out and touch someone."

Lupone just sat there.

"Is it the money you're worried about? Don't. We're better than the car companies. Full money-back guarantee. Think of the de-tox as a public service."

"Money." Lupone snorted. "Besides, I'm on scholarship."

"Scholarship!" Marcia laughed. "What're you, the prize junkie from the Sisters of Holy Charity?"

"Forget it." Lupone bit his lip and shook his head, as if he had spoken out of turn.

"Who gave you a scholarship?"

Lupone paused. Then he turned to Marcia and shouted, "You don't get it, do you, lady? Fuckin' guy's gonna *drown* me!"

"This isn't the Red Cross, William. I'm not a lifeguard. Go on. Beat it."

Lupone stared at the quarter. Then he sighed and tossed it back to Marcia. "I'll talk."

"Good."

"What you wanna talk about?"

"Trust. You don't trust people, do you?"

"Why should I?"

"Why shouldn't you?"

"Trust is for people who wanna end up in a landfill."

"Who says?"

"What they teach you, right outa the gate."

"Who's 'they'?"

"They."

"In your line of work, you mean."

"Right."

"What line of work is that?"

"Market research." He didn't smile or snigger. He just said it.

"Sounds like a tough line of work, market research."

Watch out, Willy-boy. Preston's eyes were bouncing back and forth between them as if this were a Ping-Pong game. *She's getting chatty. You're gonna die.*

"You could say."

"Stand up, William."

"Huh?"

"Stand up."

Lupone hunched his shoulders—like a turtle protecting its head—and squinted at Preston and Hector and Twist and Cheryl, and then at Marcia.

He looked suspicious, wary, trying to decide if this was a plot, to figure what would happen if he stood up. All the faces were benignly blank.

He relaxed his shoulders and rolled off one cheek and then off the other, and on the second roll his forward momentum tipped the balance of his weight out over his feet.

Marcia stood, and she kicked her chair back and broke the circle. Now the others knew what was up, so they stood and moved their chairs back.

Hector and Twist shared an incredulous glance. Cheryl took a step backward, trying to will herself to a different country. Preston cleared his throat and said to Marcia, "You're serious?"

"Shut up, Scott."

"Come on, he weighs—"

"I said shut up!"

Lupone said, "Hey . . ."

"Now, William," Marcia said, "this is about trust. I want you to stand with your hands at your sides, and I want you to close your eyes."

"What's this got to do with—"

"Do it."

Lupone treated her to a viperous glare. Then, pressing his lips together and making a guttural growling sound, he stood at attention and closed his eyes.

"When you're ready, William, I want you to let yourself go and fall backward."

"What?" Lupone kept his eyes closed.

"That's right. Just tip back on your heels and go."

"You nuts? You want I should break something? I could get a rupture."

"You'll never touch the ground, William. Your friends'll catch you."

"I got no friends."

"Here you've got friends. That's what I'm telling you."

"They'll let me fall."

"What makes you think so?"

"People always do. It's my curse."

"These people won't."

"You know what I weigh? Almost three hundred."

"Then that'll be a real challenge for them, William, won't it? They'll really have to want to catch you."

"Why should they? They don't give a fuck about me."

"We'll see."

"No. You'll see." Lupone opened his eyes and held out his hand. "Gimme the quarter."

He's bluffing. Preston tried to read Lupone's eyes, but he couldn't see them. They were hidden beneath curtains of fat. He looked at Marcia. *She doesn't know, either, not for sure.*

Marcia said, "I don't think so."

Lupone shrugged. A tight little smile puckered his lips. "Your candy store. But there's no way I'm gonna—"

"I'll make the call for you." She took a step toward the door.

Lupone paused, then decided to take the game forward. "Tell them to have my dough ready. It was about four thousand bucks they took."

"Oh, I'm not gonna call a cab." She reached for the doorknob.

"So who you gonna call?"

"There's a Mr. Ciccio."

Lupone twitched as if he'd touched an electric fence. The twitch sent ripples through the fat around his collar. "Hey . . ."

"Mr. Joseph Ciccio. Maybe you don't call him that. Maybe you use the name they put in the papers."

"You don't got his number."

He's reaching. Preston saw Marcia smile. *She's got him.*

"Gimme a break, William. You put a number in case of emergency on the form when they admitted you. I call that number. I tell them the problem. They get hold of Mr. Ciccio. Bet on it." She held the quarter between her fingertips and wiggled it at Lupone. "What I don't remember, though, is is his nickname Mamb*a* or Mamb*o*? I mean, does he have rhythm or does he bite people? I don't want to call the man by the wrong name, like, 'Hey there, Mr. Mambo,' if that's not his—"

"I'll take the fuckin' fall."

"I know you will, William." She dropped the quarter into her pocket and returned to the spot in front of Lupone. "See how easy it is to be reasonable?"

"I don't want to drown is all."

"That's reasonable." She leaned forward and placed Lupone's hands at his sides and patted them, then raised a palm to his eyes and touched his eyelids and brushed downward, the way you close the eyes of a corpse. "Trust me."

"Sure." Lupone chuckled. "You mean like they say in the movie business? In Hollywood, 'trust me' translates 'fuck you.' "

"Ssshhh." She raised a finger to Hector and Twist and pantomimed that they should stand on either side of Lupone and make a cradle with their arms down near the floor. Then she gestured for Preston to get on his knees and raise his hands in front of his shoulders. She pointed at Cheryl—frail, dark-eyed and frightened—and directed her to one of Lupone's hands.

When everyone was in position, Marcia said, "When you're ready, William."

Preston looked up from the floor. To his left knelt Twist, to his right Hector. Their arms were locked together. All he could see beyond the arms was a field of broad checks that encased enough compacted suet to crush the life out of him.

"How did your daddy die?" What would Kimberly answer? *"He was fatted to death in a drunk tank somewhere in New Mexico."*

The field of checks teetered, growing larger, then smaller, larger, smaller. Then they grew larger and larger and larger, until they struck Preston's hands and his face. Locked arms of muscle and bone were driven into his chest. He was rocked back on his knees, pressed to the floor like a limbo dancer.

He heard nothing but grunts, smelled an overpowering stench of Aqua Velva, felt his lips and nose splayed by something hard, round, bony and slick with sweat.

Marcia looked down and thought of a crèche. There was Cheryl, kneeling beside Lupone (eyes still closed) and holding his hand. There were Hector and Twist, their heads jammed against Lupone's chest because their arms were trapped beneath him. And somewhere under there was Preston.

Lupone opened his eyes and looked down at the two heads—one black, one brown—nestled against his massive breast. "Hey!" he shouted, and he beamed. "Hey!"

"Yes, William?"

"They caught me!"

"Uh-huh."

"Be dipped in shit and rolled in breadcrumbs."

"Really."

"Didn't bust a thing."

A plaintive voice, wailing like a departed spirit, wafted up through crannies in the mountain of flesh.

"Here," Marcia said, extending a hand to Lupone. "Before we have to send Scott to intensive care."

"Oh yeah," said Lupone, and he turned his head and shouted to Preston as if he were at the bottom of a mine shaft, "Sorry, pal."

There was no way Marcia could haul Lupone to his feet, so she moved to the side and gripped his hand with both of hers and braced herself and yanked. Lupone rolled and Cheryl pushed as Marcia pulled, and finally, like an overturned tortoise, Lupone tipped up onto his side. A last shove from Cheryl sent him crashing to the floor, face down.

"Mama!" said Twist, rubbing his arms to restore circulation before gangrene set in.

Hector flopped backward on the floor and gasped. The pack of cigarettes in his T-shirt sleeve was as flat as a Frisbee.

Preston was gray and twisted, like a contortionist who had gone too far and been left to die by a disappointed audience. He moaned and moved his limbs, and Marcia and Cheryl helped him to his feet.

"That was great!" Lupone said, tucking in his shirt. "But I still don't get it. How come they give a shit? Me, I'da let me fall and then laughed my ass off."

"You ever heard of John Donne, William?"

"You mean the guy writes alla time about Harps?"

"No. The one who said, 'No man is an island.' That one."

"Kinda fuckin' Einstein is that? Who ever said somebody was an island?"

"What he was saying is, we're all in this together. If you hurt, I hurt. We can't go it alone, and if we try, we go down the tubes."

"So?"

"So"—she gestured at the others—"they caught you

because they were saying, We know what kind of pain you're in because we've had the same pain and we want to help you.''

"Yeah?" Lupone looked doubtful. "Never mind. I'm not a man forgets a favor." He walked over to Twist and said, "Here." He reached in one jacket pocket, then in another. His pockets were empty. He said, "Shit. I forgot. I owe you."

"Forgot what?" Marcia asked.

"They got all my money."

"What d'you want with money?"

"Gonna give 'em some."

"Why?"

"Why?" Lupone looked puzzled. "They did me a favor."

"They didn't do it for money, William."

"So? Money's a convincer. Convinces you you did good, so maybe next time you'll do even better. Besides, I never knew a guy yet who couldn't use a couple bucks."

Preston waited for Marcia's attack. He wondered if it would be direct or oblique, savage or subtle, a club or a stiletto.

But Marcia laughed. Not a snide chuckle or a sarcastic bark but a spontaneous laugh of genuine amusement. She patted Lupone on the shoulder and said, "William, you are one hard-ass nut to crack, but I'm gonna do it."

Preston gasped. *Those are the same words she said to me! The same words! Exactly! What's going on? Does she say that to all the guys?* He wanted to call her out, to ask her, to challenge her supposed sincerity. But then he realized—amazed—that what he was feeling was not so much anger or righteous resentment as simple jealousy. He was being possessive. He wanted all the attention. He wanted to be special.

He was behaving like a baby.

Lupone winked at Marcia and said, "Good luck, sweetheart."

They gathered their chairs and formed their circle.

"I should've welcomed Cheryl back first thing," Marcia said as she sat down. She turned to Cheryl. "How'd it go?"

"I don't know. I won't know till the tests come back."

Bambi, Preston thought. That's what Bambi would look like if Bambi were a bird.

"It's out of your hands," Marcia said. "Right?"

"Right."

"No use worrying about it."

"No. But that's easy to say."

"Remember 'the serenity to accept the things we cannot change.' "

"I remember."

"You been saying the prayer?"

"Not enough."

"You like us to say it with you?"

Cheryl hesitated. "Yes."

Marcia held out her arms and they all joined hands and recited the Serenity Prayer—even Lupone, though he didn't close his eyes and didn't know the prayer and so just muttered syllables while eyeing the others to make sure they were serious and sincere and not engaged in some conspiracy to make him look like an ass.

"Now," Marcia said when they were done, "I think we should talk to Twist."

"Huh?" Twist said, evidently surprised at the sudden attention. "About what?"

"About heroin."

"What about it?"

"What does it do for you?"

"What's it *do*? Man, you *know* what it do."

"Not for you. I only know what it did for me. Where does it take you?"

"Away."

"From what?"

"From . . ." Twist looked at the ceiling. "From . . . I guess all the shit."

"That's what I want to look at. The shit."

There was a knock on the door. Marcia frowned and left her seat and went to the door and opened it a few inches.

A new arrival, Preston thought. It had to be. Therapy sessions were never interrupted except for earthquakes, terrorist attacks or new arrivals.

It was Guy Larkin. He said a few words to Marcia. She looked at her feet for a moment and then took a breath and squared her shoulders, turned back into the room and said, "Cheryl?"

For the first time since he had met her, Preston could actually see Cheryl's eyes, for they had widened so, and the skin beneath them had tightened so, that the eyes themselves seemed to be about to leave their stygian caves.

She looked terrified. She didn't speak, didn't move.

Marcia came back into the room and took Cheryl's hand. "We have to go see the doctor," she said.

Cheryl nodded and allowed herself to be gentled out of her chair.

Marcia put an arm around Cheryl and led her from the room. At the door, Marcia said to the others—and there was something awful about her voice, something stale and flat—"Everybody tell somebody else a secret."

They stared at each other. Then they stared at the floor, then at their fingernails, at their shoes, at the walls, out the window. Somebody coughed. Somebody else cleared his throat. Twist untied one of his shoes, tied it again.

Preston said, "I . . ." and everybody looked at him. He didn't know what to say. Tell somebody a secret? Tell who? And what secret? Recite his sexual fantasies? Talk about the time he padded his expense account?

They were like a car with the ignition removed. All the machinery was in place to drive the group, but the spark, Marcia, was gone.

Lupone said, "What?"

Preston shrugged, forced a wan smile. "I don't know." Maybe Lupone had a secret. *Maybe?* Definitely. The trouble was, Lupone's secrets were probably grounds for indictment. "You got something?"

"Stick it up your ass," Lupone said, hostile again. Suspicious. Closed. Marcia had opened him up a crack, but as soon as she left, he had slammed it shut.

"What the fuck . . ." Twist said.

So they quit.

Duke was sitting in the common room, struggling with a crossword puzzle. The other members of Dan's therapy group lounged around too, smoking, reading the bulletin board, eating ice cream. They never had any free time, didn't know how to cope with it, and some of them were growing anxious. Their routine had been broken, without explanation. They looked at their watches every few seconds, unconsciously desperate for the big hand to reach the top of the hour and signal their next structured experience.

"The hell's a medieval serf?" Duke asked as Preston came up and pulled out a chair.

"Esne," Preston replied, and he spelled it.

"Kinda dumb-ass word is that?" Duke filled in the blanks. " 'Help wanted: esnes? Good pay, great benefits? Make a career in esne-ing?' "

"Dan get sick?"

"He's in there." Bailey pointed with his pencil at the closed door to Dan's office. "With the fuzz."

"Why?"

"Butterball swears she heard the cop say something about Natasha Grant." Duke shook his head. "Butterball doesn't always play by the rules. Other day, she decided her drinking problem is because of her sins. She hasn't been to confession enough. Like God said, 'You don't want to 'fess up? Okay. *Zap!* You're a rummy.' So we all had to sit through a whole hour of the gory details."

"And?"

"Like Jimmy Carter. She's never *done* dick worth moaning about, but she's thought all sorts of trash. Sinned in her heart. It was a mayonnaise serenade."

Preston sat there and helped Duke finish the crossword, but he was useless when Duke began the cryptogram—finding five clues and then unscrambling the highlighted letters to make a final answer. He had never been able to do those things, his mind didn't work that way, just as he had an encyclopedic memory for phone numbers, but only one way: He could match almost any name with a phone number, if he had ever heard it, but if he was given the number and asked to dredge up the name that went with it, he couldn't do it.

He looked at his watch. Fifteen minutes till lecture time. He could go back to his room and . . . what? Read "The Big Book"? Memorize today's prayer from *Twenty-four Hours a Day*? Add to the list of outrages he had committed against others, outrages that would have to be chronicled and confessed to one of his peers for completion of his Fifth Step work? Forget it. Who were his peers here, anyway? Twist? Lupone? Duke? Yes, Duke. Close, if not on the button. And of course Priscilla. But "peer" wasn't exactly the word his mind conjured up when he thought of Priscilla.

Careful, there. Elitist thinking, Marcia would call it. Everybody's your peer, Scott. In our sickness there is oneness.

Sure. Booze is the great leveler.

What was today's lecture? He got up from the table and strolled over to the bulletin board by the cigarette machine. Probably something about how Châteauneuf-du-Pape rots your pancreas. Or another slide show on child abuse. (Christ! They'd actually shown *pictures* of a seven-year-old boy who'd been raped by his shit-faced father. That was supposed to make you stop drinking? It had made Preston *want* a drink, just so he could forget the pictures.)

The bulletin board was full of announcements of A.A. meetings, N.A. meetings (specializing in junkies), Al-Anon meetings (for the Significant Others and Codependents of the hard-core abusers), support groups, therapy groups, Twelve Step groups—all programs within the Program designed to welcome the graduate into the womb of happy abstinence. And help him or her make it through the night.

He was still searching for the little printed slip that would announce the lecture title when Marcia came in.

She stopped, surprised to see Preston, and said, "I thought you were sharing secrets."

"It doesn't work without you."

"You better learn, Scott. Can't take me home in your pocket." She pushed the door open again. "Let's take a walk. I was coming to get you anyway."

"Me? Why?"

She walked through the door and held it for him.

She didn't speak right away, just walked beside him on the path that circled the exercise area, and since sudden unscheduled private meetings with counselors, doctors, shrinks or administrators were always bad news, and since Preston wasn't in a mood for bad news, he tried to stall.

"What's this about Natasha Grant?"

"What'd you hear?"

"Duke says Dan's in there with a cop. He says Butterball says she heard the cop mention Natasha's name."

Marcia paused, then nodded and said, "They found her body on the road."

"When? What—"

"Nobody knows anything. I'm told our fearless leader intends to speak to us all tonight, fill us in."

"Banner?"

"His own self. I don't know what he'll say . . . probably just give us the party line."

What does THAT mean? There was an undercurrent of bitterness in her voice. Preston wanted to know why,

was going to ask—what the hell, all she could do was
snap at him—when she changed the subject.

"You said you'd let Lewis know about Cheryl."

The woman's got a lease on my brain! "Anything
wrong with that?"

"No."

"Then how'd you know about it? Jalapeño Pepper file
a goddam report?"

"Calm down, Scott. Lewis told me he was going to.
He *asked* me if I thought it was okay."

"He have to get a permit to pee?"

Marcia stopped walking and put a hand on Preston's
arm. "Scott . . ."

"What?"

"Shut the fuck up."

"Oh." Preston laughed. "Now that you ask me
nicely, okay."

Marcia smiled and turned back to resume walking,
and she let her hand slide down Preston's arm and in
behind his elbow, and she walked like that, with her
hand sort of drooped in his arm.

Preston felt weird, as if they were out walking on a
date, but there was nothing male-female about the gesture; it was almost affectionate, like something his
mother used to do when she'd come to see him at prep
school. And he certainly didn't feel anything male-
female about Marcia. He didn't think of her as a woman
at all. In this small world she was omnipotent and obviously omniscient.

It was like taking a stroll with God.

"Scott . . . Cheryl is going to die."

"She is?" *No!* He didn't mean that. Or not just that.

He felt a rush of adrenaline, then a fuzziness. "I mean—"

"Let me finish. You know she went for another biopsy. It came up bad. She's got almost no liver left, maybe an eighth, not enough to keep her going. Have you looked at her eyes?"

"I can't see her eyes."

"The whites of her eyes are yellow. Her skin's begun to go a kind of grayish orange. The liver's giving up. It's not processing the toxins anymore. It's shunting them by."

"Alcoholic hepatic jaundice." He remembered the lecture. God, how could he forget it? After Dr. Lapidus had spoken—or rather sermonized, for Lapidus was a thin, wiry, intense man whose every pious word chastised his audience for committing suicide, while he chain-smoked Gauloises and wheezed like a recalcitrant lawn mower—they showed a videotape of an unconscious man strapped to a hospital bed, wearing a Chicago Bears football helmet to protect his head when he lapsed into seizures, connected to machines by tubes up his nose and down his throat. His skin was the color of a spoiled banana, all speckled and blotchy, his nails cracked and rotten. And as they all watched and Dr. Lapidus stood to the side and smoked and smirked, suddenly the man's chest heaved and a geyser of blood erupted from his mouth—it must have gone four feet in the air—and spattered the camera lens. There were two or three smaller spasms that produced muddy bubbles of viscous goo, and then the man's mouth fell open and his head lolled and his eyes opened, showing nothing but yellow because his eyeballs had rolled back as he died.

Most of the audience had been paralyzed—horrified and sickened. But two jesters had jostled each other and said things like "Outrageous!" and "Far out!" Junkies, Preston guessed, whose deaths would be less spectacular if nonetheless final. They had always wanted to see a snuff film.

"Does she know?" he asked Marcia.

"Sure she knows. She has to make a decision."

"Like?"

"She can wait. She can accept it—if she *can*, and she's sedated now, so nobody'll know for a while—and say her Serenity Prayer and just wait. Sometime—in a week or a month or maybe six months—her brain will overload with ammonia and she'll start hallucinating. She'll get incoherent and she'll be hospitalized and then it's just caretaking till the varices come along and kill her. Or, she can try to get a liver transplant."

"Well, hell—"

"They have a lousy success rate. But there's a guy in Houston thinks he can do partials, give her just enough to let her get by."

"Still, that's better than—"

"It'll cost a hundred and fifty thousand dollars. At least."

"She has insurance. Won't—"

"Blue Cross, Scott? Gimme a break."

They passed the exercise area. Twist was doing push-ups. He had hung his clothes on the jungle gym and was dressed in nothing but powder-blue briefs. Whenever he had five minutes to himself, Twist exercised. He did push-ups or sit-ups or squat-jumps or he ran in place. Vanity or self-preservation—whatever it was, it worked. Twist was built like Herschel Walker; he reminded Preston of Michelangelo's *David*.

There was something to be said for heroin addiction. It screwed up your head but left your body intact. Until you OD'd.

Marcia called, "Put on some pants, Twist."

Twist didn't stop his push-ups. "Lawrence ain't no threat to nobody," he said between puffs. "He's retired. Temporarily."

Marcia let him be. They walked on.

Preston said, "Why are you telling me all this?"

"Lewis has a lot of money and a lot of friends who like to help people."

"You want me to . . ." *This whole walk is a fundraiser!* Now he felt angry, used. "Why don't *you*—"

"I can't. It's unethical . . . or illegal."

"So I'm supposed to put the arm on him."

"You won't have to. Not if you tell him all the facts. That's why I'm telling you."

"What about the joint here? This is a twenty-million-dollar facility. Banner's got friends . . . every movie star in the . . . Christ, his board could put up that kind of money out of pocket change."

"They won't."

"Why not?"

"Because Stone Banner won't ask them to, and they don't pay attention to what goes on here, they're all off playing celebrity golf, and if one of them did get wind of Cheryl's problem and offered money, Stone would turn him down. Because Stone has been lying in wait for a case like Cheryl."

"To do what?"

"He wants a poster child, wants to pull the public's

chain like with one of those pathetic kids who make the evening news begging for a kidney. He wants the public to start funding The Banner Clinic. Somebody told him about the Cousteau Society, about all those people who kick in fifteen or twenty bucks a year, which adds up to millions, so Cousteau can run his fleet and make his movies that nobody ever sees because they only run on cable. Stone thought, Hey, if the public'll throw money at that old frog they're sure to have enough left over for the Great American Hero.

"He wants the public to pay him to become the King of the Drunks, the Emperor of Addiction. And Cheryl's just the ticket.

"He wants to turn her into a freak. For publicity. For money."

They had stopped walking. Preston looked at Marcia and said, "Unless Lewis can raise enough money so Cheryl can pay for it herself."

"Right."

"That stinks."

"Yes." She took his arm again and started back toward Chaparral. "It certainly does."

Preston felt a bond with Marcia. Her hand in the crook of his arm made him feel they were in league, at least on this one issue. He was almost her equal. He said, casually, "What about Priscilla? Talk about money. You want me to—"

"No."

"All right. *You* talk to her, then."

"Nobody talks to her. People've hit on her for money all her life. She thinks that's all she is. Money. She's still too fragile. She's just beginning to feel safe, and if I so much as hint at anything to do with money, I could wreck her.'' She paused. ''I think I'd rather let Cheryl die than do that.''

When they reached Chaparral and Preston pulled open the glass door, he said, ''I never could figure why Lewis picked me.''

''Lewis sees things, Scott. He loves kindness and gentleness more than anything else. You know who he thinks of himself as? Blanche DuBois. He told me. You know: 'I have always depended on the kindness of strangers.' He saw something in you he could trust. Somewhere behind the ice-cold homophobic elitist he saw something''—she grinned at him—''Lord knows, *I* don't see it—something kind and gentle.''

When he had filled a tray with Swiss steak, cooked tomatoes, cottage cheese and iced tea, Preston headed for his usual table. There was nothing special about that table, no reason for him to feel mild resentment whenever he found it occupied by strangers. Funny how quickly people became routinized. It was the same at Mason & Storrow; he always used the same urinal in the men's room. It made no sense. He guessed it was an instinctual reflex, to reduce the number of decisions in a life packed with petty but unavoidable decisions.

Lupone and Duke were already seated. Preston didn't say hello—what was the point of greeting people you spent every waking moment with? He unloaded his tray and sat down.

''Puff and I were talking,'' Duke said. ''We didn't realize you're in such tough shape.''

''What?''

Lupone said, ''I *told* that broad there isn't a member

of the whole fuckin' human race who can't use a few extra bucks. But would she listen?''

Preston said "What?'' again.

Duke said, "How're the wife and kid making out? We could take up a collection.''

Lupone said, "I'd kick in . . . if they'd give me my money back.''

Preston saw that Lupone was having trouble controlling his fat face, so all he said was "Okay.''

"No, seriously,'' Duke said. "Maybe we oughta engrave your name on that piece of—what is it you're eating? meat?—so nobody'll steal it from you.''

"The hell are you talking about?''

Duke gave up. With a laugh, he reached in his pocket and pulled out a pack of cigarettes. It was full, but opened, and inside the cellophane wrapper was an inch-square piece of paper with Preston's name on it in ink.

"Where'd you get that?'' Preston asked.

"Table in the common room.''

"I didn't write that.''

"Sure,'' said Duke. "It's okay, Scott. You don't have to be ashamed.''

"Talkin' about shame,'' Lupone said, "we oughta take a pool on what line of bullshit Banner's gonna feed us tonight.'' As if he had suddenly remembered why he was at the table, Lupone attacked his plate, heaped his fork with mashed potatoes and stuffed it in his mouth.

Preston stripped the wrapper from the cigarette pack. The piece of paper fell on the table. Preston stared at his name. He didn't recognize the writing.

Lupone said, "I bet Stone's gonna say he don't know nothin' about nothin'.''

"I doubt he'll be defensive," Duke said. "I bet he'll spout a lot of crap about what a great lady she was."

"Ten bucks," Lupone said. "My marker's good."

Preston picked up the piece of paper and turned it over. On the back the same hand had written:

Meet me.
P.

12

"WE GOT A right!" screamed a man in a shiny jacket and string tie. "You ever hear of the First Amendment?" He made the mistake of trying to bull past Chuck, to shoulder him aside with the battering ram of moral authority.

"The only right you got," said Chuck, and he grabbed the man by the lapels and lifted him off the floor and threw him like a shot put back through the open doors, "is the right to sing the blues."

The man skittered across the sidewalk, tripped on the curb and sprawled on his back on the roundabout. His notebook fluttered into the air and landed on top of a van.

Chuck spread his legs and folded his arms and stood astride the entrance like a colossus.

"You 'spose Connie Chung is out there?" Duke mused as he watched the throng of reporters, correspondents, cameramen, field producers and drivers milling in frustrated anger, like hungry wolves before a guarded cattle pen. "Connie Chung lights my fire."

"Not yet," Preston said. "So far, Natasha's just dead. Front page, but a wire-service story and a bunch of film clips of her movies. If it turns out she killed herself, then the networks'll send some heavy hitters out to do in-depth pieces. Who they'll get to talk to them from here I have no idea. Probably good old Guy: 'Natasha Grant was a warm and loving human being. We did our best to put her in touch with her higher power, but I guess there were depths of despair in her tortured soul that even we couldn't reach. By the way, that's L-A-R-K-I-N.' But if the police think somebody pushed her, *then* you'll get the varsity. Connie Chung. Diane Sawyer. Diane Sawyer's better-looking than Connie Chung."

"For you, maybe. I like exotic." Duke paused. "Who pushed her?"

"I said 'if.' " Preston smiled. "Maybe you did it."

Duke nodded. "I did. I confess. I begged her to run away with me to Sunnybrook Farm, but she said her heart belonged to Don Ameche."

They heard a siren and saw the sheriff's car pull into the roundabout and stop. Its flashing lights reflected off the glass doors and turned the lobby into a silent discotheque. The sheriff and a young deputy as big as Chuck got out of the car and gesticulated at the gaggle of reporters, a few of whom shouted their protests, most of whom grumbled, but all of whom moved grudgingly away from the doors and to their vehicles.

As Chuck relaxed, abandoning his imitation of the classic mesomorphic Mae West stud, a small man—slight, harried and rumpled, probably in his early fifties—came scurrying up the corridor that led to the empty administrative offices.

Chuck spun on him, and the look on Chuck's face said, Why do you make me hurt you?

The man braked, stopped, held up his hands. "I'm no reporter!" he said. "I've got a *prob*lem!"

"Nothin' like the problem you're *gonna* have." Chuck advanced on the man.

"No! I mean, I'm a patient."

"How'd you get in? There's security guards all over the place."

"I couldn't get near the front door, so I went around back. The guard was busy with a camera crew trying to sneak in a window."

"Yeah?" Chuck stepped to the reception desk and reached down for a looseleaf notebook. "What's your name?"

"Parkinson. But I wouldn't be in there. Not yet. See, I was in jail on a DWI till this afternoon, and I had my court hearing, and the judge said if I didn't check into a rehab by tonight he'd put me back in jail and make me serve the whole thirty. I can't serve any thirty days! I'm a . . . a CPA!"

"Right." Chuck replaced the notebook. He looked at Duke and Preston and raised his eyebrows. They looked at each other. Duke shrugged.

Preston stepped forward, held out his hand and said, "Mr. Parkinson, my name's Scott. I'm a counselor-tech here at Banner." He glanced at Chuck, who frowned but didn't interfere. "What's your poison?"

"Poison?" Parkinson shook hands. "Oh, you mean . . . Anything. As long as it comes in a bottle."

"What makes you think you have a problem?"

Parkinson smiled and shook his head. He didn't hesitate. "My wife and I . . . well, when we got married, she didn't drink, but pretty soon she started, just to keep me company, and before long we were tying one on pretty regularly. Terrible.'' He grimaced at the recollected pain. ''Her father ran a greenhouse, and one night we got smashed and wrecked it, broke every pane in the place. After a while, I stopped, actually joined A.A., but she never did. Couldn't, I guess. I don't know where she is now. Anyway, I stayed sober for a couple of years, but then . . . Well, you know how it is.''

''I sure do.'' Preston put a sympathetic hand on Parkinson's shoulder. Then he turned to Chuck and shook his head.

Chuck grinned.

''Chuck'll take care of you,'' Preston said, and he turned Parkinson toward Chuck.

''Thank—'' was as far as Parkinson got before Chuck, in a single magical motion, ripped off his shirt and jacket, leaving him standing there in a sleeveless undershirt, with the two ends of his necktie flapped back over his shoulders . . . and a tiny remote microphone taped to the pocket of skin between his clavicles.

Chuck leaned down and shouted into the microphone, ''Say hey, motherfuck!''

Parkinson tried to smile. ''Can't blame a fella for trying.''

''Hell, no,'' Chuck said.

Parkinson reached down for his shirt. ''I guess I'll be on my—''

''Don't tell me you're leaving already?'' Chuck grabbed Parkinson by the hair and straightened him up like a Marine recruit. ''You said you want to check in. Shucks, a fella as resourceful as you oughta get his wish." He looked at Preston and Duke. "Right, gentlemen?"

"Absolutely," said Duke.

"By all means," said Preston.

"Joke's over," Parkinson said, suddenly a tough guy. "You won. Now let me the hell out of here, or—"

"No way, Mr. Parkinson," said Chuck, and he marched Parkinson to the door of Nurse Bridget's office.

Nurse Bridget sat at her desk, interpreting EKG results and making notes in patients' files.

"Nurse Bridget, this here's Mr. Parkinson."

"Hello, dearie." Bridget smiled until she saw the fear on Parkinson's face and the grip Chuck had on his hair.

"Nurse Bronsky here?" Chuck asked.

"Nurse Bronsky's always here."

"Get him," Chuck said, shoving Parkinson toward the door at the back of the office. "Mr. Parkinson wants to see Nurse Bronsky something fierce."

Preston and Duke peeked around the door as Nurse Bridget punched a number into the telephone intercom.

Just before the door at the rear of the office closed, they heard Chuck say, "You'll like Nurse Bronsky. Some patients actually fall in *love* with him . . . damnedest thing."

Preston and Duke started down the corridor toward the assembly hall, where Guy Larkin was waving his arms and scurrying about like a den mother shepherding her Cubs and Brownies into chapel.

"How did you know?" Duke asked.

Preston smiled. "Stupid bastard tried to sell me the plot of *Days of Wine and Roses*."

* * *

Their names were checked against a list as they entered. The hall was already packed, for all sixty patients were there, as well as every counselor and counselortech, the doctor, the shrink, the chaplain, the rabbi and assorted maintenance personnel.

From their place standing in the rear of the room, Preston tried to find Priscilla, but spotting one blond head in a kaleidoscope of moving, bobbing colors was impossible.

"Meet me," her note had said. But where?

Outside. Of course.

Tonight? Of course. Even though tonight, of all nights, was not exactly the smartest night to meet, since every security guard in the county would be patrolling the grounds.

Never mind.

"Meet me," she had said. And meet her he would.

He felt like Romeo plotting to spirit Juliet away from her parents.

Remember how that romance turned out?

Shut up!

Lupone squeezed past several standees along the wall and forced open a space beside Preston. "This's gonna be a gas," he said.

Larkin made sure there were no stragglers in the corridor, then closed the doors and walked to the podium. The room fell silent.

"This is a sad night for all of us," he said. He turned to the side door. "Ladies and gentlemen . . . Stone Banner."

Banner entered slowly, his pace barely faster than a pallbearer's. He wore black boots, black jeans and a buff buckskin jacket with a black armband wrapped around the left sleeve. His hair was perfect, but his face—even under the obvious makeup—was puffy.

There was scattered applause, which Banner cut off with an irritable wave.

"The guy's got *balls*!" Lupone whispered.

"What d'you mean?" Preston asked.

"Watch. . . . I'll be goddamned!"

Banner reached the podium and stood for a moment, looking down. Then he raised his eyes to the audience. His hands seemed to have lives of their own. They gripped the podium, touched his pockets, smoothed his hair, straightened his belt buckle, moved the little light on the podium, clasped one another.

Lupone grinned. "Is he gonna do it? Is he gonna go for it?"

Preston shushed him. He was sure Lupone's hoarse whisper would carry to the front of the room. But there was so much ambient noise—throats being cleared, feet shuffling, chairs squeaking—that no one noticed.

Banner sniffled and touched his nose.

"Yes!" said Lupone. "He did it! Now . . . the excuse."

"I'm sorry." Banner sniffed again. "This has been a terrible, terrible day." He touched his nose.

"Five points!" Lupone nudged Preston. "*Much* better'n blaming it on the flu."

"What's this about?" Duke said, leaning across Preston.

"He's wasted," said Lupone. "Coked right up to the fuckin' ozone."

"Bullshit."

"Yeah? You the expert on blow alluva sudden? I *been* to that party, man. A thousand times."

Preston said, "He's upset."

"He's blasted, what he is. Ten bucks says this is how it goes: He cries, he sniffles, he touches his nose, he gets all emotional, he sniffles, he goes to his nose, he calls us all his best friends, he cries s'more, sniffles, back to his nose again." He pointed at Banner. "A gas. Guy's a fuckin' riot."

Banner looked their way, so Lupone wiped the mask of mirth off his face and shut up.

"America has lost its leading lady," Banner said. "I have lost my dearest friend." He sniffled and squeezed his nostrils. "You've seen the vultures outside. They will not get in here." He slammed his hand on the podium, knocking the light loose, and he lurched against the podium and grabbed it before it could crash to the floor. "But some of you will be graduating tomorrow or the next day or next week, and people'll ask you what went on here, what really happened to Natasha G., so I want you to know the truth. Or at least everything *I* know."

"Sure, Stone . . ." Lupone whispered.

"You don't *know*," said Preston. "You just *want* him to be coked up."

"Right." Lupone glanced at Preston. "Asshole."

Banner took a handkerchief from his pocket and blew his nose. "As far as I knew, she was doing great." His hand made three attempts to stuff the handkerchief back in his pocket, but he kept missing, so he clutched it in his fist and continued. "She'd really gotten with the Program. I hadn't seen her since she left, till last night she showed up—just showed up—at Xanadu. Something was wrong. She looked awful. There was pain in her eyes . . .'' He paused for effect, and touched the handkerchief to his eyes and nose. ''. . . the pain of guilt and failure. We've all seen it. I knew right then she was on something.''

''I bet you did,'' said Lupone.

''Give him a break,'' said Preston.

Banner went on. ''I didn't know what, of course . . .''

''Nooo,'' said Lupone. ''How could you?''

He smiled at Preston, and now Preston knew that Lupone was needling *him*, not Banner. He tried to step away from Lupone, but there was nowhere to go.

''. . . and she denied it, said she was just out of sorts, maybe coming down with something. I asked her why she had come back, but she couldn't answer. *I* knew, though, and I told her: God had brought her back, for help. He had guided her footsteps to my door. I don't know, maybe that was my mistake . . .'' Banner wiped his eyes and sneaked a dab or two at his nose. ''. . . because I left the room to get my car keys to drive her down here and check her in, and when I got back she was gone. I looked for her. I scoured the whole top of the mountain, calling out to her. But it was pitch-dark, there was no moon, she could have been any-where. After about half an hour, I went back inside. I figured she'd had a cab waiting for her. I never saw her again.'' Now he was weeping openly.

Larkin jumped up from his seat and stepped to the podium and put his arms around Banner. He nodded to a couple of people in the front row, and they joined him, and the three of them surrounded Banner like a chrysalis.

Larkin raised a hand to the audience and, like Zubin Mehta, led them in a chorus of "We love you, Stone!"

Lupone said, "I'm gonna puke."

Watching, Preston felt an impulse to be genuinely moved. This was what it was all about. Comfort. Solace. We are not alone. But Lupone's cynicism throttled the impulse, confused it with doubt. So Preston felt anger, too. At Lupone.

But what if Lupone was right?

Banner untangled himself from the loving arms. He wiped his face and blew his nose and snorted, then gave each of his comforters a hug and sent them back to their seats. He stood at the podium and after a moment, composing himself, smiled for the first time.

"You are my rock," he said to the audience, "my higher power. I need you. I love you. I thank you."

This was the old Banner. He waved and grinned and accepted pats of congratulation from people who swarmed around his feet. He didn't step down and join them, though, nor did he invite them up to him.

He's like a president, Preston thought. Affection, yes; familiarity, no; intimacy, never.

He turned to say something to Lupone, but he wasn't sure what: to concede, perhaps, that Lupone had forecast Banner's every move, had predicted his every utterance. But perhaps to argue, too, to contend that Banner's behavior might, just might, have been more than a strung-out performance. Why couldn't it have been real?

Lupone was gone.

The crowd around Banner parted, as if pressed by a subsurface current, and Lupone's bald head, glowing with sweat, appeared at Banner's knees.

Preston saw Lupone tilt his head back and say something to Banner. Banner didn't see him right away, kept smiling and patting shoulders and wiping his nose.

Then suddenly Banner did see Lupone and heard what Lupone was saying, and he jerked upright as if he'd been goosed, and turned and rushed off the platform and out the side door.

There was a brief commotion up there. Somebody must have mouthed off to Lupone, and Lupone must have decked him (or her) or maybe called his opponent a cocksucker or something and gotten hit himself, because suddenly people were scrambling to get out of the way, knocking each other into chairs and falling down and being trampled. And then, wading through the mass, swatting people aside like gnats, came the great black form of Chuck.

"What say we retire for a glass of port and a quiche?" said Duke.

"Timely," Preston said, "very timely," and he followed Duke out the door.

They waited for Lupone in the corridor. He was one of the last to leave the room, and he sported a rosy bruise on one cheek and a couple of new lumps on the terrain of his lips.

"Ungrateful fuck," he said as he walked past them without stopping.

"What'd you say to him?" Duke asked as he and Preston fell in step beside Lupone.

"Nothing! 'Hey, Stone, you're lookin' great.' That's all."

"Man, he took off like a white-ass deer."

"No wonder he got no friends." Lupone touched his lip. "Dick-head!" He aimed a kick at a standing ashtray and sent it careening down the corridor into a wall, where it fell apart with a raucous clang.

"What should . . ." Preston sought words that would give no offense. "What is it he should be grateful for?"

"Where you think he gets his fuckin' coke?"

Duke laughed. "Get off it, Puff. You were begging *us* for blow."

"Not me. Don Ciccio. The fuck you think I got a scholarship here? They like my clothes? Everybody scratches everybody's back, that's the way the world is." He turned on Preston. "I forgot. You don't buy any of it. That was all *Guiding Light* shit in there, straight from the heart. Keep believing it, pal. You'll live to be a thousand."

Lupone veered off, into a lavatory at the end of the corridor.

"You believe him?" Duke asked as he and Preston walked along the dark path to Chaparral.

"No. I think he can't stand the stripping process. What Marcia says: We all make our excuses because we're special. He can't stand being told he's like everyone else, won't join the common denominator, has to have the inside scoop, has to know things nobody else knows. If you don't have any self-respect, you have to make up things so people respect you."

"You mean, Nobody knows the troubles I've seen."

"Yeah."

After a few more steps, Duke said, "Banner sure looked wrecked."

"Yeah, but—"

"Puffguts sure did spook him."

"Who knows what he really said? Probably asked Banner if he knew where he could score some blow."

* * *

The meditation walks had been canceled. Sandra, the counselor-tech, said it was because there might still be reporters creeping around in the bushes. The security guards had been told to arrest anything that breathed.

The patients sat around the common room, speculating about the possible causes of Natasha Grant's demise. Someone conjectured that she had been killed elsewhere and dumped on the road. Someone else guessed that she had had a slip, got stoned at a Beautiful People party and, in grief and remorse, been hitchhiking back to the clinic when she was struck by a truck. Nobody talked about how Banner had looked at the meeting.

Preston noticed that Lupone contributed nothing but sat back and chuckled knowingly at the various theories.

I'm right. I know I am. He just wants to feel superior.

He noticed, too, that Priscilla wasn't there. Either she had gone to bed or she had gone out and was waiting for him.

He hung around for a few minutes, smoked a couple of cigarettes, then mumbled something about being tired and slipped away down the hall to the row of bedrooms.

There was a light under Priscilla's door. He knocked. No answer. Maybe she was in the john. He listened for the sound of running water, heard nothing, and knocked again. Still no answer.

He went to his room, wondering what to say if Twist asked him questions. But Twist wasn't there. Preston turned out the light, opened the window and climbed out into the cool night.

He stood with his back against the wall and let his
eyes adjust to the darkness.

He heard a scratching noise from a far corner of the
building. A match flared and was cupped in some
hands. Then the match fell to the ground, and the orange glow of a cigarette end hovered like a firefly. The
smoker coughed and disappeared around the corner.

Where was she? She couldn't be waiting in the open.
There were no trees out here, no bushes large enough
to conceal a human. He replayed in his mind the walks
they had taken. There was only one possibility, at the
very outer limit of the path surrounding the clinic
grounds, where sand had been pressed into a bulwark
to stop erosion. One night they had lain behind the bulwark and gazed up at the stars, and because neither of
them knew anything of the heavens, had perceived private constellations and awarded them silly names.

She was there, pointing up at the sky and outlining
their constellations and whispering the names to herself.

She didn't hear him approach, for he had trod delicately through the soft sand, avoiding sticks and stones
and clumps of low brush. He stood over her for a moment and watched, trying to still his heart. He hadn't
spoken to her in days, and the longing had festered in
him, until now—against his mind, against all reason—
he was convinced that he was actually, truly, profoundly
in love with her.

Which, as soon as the thought coalesced in his brain,
he condemned as arrant bullshit.

He stepped off the bulwark and slid down beside her
in the sand and said, "Hi."

"Hi." She smiled.

"Sorry I'm—"

She kissed him. She reached up and put a hand behind his head and pulled it down to her and put her lips on his and . . .

And nothing. That was it. There was no moving, no tonguing, no urgency, no passion. It wasn't a kiss; it was a smooch.

She let him go and said, "That was for when we were so rudely interrupted."

"I see." He wanted to try again, to lean over her and open his mouth and look into her eyes and enclose her mouth in his and encourage her to . . .

Stop it!

He said, "That was nice. We should do it again sometime."

"I went up the mountain."

Wham! *I told you not to! Are you nuts?* He said, "Why?"

"He asked me to an A.A. meeting, I told you that. Then he asked me to another one. I asked Dan and he said it was okay. So I went. I thought it'd be fun."

You drag me out here in the middle of the night to tell me about fun times at Stone's?

"Was it?"

"No. It was . . . I guess weird is what it was."

"Tell me."

"An A.A. meeting is supposed to be a lot of people telling about their experiences and helping each other, but when I got there it was just the two of us. He said a couple of others would be coming along, but nobody ever did."

"So you left."

"We had some sodas, and he'd put out cookies and

things as if there *were* other people coming, and suddenly he started telling me how lonesome he was and all he needed was a friend, a real friend . . .''

The ballad of the lonely satyr.

". . . and I told him I'd be his friend, and he asked if he could hold me . . .''

"*Hold* you!"

". . . just like a friend, and I had to think about that, but before I could say anything the phone rang. He went to get it. I think it was from one of his cars."

"Why?"

"I heard him say, 'Where are you now?' and then 'Ten minutes! Holy shit.' Anyway, when he came back he was a different person. He said he was sorry, this had probably been a mistake, maybe we'd get together sometime soon, he really did want to be my friend . . . a lot of junk like that."

"*Then* you left."

"He had picked me up, but he said he didn't have time to drive me back, he had an important meeting, did I mind walking. That's two miles. But it was a nice night and all downhill, so I said okay and started walking. I wasn't too far from the house, just at the top of the hill, when I saw these headlights coming up the mountain, coming fast. I didn't know if he could see me, so I got off the road behind a big rock. This limo zoomed past and stopped in front of the house. The driver got out. He went around to open the back door, but she was already out of the car."

"She?"

"Natasha. I heard him ask her if she wanted him to wait, and she said, Yes, please, she'd only be a few minutes."

"How did she look?"

"Great. It was dark, but she was all lit up by the floodlights from the house. Her hair was done, she was made up, she didn't slur her words or anything, didn't stagger around. She was fine."

"Then what?"

"She went in the house and I walked down the mountain."

"And her driver waited for her."

"It wasn't her driver."

"What d'you mean?"

"It was Chuck."

Preston leaned back on his elbows and looked at the sky, at the constellation Priscilla had named Eloise because it looked like a little girl (he didn't see it at all) and she liked the story of Eloise who lived in the Plaza.

Priscilla said, "I don't think Stone was telling the truth tonight."

"No," Preston said. "Neither do I."

Twist was asleep and snoring like a diesel bus when Preston crawled through the window, so Preston let his clothes fall by the side of the bed and slipped between the sheets.

He would have liked to call Marcia, but the only phone he could have used was the coin box in the common room, and eavesdropping was a favorite pastime.

Besides, there'd be time enough to speak to her in the morning. He'd ambush her on her way to the cafeteria.

PART THREE

13

"WHERE'D YOU GET to last night?" Twist asked as Preston pulled out a chair and unloaded his tray.

"Nowhere." Preston mashed pieces of banana around in a bowl of All-Bran and watched Twist tuck a napkin into the neck of his T-shirt (its fibers stretched nearly transparent by his pectoral and deltoid massifs) and survey his breakfast tableau: four fried eggs lying on a bed of buttered grits and surrounded by a bulwark of bacon, sausages and ham.

"I don't know why you bother exercising, Twist. Save a lot of time and effort if you started every day with a heart transplant."

"*You* grow up so hungry you eat wall paint and bush berries, *then* come talk to me 'bout what I eat." Twist dropped a sausage onto the yolk of an egg and folded the white around it—like swaddling a baby—and aimed the package at his mouth. "What's up *your* nose this morning?"

"Nothing."

Duke came to the table, followed by Hector, and because Twist was the only person in the Western world who hadn't heard about the paparazzo's rendezvous last night with Nurse Bronsky, Duke felt obliged to tell him the whole story, embellished with sound effects.

Preston was grateful that he didn't have to talk. He could sit with his back to the wall and let his eyes drift around the staff section of the dining room, then to the door, then back again.

Where the hell was Marcia?

He had risen early and gone to wait for her in the parking lot. He had checked her office, in case she had had to take her car for servicing and someone had dropped her off. He had been the first patient in the cafeteria.

Other people trickled in, and everything seemed normal. The serving women called the patients honey and lovey; the patients made lame jokes about the ingredients in the coffee.

But when the staff section began to fill up, with Larkin and Nurse Bridget and Nurse Bronsky, with the counselors from Bandito and Geronimo, with the shrink and the doctors and the others who kept the engine of the clinic running, Preston sensed a difference. None of them ate alone, as some usually did, reading newspapers or whatever. They appeared to huddle around their tables. They spoke very little, and what they did say was uttered very quietly.

It was as if someone had died during the night.

Someone *had* died, of course—Natasha—but that hadn't happened last night, and it wasn't a secret. No one had to whisper about it.

Then Preston noticed something else.

Dan wasn't here either.

* * *

They waited in Marcia's office, in their circle—Preston, Hector, Twist and Lupone, and an empty chair that Preston had set up for Marcia.

Preston looked at his watch. Five after. Marcia was never late for therapy.

He wondered if the others felt the same uneasiness. But then Lupone let go a noisy fart and made a comment about needing more fiber in his diet, and Twist said he didn't need fiber he needed a cork, and Hector said something in Spanish and laughed, and Preston concluded that none of them noticed anything, ever.

The door opened, and a woman strode in and shut the door behind her and walked over and dropped a pile of patient folders onto Marcia's desk.

She was big—probably five ten, a hundred and sixty pounds—and solid. She wore a plain black dress, no jewelry and practical black lace-up shoes. Her hair fit her head like a tightly curled champagne-colored bathing cap.

She turned and stood behind Marcia's chair and looked down at them and smiled.

She had terrible teeth—snaggled, askew and spotted brown and black.

"Good *mor*ning!" she said cheerily. "My name is Gwen, and I'm an alcoholic and an addict."

There was some South in her accent, but Preston couldn't place it. It didn't have the warm roundness of the Deep South, or the casual elisions of the Southwest. It was probably Tennessee or North Carolina, but whatever it was wasn't natural. It had been studied, either to get rid of something or to acquire something. Her teeth spoke of poverty, her clothes of determination, or bitterness.

Suddenly Preston was frightened.

Twist and Hector looked at each other. Lupone eyed the woman through his little slits, as if deciding whether or not to have her erased.

''Well?'' Gwen said. ''What do we say?''

No one said anything.

''We say''—she raised her arms and shouted, grinning—''HI, Gwen!''

Silence.

Lupone shifted his weight on his two chairs. ''What we say is, who the fuck are you?''

The smile didn't vanish, didn't even shrink. ''I told you. My name is—''

''Where's Marcia?'' Preston said, hoping to hear—willing her to say—that Marcia had a cold. Or pneumonia. Or a broken leg. Something finite.

''Marcia won't be with us anymore.'' She glanced at the folders on the desk. ''Let's see, you must be—''

''What?'' Lupone said. ''She croaked?''

''Heavens, no.'' Gwen laughed. ''I guess she just got another position. Moved on. We all must, sooner or later.''

''Bull*shit*!'' said Twist.

Gwen paused, still smiling, always smiling, as if the smile was stitched onto her face and anchored there by those rotten teeth. ''One of the little changes we'll be making, Khalil, is—''

''Name's Twist.''

''I don't like nicknames, Khalil. I think they're escape mechanisms, ways of hiding who we really are. So I'd like to call you by the name God gave you.''

"No God gave me that dumb-ass name. Louis fuckin' Farrakhan gave me it, forced the old man to call me it. Mama called me Junius."

"Fine. Junius, then. One of the—"

"Name's Twist."

Hector laughed and nudged Lupone.

"—little changes we'll be making is that we're all going to try, honestly try, to clean up our language. Gutter language is lazy language. You don't want people to think you're just a lazy nigger, do you, Junius?"

Preston saw Twist start, had a second's horror of Twist launching himself out of his chair and throttling the grinning cow.

But all Twist did was straighten up and lean back in his chair and look at her and say, "Keep it up, honey-bun, and all people gonna be sayin' 'bout *you* is you're a dead cunt."

"So it's threats now, Junius?" Smile, smile. Not a hint of fear.

This woman is hard as spikes.

"Well, I guess we have to wallow at the very bottom before we can reach upward for God's sweet light." She stepped around Preston and sat in Marcia's chair. "Now," she said, looking from face to face, "the quickest way for us to get to know each other is for us each to take a turn on the Hot Seat. Do we agree? . . . Scott?"

"The what?"

"Marcia didn't put you on the Hot Seat? Naughty. It's so effective."

While she looked at the other faces, Preston sneaked a glance at his watch. Half an hour to go. *Keep her talking. Keep her from* doing *anything*. All he wanted was to get through the session, survive it, so he could get out of here and discover what had happened to Marcia.

"Let's begin with you, Guglielmo," Gwen said.

"Let's not," said Lupone.

"Why do you keep scratching yourself?"

"I don't."

"Yes, you do." She pointed at him. "There."

Preston had been in Lupone's company for twelve or fifteen hours a day, more or less, for a week and had never noticed it, but as soon as she pointed it out, it was as obvious as a goiter. Every few seconds, Lupone scratched a spot just above his belt on his right side.

"It itches," Lupone said.

"Why?"

"The fuck do I know why it itches? It itches."

"Are you allergic?"

"Yeah," he snorted. "Allergic. To ninety-eight-grain thirty-eight police-special plus *P*s."

"What are they?"

"It's a *bullet* hole, lady!"

"I don't believe you."

"I care."

Lupone looked at Preston, then at Hector and Twist. They were all staring at him with a kind of strange reverence.

He loves it.

Gwen said, "Somebody shot you?"

"No way." Lupone's voice dismissed the very possibility as unthinkable *lèse-majesté*.

"What happened?"

"I shot myself."

"What ever for?"

"I was in the shithouse." Offhand. Casual. No big deal.

"The where?"

"I had a tough day coming up, so I took a bunch of bennies, eye-opener, and after a while I had a few seven-and-sevens that put me in a shitty kinda no-man's-land, so when some guy said here, have a Valium, I had a coupla them, which put the brakes right on it, but just about the time I hadda go to work I was really fucked so I did a coupla lines. I don't even 'member thinkin' about it, but I was checking to make sure I had all six in my Smith and I musta said aw shit on it, 'cause next thing I knew I was in the doctor's office and he was diggin' the sucker out."

Lupone looked at Preston and smirked, and Preston felt cool on his teeth and realized that his mouth was open.

Gwen said, "You tried to kill yourself."

"Hell no. An accident is all."

Gwen said to Hector, "Do you believe him, Hector?"

"Believe him?" Hector started. "You mean, believe him? He say that the way it is, that the way it is."

"I don't."

Lupone lurched forward and almost toppled off his chairs. "I give a *fuck* what you think, lady! Why would I lie?"

"That's what we're here to find out, Guglielmo." Gwen smiled sweetly.

Preston sneaked another glance at his watch. Its hands were paralyzed, quick-frozen by the menace of Gwen. *My treatment is over. This woman has nothing to offer me but pain.* He felt a sudden rush of anger at Marcia.

How could you do *this to me*? She had broken him down
and begun to build him up and then abandoned him.
He began to salivate, and a familiar taste permeated his
spittle. More than anything else right now, he wanted
a drink.

The flash of recognition made him sweat with fear.
How could it be happening? One tiny *frisson* of fear,
and the boozing reflex kicks into gear? If it could happen here, in this sanctum of sobriety, what would it be
like the first time something went wrong in the real
world?

He would never make it on his own.

"What do you think, Scott?" Gwen said. "Is Guglielmo telling the truth?"

Marcia rode Dan as if he were a Brahma bull, bracing
herself with her hands to keep from falling off as he
bucked and whinnied.

They hadn't made love in the morning for weeks, and
she was tempted to roll away and tease him for a while,
to prolong her pleasure. But she sensed no urgency to
his writhing, he wasn't ready to fire quite yet. This was
their second go-round in the past two hours, and his
trigger wouldn't be as sensitive this time. If she was
wrong, too bad; they'd try again in another couple of
hours. They had plenty of time.

They had nothing *but* time.

The bulletin had come at six-thirty. She was up, had
taken a shower and was having a cup of coffee when
the doorbell rang.

It wasn't a telegram, not a Federal Express envelope
nor a UPS night letter. It was a plain white envelope
with the clinic's logo in the top left-hand corner . . .

delivered by a *state trooper*, for Christ's sake! (What, were they worried she'd attack a Western Union messenger?)

As soon as she looked at the envelope, she knew what it was. She didn't have to read the message inside.

It was addressed to her and Dan.

Both of them.

At her address.

But the smokey insisted that she open it and read it in front of him, and when she had finished, he asked if she understood it, did she have any questions.

Yes, she said, she understood it; no, she had no questions.

The smokey tipped his hat and said, "Have a nice day," and left.

She sat in the kitchen and read it again while she finished her coffee. She had to lay the sheet of white bond on the table, for her hands were shaking so badly that she couldn't hold it steady. At first her rage was wild and unfocused, like a hive of frantic bees. She tried an old trick and imagined that she was plucking her angers from the sky one by one and examining them and crushing them, and she was interested—and mildly amused—to discover that one of them was Martin Luther King. She was furious at him for leaving her.

She went into the bedroom and sat on the bed and touched Dan's cheek and said, "Hey." When he was awake, she read him the message. It was in the form of a memorandum (to both of them, conspicuously at the same apartment number, let's not kid ourselves, we've known all along) from Lawrence Victor Tomlinson, chairman of the board of trustees of The Banner Clinic and (unnoted but well known) chief executive officer of

a chemical conglomerate and bosom buddy of several
U.S. presidents:

> *You are, hereby and effective immediately, dismissed*
> *from the staff of The Banner Clinic for conduct un-*
> *becoming employees of the Clinic. You are banned*
> *from the Clinic grounds. Your personal effects will be*
> *sent to you. You will receive by mail two weeks' sal-*
> *ary. Your health benefits will terminate at the end of*
> *the current month. You are reminded of the declara-*
> *tion of confidentiality signed upon your employment,*
> *any violation of which may occasion civil or criminal*
> *prosecution, or both.*

"Conduct unbecoming?" Dan said. "What does that
mean?"

"It means"—Marcia kissed him—"that in this white-
bread world, nobody likes Oreo Cookies."

"That's ridiculous."

"*You* tell *me*, then."

Dan was silent, and Marcia imagined that she could
actually see gears mesh in his head. After a moment he
said, "What are we going to do?"

"First thing, I thought we'd go downtown and find
the scraunchiest dealer we can and buy all his worst shit
and eat it, and when we got a really *bad* buzz going,
we go machine-gun Mr. Lawrence Victor Tomlinson
and the rest of the board. Is that a great idea or what?"

Dan didn't smile.

Mistake. Irony isn't his long suit. "Don't worry,
baby"—she touched his cheek—"I'm kidding." She
paused. "But we *are* gonna have to be there for each
other. There's a little bastard inside me right now, and

he's saying, 'C'mon, Marcia, let's go grab a couple of yellows, maybe a red or two, pop 'em down and forget the whole thing.' "

"What about the Human Rights Commission?"

"And say what? You think they'll admit they canned us 'cause I'm a jungle bunny? Forget it. They canned us 'cause we're living in sin, sets a bad example for unstable patients, et cetera, et cetera, et cetera. They have the right."

"We'll get married."

"Sweet, Daniel, but too late." She leaned across his legs and propped herself up on one elbow. "You want to hear sick? We've just been run over, no prospects of anything, about six bucks between us, and I'm wondering how some of my drunks are gonna make it. They don't know how dependent they are, and they're gonna get a new counselor who could be Joan of fuckin' Arc and won't be able to get through to them, and they won't know why and she or he won't know why, and they're gonna think, Hey, I've just been shafted here, and they're right. There are some of them right on the edge, like Preston, they're just putting their bricks in place and there's no mortar to them yet. A little push, they can go either way."

Dan said, "They've *got* to give us references. I mean, we're *good*."

"Good doesn't count, baby."

"I don't get how you can be so damn cool." He was annoyed. "You're just gonna give up?"

"No."

"Aren't you mad?"

"Sure."

"So what are we gonna *do*?" He threw back the covers, but Marcia didn't move off his legs, so he was forced to lie there, naked.

"You're so pissed," she said and touched him, "let's see you loose the fateful lightning of your terrible swift sword."

When they were finished, they sprawled on their backs on the bed. Marcia left a leg draped across Dan's midriff, and she stared at the ceiling.

When her pulse had slowed to nearly normal, she said, "What's your pleasure—professionally, I mean—survival or revenge?"

Dan considered. "We can't have both?"

"Maybe. Probably not. I vote revenge. Survival is just survival. I gotta do something makes me *feel* good."

"Like?"

"What say we try to bring down the temple?"

"Dream on. How?"

"You knew Natasha better than anybody. Did you swallow that line of Stone's?"

"She was pretty together when she left. But you never know what—"

"I think it stunk. Like he had a dead fish in his pocket. Where were you sitting?"

"Last night? Off to the side. Why?"

"I was way in the back," Marcia said. "I couldn't see too well. But the way he was fumbling, it sure looked to me that either he had a bad cold and was juiced on decongestants, or else he'd been putting some goodies up his nose."

"Stone?" Dan huffed. "Be serious. You *want* to believe that. What're you saying? We should blow the whistle on him? We can't even set foot in the place."

"True." She rubbed her foot on his stomach. "But we have spies. Oh *my*, do we have spies."

"I don't think you people want to get better," Gwen said, her smile by now a caricature of a death rictus. "You know why? You're all still lying and still denying."

Lupone had refused to retract his story about the source of his itching, despite Gwen's insistence that it was a fantasy made up to glamorize his drab life as a low-level marketing executive.

By the time she turned to Twist, a tacit understanding had spread among the patients that since truth had no value in this forum, since Gwen had no intention of believing anything they said and was interested only in proving them all liars, they would each invent a fine lie that would be supported by all the others.

All this they agreed with their eyes.

Gwen asked Twist why he persisted in denying his Arab-African heritage, which was obvious to her because he had refused to accept either his Moslem name or his black name.

Feigning remorse, Twist said that his drug problem was grounded in sex. "My aunt, she fell in love with my . . . weapon . . . took to callin' it Lawrence of Arabia 'cause it conquered all that come before it, and I knew God would strike me dead for porkin' my mama's sister so I started sniffin'."

Preston attempted to corroborate Twist's story with a colorful description of Lawrence's magnitude, but Gwen cut him off and said, "Junius, your problem isn't sex. It's mendacity."

Hector, confronted with the accusation that the reason he spent his life in treatment centers was that he was obsessed with the attention lavished on him by doctors, psychiatrists and counselors, that his problem could be reduced to one word—"egomania"—said, "Wrong. If you knew to read my record, you'd see my real papa is Cesar Chavez, and them grape pickers is worried that if it gets out he's been fuckin' around, no more *huelga*. So they gotta keep me locked up. You think I *like* it here?"

Preston opted for simplicity. When Gwen asked him when he had first known he was an alcoholic, he said, "I'm not. I've been trying to tell people for three weeks, especially Marcia, but will she listen?" He spread his arms: Saint Sebastian at the stake.

Gwen sat stonily and looked at each of them, and each of them looked at the floor, like twelve-year-olds caught peeping into the girls' locker room.

"None of you," she said at last, "none of you will get your medallions. You'll leave here and go out in the world without that symbol of success, and I guarantee you within a week you'll all be in the gutter. I could give you that medallion, that comfort, but I won't. Do you know why? Because God is not pleased with you, not pleased at all." She stood up. "Now get out of here."

At the door, Preston looked back and said, "Hey, Gwen, do me a favor? Next time you talk to God"— he winked—"give Him my very best. I think He's aces."

"What an asshole," Duke said to Preston as he watched his new counselor—a young man in a dark suit, white shirt and dark tie, who looked like a Seventh Day Adventist canvasser—walk from Dan's office (now his) into Marcia's office (now Gwen's) and close the door. "The guy tried something called the Hot Seat."

"Yeah, so did Ilse Koch."

"You should've heard Priscilla. This dude gets on her case about being a rich bitch and all, and she gives him that look like he's something the toilet forgot to flush and says, 'Mr. Crippin, I don't know who you are or why you're here, but if you think you can intimidate me with your petty proletarian snobbery, you're very much mistaken.' "

"You know what happened?"

"You mean *happened* happened? No idea."

"Let's go find out."

Guy Larkin wasn't in his office.

Nurse Bridget was typing labels for blood samples.

Preston poked his head in the door and said, "D'you know what happened to Marcia?"

Nurse Bridget kept typing. "Did something happen to her?"

"Her and Dan," Duke said. "Where are they?"

She shook her head. "Nobody tells me anything."

She knows. Preston said, "What you mean is, they told you not to say anything."

"Have it your way, dearie."

They walked down the corridor of administrative offices, hoping to find an unsuspecting secretary they could surprise into revealing something.

A voice behind them said, "You haven't been murdered in your bed yet."

It was Sandra, the counselor-tech. She wore slacks, not shorts, a blouse, not a T-shirt. But she still carried her dog-eared copy of *Beyond the Chains of Illusion.*

"Hey," Preston said. "Working days now?"

"Promoted. Assistant counselor." She smiled. "One more step and I'll have a license to get inside your head."

"Somebody leave?" Preston asked, all innocence.

"Nice try, Scott." She punched him lightly on the shoulder.

"C'mon, Sandra. Tell me what happened."

"Not sure. All I *know* is they moved Crippin up and that Gwen, thank God. She was on me like fleas."

"But you hear things," Duke said.

"Everybody hears things."

"Like what?"

"Like"—serious now—"like, they're paying me more money and giving me more to do, and I don't want to blow it by shooting off my mouth. Have a great day."

The psychologist was sitting at his desk, reading. Preston tapped on the open door and said, "Dr. Frost . . ."

Frost looked up. "Ah! Preston, isn't it? Scott Preston?"

"Right." Preston took a step inside the office. Duke followed.

"And . . . ?" Frost looked at Duke.

"Duke Bailey. Self-loathing. Probable suicide. You remember."

"Of course. What can I—"

"Two counselors," Preston said, realizing suddenly that he had never known Marcia's last name. "Marcia and Dan. Do you know what happened to them?"

Frost hesitated, clearly—obviously, no question—deciding whether or not to lie.

At last, he said, "I do."

Bless the headshrinker's oath, Preston thought: I will dissemble, I will circumlocute, I will refuse to answer, but I will never lie.

"Tell us."

"No."

Die, shrinks!

"Why not?"

"You don't need to know. All you need to know—"

"She's my counselor!"

"—is she's gone. You have a new counselor. Develop a relationship with her. You've become too dependent. Both of you."

"How do *you* know?"

"It's common. Everybody does."

Duke said to Preston, "Shall we beat the shit out of him?"

Frost tensed, and his hand went behind his desk.

"No satisfaction," Preston said. 'You can't make a shrink beg. They just lie there and bleed and say"— here Preston raised his voice to a falsetto whine— " 'How does this make you *feel*?' "

They quit. Who else could they ask?

They walked back toward Chaparral, wondering aloud what transgressions Marcia and Dan could have committed (for Frost had as much as acknowledged that they had been fired). Had they refused an order? Had they been judged too hard or too soft on their patients? Had they (Jesus!) been caught drinking? As they passed the staff parking lot they saw Chuck buffing the hood of a fire-engine-red Porsche.

They drew closer, and Preston said, "He's not polishing that car. He's punishing it."

Chuck was rubbing one spot about two feet square—

rubbing and rubbing and rubbing. The muscles in his shoulders rose and fell like ripples in a pond.

"Hey, Chuck," Preston said.

Chuck turned his head an inch, saw them and grunted.

"There's quicker ways to take paint off," Duke said.

"Fuck do you care?"

"Right. Right you are."

Preston said, "D'you know what happened to Marcia and Dan?"

Chuck didn't answer.

"I mean, they're gone."

Chuck rubbed some more, then muttered, "Nobody's damn business."

"What isn't?"

"What they do."

"What *did* they do?"

"Nothin'. Not a Christ thing they didn't have a right to."

"Then what—"

Chuck spun on them then and raised the leather-backed buffer and, as if it were a Kleenex, tore it in two before Preston's eyes. "You're all the same! Matter what nobody says, all the slick talk and smooth bullshit, you're all the *fuckin'* same!"

Duke took a step back and started to speak, but Preston grabbed his arm, and shushed him, for now he knew. In his mind he saw Marcia and Dan in the cafeteria line, saw them whispering, felt the intimacy he had felt that day, and he knew.

Here, in this backwater in the land of the free and the home of the brave, lived a nasty little creature named Apartheid.

He closed his eyes and forced the bile in his throat to reverse its course and return down his gullet.

"Sorry," he said to Chuck. "I'm really sorry."

Duke didn't know, of course, had no idea what had caused Chuck to detonate, so all he wanted to do was mollify him.

"That's a really nice car," Duke said. "Where'd you get it?"

"Oh yeah?" Chuck shouted, and he stepped at Duke and actually took a swing at him, and when he saw that he had missed by three feet and that Duke was back-pedaling like a guy in some cartoon, he added, "So what? Not jigaboo enough? So fuckin' what?"

Preston told Duke when they were safely on the path back to Chaparral.

At first Duke didn't believe it, but then, because he couldn't think of anything more plausible, he did believe it, and he said, "They can't do that."

"Who says?"

"It's gotta be a violation of . . . I don't know, the Helsinki agreement."

"They can do whatever they want."

"No way, man. I'm going on strike."

"Sure. *That'll* show 'em."

They walked in silence for a few steps. Then Duke said, "What d'you guess Chuck makes?"

"Twenty-five? Thirty? Why?"

"That's a nine twenty-eight S-four . . . a sixty-thousand-dollar car."

Guy Larkin stopped them as they crossed the common room. He had a sheet of paper in his hand, and he consulted it and said to Duke, "Family Week. Clarisse is still a 'maybe.' She'll try to make it."

"Great!" Duke grinned. "Two weeks ago, she was a definite 'piss on you.'"

Larkin looked at the paper again and said to Preston, "Margaret will be here, with Kirk."

Preston started, then realized what had happened and said, "That's a typo."

"What is?"

"It should be 'Kim.' My daughter's name is Kimberly."

14

THEY COULDN'T AGREE on anything.

They talked at meals, after lectures, during walks. Some of them even tried to discuss it during therapy, but Crippin (whose given name was Melvin but who wanted to be called "just Mel") and Gwen cut them off, declaring the routine departure of two counselors to be an unfit topic for therapy because it had nothing to do with recovery. It was over and done with, whereas their recovery was just beginning.

Everybody had his or her own ideas about what should or shouldn't be done.

Lupone said the thing was, Don't make waves. What had happened to Marcia was none of his business, and in his line of work people who got too nosy ended up as snapshots in their mothers' scrapbooks. "Besides, I got less than three weeks to serve, so I don't care they give me Pee Wee fuckin' Herman for a counselor."

Twist said that even though he had nothing against Marcia, in fact she was pretty righteous, she should've known she'd get in trouble for balling a honky, specially since all the big shots who ran this place were the kind of folks who didn't think of black people as people but just as *things* who made beds and served little tiny sandwiches with no goddam crust on the bread.

Priscilla said it wasn't fair.

Clarence Crosby said he agreed but he was dipped if he knew what they could do about it, since a bunch of drunks and junkies weren't exactly the U.S. Congress that anybody'd listen to.

Hector said he'd been in so many joints in his time and seen so many counselors come and go for so many different reasons that he thought of them as interchangeable, and while he felt sorry for Marcia and agreed that it was nobody's business what you put where on your own time, she'd probably get another job in a day or two and chances were he'd run into her at the next joint he went into, or for sure the one after that.

Duke said they were all chickenshit assholes and why should they let some two-bit cowboy has-been and a bunch of fuckheads who if they didn't have so much money they could buy off judges and get free prescriptions from tame doctors would all probably be patients themselves tell a class broad like Marcia how to run her life? They had to *do* something.

Like what? Preston wanted to know.

Priscilla said it wasn't *fair*, darn it, and she was tempted to call her father, except that her father probably agreed that people of different races should fraternize with their own kind.

Twist said he'd never heard anybody call it fraternizing.

Lupone said he could probably make a call and get

somebody's knees broken, but they'd have to figure out whose knees deserved breaking.

And so on and so forth, with nobody agreeing on anything and nothing specific being suggested, let alone done.

Preston began to avoid the conversations, not only because they didn't lead anywhere but because he had worries of his own. Family Week was coming up, and even though it wasn't really a week but only a couple of days, the prospect of confronting Margaret and Kimberly panicked him.

What would they think of him? He was a different person from the self-deceiving, self-pitying cripple they had last seen weeping over a wastebasket almost four weeks ago. He wasn't sure exactly *how* he was a different person, but he knew he was different. He looked different—at least, he felt he looked different—eight or ten pounds lighter, no longer bloated in the gut and puffy in the face, no more milky pink in the eyes, no more ragged patches of torn skin around the base of his fingernails. But the real difference, if there was a difference, was inside. He had a new perspective on himself, on his disease. Yes, he was actually coming to see a truth in what he used to think was facile, exculpatory nonsense: It *was* a disease, not a character flaw, because it was something he couldn't help, like hemophilia. He drank not because of professional pressure or financial pressure or to escape but purely and simply (and how pure it was in its simplicity!) because he couldn't *not* drink.

And the rationale wasn't just escapism, either, not just a way of avoiding guilt, because if he had hurt people, and he had, himself included, there was nothing he could do about it now except apologize, which he would do, and try not to hurt them again. Which made it easier to deal with what Margaret and Kimberly and Warren Storrow and anyone else might think of him, because he had no control over what they thought of him. He was responsible for what he did, how he acted, not for how people reacted. If they didn't like him, couldn't accept him, too bad.

We do the best we can, and if that's not good enough, well . . .

What would *he* think of *them*? Had they changed? Had they concluded that part of the blame lay with them? It didn't, not really, except insofar as they might have been "enablers," somehow subconsciously behaving in ways that encouraged his drinking, like making excuses for him or going along with his own pathetic excuses for himself. He would tell them it wasn't their fault, especially Kimberly.

Why did she have to be put through this? If anyone was an innocent victim, it was Kimberly. What did Margaret hope to accomplish by bringing her along, exposing her to all the sordid details of a world she should never have to know? He guessed that that Chris Evert woman at his intervention, what's her name, had kept in touch with Margaret and had pressured her to bring Kimberly along, had convinced her that only by forcing *all* members of the family to face the *whole* truth could true honesty and openness be achieved, without which the integrity of the family unit could not survive.

Whatever the hell that meant.

It was all a lot of sophistic cant.

Kimberly was a *child*, for crissakes.

But she'd learn something, that was for sure. She'd have something special to bring to show-and-tell.

What I did on my spring vacation.

For "Family Week" was a misnomer, and not merely because of the duration of the event. It wasn't designed to bring a family together to mend ties that had been shattered by booze or pills or needles. It was bringing families together with other families, with the patients like baited bulls in the center of the ring, so that aggrieved wives and abused children, resentful husbands and confused parents could spill their venom and vent their hatreds and air their horrors—all for the edification of complete strangers, so that (he guessed) they could go home thinking either, "Holy shit! And *I* thought *I* had it bad!" or "Holy shit! I must be out of my mind to have hung around as long as I did!"

That, at any rate, was the portrait of Family Week painted for Preston by other patients as they lurched, wan and trembling, from the meeting rooms and rushed back to the comfort of their common rooms, the kind words of their fellow outcasts and the solace of a pint of ice cream.

The first they knew that the day had arrived was when Larkin made the rounds of the breakfast tables and told them—Preston, Duke, Twist, Crosby, Hector and Lupone—that they were excused from lecture and were to report to rooms in Peacemaker. He suggested that they make themselves "presentable."

"Me?" Lupone said. "What I got a visitor for?"

"Your brother," said Larkin. "He asked permission to come, even though it's early for you. We thought it would be okay."

"My brother."

Larkin checked his clipboard. "Raffi."

"Oh." Lupone said softly. It was the first time Preston had heard Lupone say anything softly.

"Anybody seen Priscilla?" Larkin asked.

No one had.

"Never mind, I'll find her. She's probably making herself look fabulous for Mom and Dad. Have a *great* day."

"You don't like your brother?" Duke said to Lupone.

"I don't got no brother."

"So who's Raffi?"

"*Vindicatore,* like Li'l Bit. They sent him to check up on me. If he decides I ain't doin' so good . . ."

"What?" Duke laughed. "You get demerits?"

"You could say. He arranges for me to swallow my tongue."

Preston put on a clean Brooks Brothers button-down shirt, pressed slacks and loafers. He had taken a jacket and tie from the closet and was about to tie the tie when he thought, No, don't look like the same tight-ass you were when you left. You're an inmate, a patient, a changed man.

Let your eyes reflect the agony of self-knowledge.

"Who you got comin'?" Hector asked Twist as they walked down the corridor.

"The old lady. She said if they give her the day off."

"Where she at?"

"Runs payroll for a Bob's Big Boy."

"Hey, smart."

"Yeah." Twist smiled. "Only dumb thing she ever done was hang out with me. Wh'about you?"

"Surprise," Hector said. "Got a buddy runs hookers. I never know who he's gonna send to play Corazon. That's my honey on the admission form. Sometimes it's a big fat mama painted up like a subway car. That kind likes to give me all sortsa shit about how I slap 'em around. Sometimes it's a skinny little thing like she's been eatin' lizards. That kind hassles my ass 'bout walkin' out on her and the twins.'' He laughed. ''One time one a them played it up real fine and got all teary 'bout how I prob'ly couldn't remember the names a the goddam twins. Fucked if I could, either, I couldn't think up names fast enough. *Did* they rip my ass for that!''

''What you bother for?''

''Hey, man, you gotta have a family on Family Week. That's all part a the game.''

Walking beside Duke, Preston saw him light a third cigarette from the butt of the second one. ''You love her, don't you,'' Preston said.

''Who knows?'' Duke said. ''What's love? All I know is, she doesn't come, it means I got no one.'' He sucked enough smoke into his lungs to asphyxiate a bison. ''You know what my social life was before I met Clarisse? My friends were a TV set, an eye patch and a little fridge I kept a bottle of vodka in. I'd sit in bed and watch TV and drink the vodka. After a while, I'd start to see double so I'd put the eye patch on, go from stereo to mono so the double image'd go away. I'd wake up in the morning with the eye patch on and a big puddle of cold vodka on my chest from where the glass spilled, and the TV set playing *Sunrise Sermonette*. Yessir, good times were had by all.'' He dragged the cigarette down to a nub and tossed it in an ashtray. ''Nobody should have no one.''

''I don't know,'' Crosby said. He was walking a few

paces behind them. "If you don't love nobody, you got nobody to lose. A fella can stand just so much pain."

"Who've you got coming today, Clarence?" Preston stepped to the side so Crosby could walk between him and Duke.

"Not sure. But I tell you one thing: That bitch brings my little boy, I'm cutting her legs off and feeding them to the alligators. He's six."

Duke said, "He wouldn't understand anyway."

"A lot more'n you think. His memories of me are sweet, playing ball in the backyard, taking my at-bats with fifty thousand people hollering my name and going apeshit when I stroked one. He thinks I'm great. No *way* he's gonna know the truth."

The two rooms were across the hall from each other. Larkin directed Duke and Crosby into the one on the right. Preston looked through the doorway and saw Butterball and a bunch of people he didn't recognize. And Gwen.

Larkin must have seen him start, for he said, "We shuffle up the counselors for Family Week, Scott. Get rid of all assumptions and attachments."

"You'll get real attached to her," Preston said to Duke. "She's a person who attracts attachments."

"Yeah," Duke said. "Like a leech."

Larkin looked at his watch and said, before Preston could turn into the other room, "Have you seen Priscilla?"

"Still haven't found her?"

"She'll be along. I'm not worried."

Just Mel (as Duke insisted on calling him) was waiting for them. He was wearing his black suit and white shirt and dark tie and a pair of Corfam brogans, which made Preston assume that Just Mel's father had been a policeman or a professional soldier, because nobody else ever wore Corfam.

The room was divided into two sections of seats, families on the left, patients on the right. Confrontational.

There were three people in the seats on the left: a pretty black woman in a sedate skirt and blouse (Twist's old lady), who was knitting; a sallow-faced, red-haired woman in high heels, a short skirt and a toreador jacket, holding a cigarette between talons as long as an eagle's (playing the role of Hector's Corazon), and a short, slight, dark man in a gray suit, whose hair was brushed straight back and pomaded in place (this had to be Raffi).

As the four patients entered the room, like medical specimens, Raffi stood up and intercepted Lupone, and the two of them embraced ritualistically, bussing both cheeks, holding each other's shoulders, looking into each other's eyes.

"Puffguts." Solemn.

"Raffi." Forcing a smile.

"How's it goin'?" Concerned.

"Great, Raff! Couldn't be better." Like a game-show host.

"Stop it!" Just Mel shouted. "Stop it! Stop it! Stop it!"

Raffi turned his head slowly toward Just Mel. "Fuck is this, Puff?"

"There's turkeys the world over, Raff."

Like a referee breaking up a clinch, Just Mel stepped between them and pushed them apart.

"I know what it's like, I really do," Just Mel said as

he escorted Raffi back to his seat. "Our Significant Others are the dearest things in the world to us. We've been apart for weeks. But we must have patience."

Raffi used two fingers to pluck Just Mel's hand from his arm. "Touch me once more, pal, you'll be playin' the harp with fuckin' stumps."

"Now, now," said Just Mel, and he shut the door and returned to the center of the room.

She's not coming. She changed her mind. Preston felt a split second of anger, followed by a flood of relief. Let Kimberly grow up just a little bit more without having to know about hit men and whores. He and Margaret would work things out when he got home. Or they wouldn't. Whatever, Kimberly wouldn't have to witness a community of abasement.

"Now, let's get to know each other." Just Mel consulted a list and pointed around the room. "This is Hector and Hector's Corazon. This is Khalil and his friend, Desiree. This is William and his . . . his . . ."

"Brother," said Lupone.

". . . his brother, Raffi. This is Scott and . . . oh, I guess she isn't here yet."

She's not coming, Mel. Believe it.

Just Mel had another name on his list, and Preston heard him start to say "Where's Cheryl?" but then eat the words.

Preston said them. "Where's Cheryl?"

Just Mel turned pink as a flamingo. "I made a mistake."

"Where is she?"

Just Mel murmured, "Deceased."

It was as if all the air had been sucked out of the room.

"Say what?" Twist said after a moment.

"You say 'dead'?" said Hector.

Just Mel nodded. "This morning."

Dead. Just like that. Where's Cheryl? Cheryl's dead. Oh yeah? Pass the salt. Preston felt dizzy.

"Let her not have died in vain," said Just Mel. "Let's take a lesson from her. Let's let her weakness be our strength. Let's all say the Serenity Prayer in her memory."

He started to recite the prayer. Hector joined in, sort of, and Preston mouthed the words.

The people on the left side of the room looked uncomfortable. Desiree knitted faster, and the red-headed Corazon smoked faster. Raffi pared his fingernails.

"There!" Just Mel said when he had finished the prayer. "I don't know about you, but *I* feel better."

Glad to hear it. In his mind's eye, all Preston could see was an image of Cheryl, tiny and frail and gray, lying on a metal table. Cold. So cold.

"Desiree," Just Mel said, and he went and stood in front of her, "tell us what life was like with Khalil."

"He took dope," Desiree said, and kept on knitting.

"Yes, but what did he *do*?"

"Smiled a lot."

Just Mel sighed. "All right, then, what *didn't* he do? He didn't go to work, did he, didn't help out around the house?"

"He worked. If something was broke, he fixed it."

"But how did it make you *feel*, him spending all your money on dope?"

"Didn't spend my money. Spent his own." She performed a fancy maneuver that made the knitting needles click like a ratchet.

"But didn't you feel alone? Wasn't it like living with a dead person?"

"Sometimes." Desiree's eyes never left her knitting, but she smiled at some secret memory. "Not always."

"Why didn't you leave him?"

" 'Cause sometimes with him is better than always with most people."

"I see." Just Mel looked grim. He couldn't open any wounds. She wasn't playing the game. He turned to Corazon. "Is that how you felt about Hector, Corazon?"

She had been gazing fixedly at the ash of her cigarette—lost, it seemed to Preston, in some chemical reverie. It took a beat for the name to register. Then her head snapped up and she said, "He was *bad*. That is one sick motherfucker."

"How so?" Just Mel sat back and smiled.

Hector compressed his lips to suppress his own smile, and squared himself to meet the challenge, ready to dissolve in grief or explode in outrage, depending on what accusations had been mischievously programmed into the doxy by his buddy the pimp.

"You ever heard of Wesson Oil?"

"Of course. What does—"

The door opened. Margaret's head peeked in. She said, "Is this . . . ?" Then she saw Preston.

Shit!

As she stepped into the room, she said, "I'm Margaret Preston. Excuse me for interrupting. Please go ahead."

There was a man with her. He was middle-aged, middle-weight, middling tall, a middle American, like the man on the television commercial who gets heartburn after dinner and his wife brings him Maalox and then he wants to go out for a banana split. He wore a brown jacket and beige slacks and brown cordovans and an ivory shirt and a brown tie with subdued yellow stripes in it. And a completely unnecessary collar pin.

Margaret found a seat and sat down and held her head up and looked directly—defiantly—at Preston. And this guy sat down beside her and . . .

Jesus Christ! He's holding her hand!

Just Mel consulted his list. "And you are . . . ?"

"Kirk," said the man.

"Great! Welcome, Kirk. This is Hector and Hector's—"

"Just a second," Preston said. He glared at Margaret. "Who the hell is Kirk?"

"It's not your turn, Scott," said Just Mel.

"I wasn't talking to you." Preston didn't take his eyes off Margaret.

"It's Hector's turn, Scott. You'll have to wait your—"

"Fuck you, Mel."

Kirk said, "I say!"

Margaret shook her head.

Just Mel said, "That's uncalled for, Scott."

Preston said to Margaret, "Who the hell is Kirk?"

"Kirk is my friend, Scott," she said, head even higher. "Kirk cares for me. I think the term you use is . . . Significant Other."

"See?" said Just Mel. "That's who Kirk is."

Preston ignored him. "I'm your *husband*! What the hell does that make me?"

Lupone chuckled and nudged Hector and put his

hands up to his temples and extended an index finger on either side of his head, making horns.

Preston saw it and didn't care. "Yeah," he said, "I mean, except for a cuckold."

"What's that?" Hector whispered to Twist.

"Must be like the shaftee," said Twist.

"Scott," Margaret said, "I thought it would be a kindness to—"

"I'm out of the house—I'm in a *hospital*—for three and a half weeks and already you're boffing your brains out with a stranger?"

"Hold on there, mister!" Kirk was on his feet. "You can't—" He turned around, for someone was tugging at his coattail. It was Raffi. Raffi didn't say a word, just pointed at Kirk's seat and smiled the smile of Kipling's snake, and Kirk, who must not have been a thoroughly stupid man, sat down again.

Margaret said, "You're disgusting. I should've known . . ."

"Known what?"

Just Mel stood up and went to the center of the room. "Scott," he said, "let's analyze the space you're in now."

"It's the space *you're* in, asshole," Preston said. "You're in my way."

Margaret said, "I could've written you, Scott. I could've told you on the phone. But I thought it would be a kindness to tell you in person, here, where you have friends and support and people to talk to. People who'll help you understand."

"Tell me? What, that you and—"

"That I'm leaving you."

"For"—Preston pointed at Kirk—"for *him*?"

"Very wise," Just Mel said to Margaret. "Very wise to share it with us. That's why we're here."

"Mr. Larkin thought so."

Larkin! The bastard! He might've warned me. Preston exhaled. "Okay, Margaret, make me understand. Make me understand why you're leaving me for a . . . a shoe clerk."

"Typical." Margaret sneered. "Kirk is an arbitrageur."

"Holy shit," Hector said. "What's *that*?"

"Shaf*ter*," said Twist.

"Kimberly?" Preston said. "I don't s'pose she has anything to say about this."

"Kimberly is very fond of Kirk, Scott. He's already like a father to her. . . ." She paused, dagger poised. "The father she—"

"Nice, Margaret. Very nice."

"Kirk doesn't drink. Doesn't touch a drop. He can't. You see, his mother was . . . was . . ."

Kirk squeezed her hand and said, "It's all right, honey." He looked around the room and said (the bravest man in the world), "Mother was a drunk."

"No shit," said Lupone. He elbowed Hector. "Ain't that disgusting?"

Just Mel frowned at Lupone and said, "Thank you, Kirk, thank you for sharing that with us." He had an idea. "I think we should all thank Kirk, don't you?"

Kirk smiled humbly.

Just Mel raised his hands to conduct the chorus.

Lupone nudged Hector, who nudged Twist, who nudged Preston, and before Just Mel could mouth the first consonant they shouted in concert, "FUCK YOU, KIRK!"

The silence that followed was broken by Corazon's coda to Kirk: "What a flamer."

Kirk's smile collapsed. Margaret's face had the reddish-purple color of a cheap Beaujolais. The veins in her temples throbbed as if beetles were in there trying to escape. She and Kirk stood up and, holding hands, walked to the door.

"I'm glad I came, Scott," she said. "It makes me feel much better about my decision. You've made it very easy for me. You'll be hearing from my lawyer when you get out."

She opened the door and went out. Kirk followed her, and before Kirk shut the door behind him Preston heard him say, "*If* he gets out. He is very, very ill."

"Well!" Just Mel said when they had gone. "We certainly have something to talk about now. Scott, let's look at where your head is. How does all this make you feel?"

How do I feel? How about "like I was hit in the head by a hammer"? Or "slugged in the stomach by Mike Tyson"? How should I feel when seventeen years of my life have just been declared invalid . . . worthless . . . expunged? How about "punched in the soul"?

But all Preston said, evenly, as he pulled his eyes away from the door, was "Get off my case, Mel."

"That's alcoholic thinking, Scott. We have to—"

"Hey, Just Mel!" Lupone cut him off. "Fuck off, why don't you. I wanna get back to what's-her-face and the Wesson Oil. That sounded good."

Preston heard nothing for the rest of the hour. He was pretty sure there was some laughter, and he remembered a couple of shouts, but he spent the time inside himself, doing exactly what Just Mel wanted him to: examining how he felt.

The anger didn't last long, only a few minutes of routine, predictable reactions: hurt pride, the bitter taste of betrayal, the bruise to his ego at the thought of Kirk preferred in his bed.

Guilt came next, the kind of searing, sweat-inducing remorse that he recalled as the companion of his worst hangovers. *What have I done? I have embraced drink, destroyer of love. Why couldn't I have quit last year or the year before that?*

When had the balance tipped? When had the damage become irreparable?

He would never know.

Then sorrow, a dead weight of grief at all the times of joy that would be forever shrouded by the black cloak of his disgrace. What was left to him? What was the point of—

Stop it!

He recognized the progression, envisioned the seducer waiting for him to take the next step, over the threshold into the realm of Who Cares? Forget it. Have a drink.

Today is the first day of the rest of your life.

And what would the rest of his life bring?

Interesting question. Exciting, even.

He felt a sense of adventure.

New things were going to happen to him. Good or bad, it didn't matter, they would be new.

Freedom.

Freedom to do what?

Priscilla. Oh, how natural the progression!

But what about Priscilla? For that matter, what *was*

Priscilla? An adolescent trapped in a woman's body. But an adolescent with the apparent capacity to turn hard as concrete when the going got tough.

How would their relationship change now that he was free? Would he still be her dearest, truest friend, or would she be tempted to insert into their chaste goodnight kisses the tiniest slip of tongue?

Talk about adolescence! he chastised himself.

The patients were permitted five minutes with their Significant Others at the end of the hour. But since Preston's Other had become quite Insignificant now that she had run off with this guy who she said was Ivan Boesky but who looked like Willy Loman, he wandered into the hall and smoked a cigarette while he waited for Duke to come out of his group.

He was staring at a framed cartoon poster of two pigs kissing beneath a balloon that said "K.I.S.S."—an acronym for "Keep It Simple, Stupid"—when he heard footsteps behind him and felt a tap on the shoulder.

It was Lupone. He put an arm around Preston and guided him down the corridor and spoke in a voice as low and rumbling as a freight train on a faraway track. "I got a deal for you. Raffi says he'll whack this Kirk if you want."

"Oh?" Preston croaked.

"It's a shitty thing, jump the missus' bones while a guy's inna joint."

"That's . . ." *What should I be? Grateful? Surprised? Appalled? Outraged? No! Not outraged. The man is offering you a favor.* "That's very nice of him. But why should he—"

"Call it professional courtesy."

"How can I—"

"Who knows? You run this publishing house, right? You say what gets printed and what gets squashed. Maybe someday some guy inna witness-protection program wants to narc on us, make a buck stabbing his family inna back with a kiss-and-tell book. You remember your friend Raffi who whacked that prick for you. Maybe you work it out so the book dies of natural causes. Whattaya say?"

What do I say? I say I've been drugged by Jivaro Indians and am having a hallucination.

What he said was "Puff . . . I'm grateful. Please tell Raffi I owe him one, just for the thought. But I figure it this way: If that's what her taste runs to, guys like that, then I'm better off without her."

"Yeah, but the insult . . ."

Think! "She'll pay for the insult."

"How?"

"With regret."

Lupone seemed to absorb the words like a sponge. Then he grabbed Preston's chin in one of his Smithfield hams and looked deep into his eyes and said, "I heard a Christian charity. The Sisters of the Rosy Sepulcher told me all about it. But you! You make the pope look like a shylock."

Then he kissed Preston. On the mouth. And walked back and told Raffi, who looked like he'd just heard that the Martians had landed at Grover's Mill.

Duke's group still hadn't gotten out, so Preston went outside and sat on one of the benches in the exercise area and had another smoke.

He replayed the scene with Margaret, waiting for the inevitable surge of pain. It didn't come. He guessed he was in a kind of shock. The pain would come later.

He wanted the pain *now*, wanted to know what it would be like, so he reached for it by summoning the image of Kimberly. His baby. He had lost her. Never again would he—

Balls! You don't *own* your children. How do you lose something you never had? Whatever he had with Kimberly wasn't lost. It was changed, maybe, but there was nothing he could do about that. And—who could tell?— maybe the changes wouldn't be all bad.

The pain wouldn't come. But sometime it would, sometime when he didn't expect it. He prayed it wouldn't be on some lousy day when he was all alone and found himself passing a dark and welcoming saloon.

To his surprise, he felt admiration for Margaret for having the guts to read the death sentence over the corpse of a marriage that had probably been clinically dead for a long time. If she could find happiness with Kirk, good for her.

A couple, visitors, came out of Peacemaker and saw him. The man said something to the woman, and the woman nodded and said something back, and they started toward him.

Preston knew right away who they were, and the first thing he thought was, I wish I'd put on a tie.

They were the Ralph Lauren twins, she in a casually tailored Ultrasuede suit and a casually cut silk blouse with a silk scarf tossed casually over one shoulder and an anchor-link gold chain around her neck and a gold Rolex on her wrist, he in jodhpur boots and a pinch- waist tweed jacket and a shirt that looked as if it used to be a tablecloth at "21" and a wool tie and a paisley handkerchief in his breast pocket and a gold Rolex on his wrist.

"Mr. Preston?" said the man.

"Mr. and Mrs. Godfrey."

They weren't surprised that he knew who they were. They were accustomed to being recognized, entitled to be known.

They shook hands, and Mr. Godfrey said, "They said inside there—"

". . . in group," Mrs. Godfrey interjected, evidently pleased to know an "in" word.

". . . that you have been particularly—"

". . . close to Priscilla."

Preston wanted to throttle her. She was one of those discreetly arrogant women who never say anything out of place, never raise their voices, but express their innate superiority to their husbands by never letting them finish a sentence.

"I like to think we're friends," Preston said.

"Do you have any idea—"

". . . where she could be?"

"She didn't show up? At all?"

"We wondered if perhaps she's—"

". . . afraid to face us."

"I saw her last night. She was looking forward to seeing you."

"I must say, we find their attitude quite—"

". . . irresponsible."

"They say if she ran away—"

". . . there's nothing they can do about it." Mrs. Godfrey kept the ball and ran with it. "They showed us their idiotic form that absolves them of all responsibility. I assured them that their form would be dross in the hands of our Mr. Preble.''

Mr. Godfrey explained. ''Of Preble, Plunkett and Twyne?''

Preston said, ''I don't think she ran away. She would've told me. Or somebody. I know she would've.''

''Then where—''

''. . . is she?''

''I don't know.'' Preston reached for his cigarettes. He offered them to the Godfreys, who reacted as if he were serving a pâté of cockroaches. ''But I'm going to find out, I promise you.''

''If you'd call us,'' Mr. Godfrey said, handing Preston a business card, ''even if Priscilla won't—''

''. . . any time, day or night . . .''

''. . . we'd be extremely grateful and, you may be sure—''

''. . . our gratitude will not be simply a handshake and a pat on the back.'' Mrs. Godfrey smiled at Preston and took her husband's arm and turned him back toward Peacemaker.

Preston looked at the card and tucked it into his shirt pocket. He felt disheveled—hell, he *was* disheveled, compared with them—and dirty. The ''dirty'' was their fault.

Forget it. And since he had recently been proclaimed a paragon of Christian virtue, he added to himself, They know not what they do.

The Godfreys were almost at the door when Mr. Godfrey said, ''You know what I need, Bunny?'' and put a hand inside his jacket.

''Not here, Dillon.'' She pulled his hand out of his

jacket and glanced Preston's way. "It isn't fair . . . to *them.*"

"But Bunny, I need one. I need a drink."

So do I, Dillon. So do I.

15

GUY LARKIN HAD retreated to his bunker. His door was closed, and when Preston knocked all Larkin said (snapped, really) was "Come!"

Larkin had even removed his "Have a *Great* Day" button. His voice said he resented the interruption. "What is it?"

A man sat across the desk from Larkin, wearing an outfit with more parts than a Mercedes (all it lacked was spats), making notes on a yellow pad. An expensive briefcase was open on the floor by his feet. This was a lawyer, had to be, a gladiator summoned to do battle with Mr. Preble of Preble, Plunkett and Twyne.

"*You* called *me*," Preston said.

"Oh. Yes. This is Mr. Bixler." He looked at the lawyer. "Scott Preston."

"Just a couple of questions, Mr. Preston," Bixler said pleasantly. "When did you last see Priscilla Godfrey?"

"Last night. I've already been through this with her parents."

"You *what*?" Larkin came out of his chair.

"Guy . . ." Like a dog trainer, Bixler motioned Larkin to sit down.

"They asked," Preston said. "What'd you want me to do, lie?"

"No," said Bixler. "Not at all." He cleared his throat. "It might be better, though, if you refrained from discussing the matter with them. Now: for my records, are you aware, Mr. Preston, that all patients check into The Banner Clinic of their own accord, that they are free to leave at any time?"

"Sure. But what does what I think have to do with anything?"

"Just answer the questions, Scott!" Larkin said.

"I did." Preston favored Larkin with what he hoped was a patronizing smile. "Guy."

Bixler ignored Larkin. "A precaution, Mr. Preston. There's a chance, I'd say remote, that you might be asked . . . in the event Miss Godfrey doesn't . . . I don't think there's any likelihood, really . . . to give a deposition."

"Okay," Preston said. "Go for it."

Bixler looked at his pad. "Are you further aware that under its charter from the State of New Mexico, the clinic—unlike, say, a hospital—has no more liability for the welfare of its clients than a hotel?"

"No."

"No?"

"Look, you think people come in here looking to sue somebody? They come in here looking to save their lives. Nobody reads all that crap they make you sign."

Bixler did not look pleased. "Did Priscilla Godfrey

say anything to you about wanting to leave, intending to leave, wishing she could leave?''

"No."

"Did she ever talk about wanting to be alone, get away to think, that kind of thing?"

"No."

"Are you the only person she confided in?"

"How would I know?" Preston was beginning to enjoy this. "If she confided in anyone else, she wouldn't tell me, would she? That's what confiding means."

Bixler gave him a hard look. "So it's possible she told someone else she was intending to leave."

"Not likely."

"I didn't ask you if it was likely. I asked if it was possible."

"Sure, it's possible. It's also possible she was kidnapped by a sex-crazed jai alai player. But it's not likely."

"Look here!" This time Larkin came all the way to attention. "You think this is a game, Scott? You think you're back in Skull and Bones? This is serious business, mister, and I don't like your attitude. In fact—"

"Guy . . ." Bixler raised his hand again.

Larkin would not be denied. "I haven't liked your attitude from day one. Let me tell you something: I would say the chances are slim, very slim, that you will ever . . . *ever* . . . receive . . . your . . . medallion!" Thus delivered of his thunderbolt, Larkin sat down.

Bixler said, "Thank you, Mr. Preston."

"Have you called the police?"

"For what? No crime has been committed. People have gone AWOL before. Sometimes they hitchhike into town and get drunk or take drugs. Usually they come back.''

"And if they don't?''

"Get out, Scott!'' said Larkin.

Preston was tempted to wish Larkin a great day, but he suppressed the impulse and left without saying anything.

When he had closed the door behind him, he heard Bixler say, "Not smart, Guy,'' and Larkin reply, "I hate Yalies.''

Priscilla had said nothing to anyone about doing anything or going anywhere. The last person with a recollection of seeing her—and it was easy not to recall seeing someone, because in the evenings everybody milled in and out, watching television, eating ice cream, chatting—was Twist, who told Preston he had been watching a movie on TV, *Cry Freedom*, and Priscilla had wandered in and watched for a few minutes, but when someone hit the Steve Biko character with a club she had left, saying something about there being too darn much pain in the world.

"I wouldn've remembered it,'' Twist said, " 'cept for 'darn.' Here's this dude gettin' the shit kicked outa him, and here's little Gloria sayin' 'darn.' ''

"She went to bed?''

"Beats me where she went. She split, 's all I know.''

It was dark, long after the evening lecture, before Preston had a chance to slip away and go into Priscilla's room. He shut the door and turned on the light and stood and looked. Everything was in place. Her clothes hung in the closet, her cosmetics lined a bathroom shelf, a copy of ''The Big Book'' was open on the desk beside a pad and a red pencil with which she had been underlining passages.

He went to the desk and opened the top drawer and found her wallet, full of credit cards, her driver's license and $385 in cash.

This was not a woman who had run away, not a woman who had gone into town for a few drinks.

Because he didn't know what else to do, he went to the dresser and opened the drawers. He didn't know what he was looking for. Something missing. But how would he know if something was missing? He paid no attention to what people wore.

Except for the Godfreys.

Except for Priscilla.

The first two drawers were full of lingerie. The third held blouses and a couple of T-shirts and a pair of exercise shorts.

The fourth was packed with sweaters. He was about to close it when, for no reason at all, he remembered what she had been wearing the night she arrived. A linen skirt and navy blue pumps and . . . a blue cashmere sweater.

It wasn't there.

All right! Wherever she had gone, she had worn a sweater, which meant she had left at night, because no one would wear a sweater in the desert in the daytime.

He examined the closet. Two dresses and half a dozen skirts, including the linen one, hung on hangers. Amid them was an empty pants-hanger. Did she ever wear slacks? Jeans? He couldn't remember.

Shoes. The blue pumps were there, and a beige pair and a black pair, a pair of shower clogs and a pair of Topsider moccasins.

But no running shoes, the shoes she wore on their walks. Her Nikes were gone.

Okay. She had gone out at night and had planned to do some walking.

She had had an accident, maybe been bitten by a snake or hit by a car.

No. There were security guards all over the place, and cars passed by all the time. Somebody would have found her.

She had gotten where she was going but had been unable to get back.

Why?

Because they wouldn't let her.

Who was "they"? *How the hell do I know who "they" is? Nobody lives around here except . . .*

Banner.

Preston felt sick. *Don't avoid it. Look at it.*

Okay. Banner invited her up the mountain again, and she went and—*Go ahead, torture yourself!*—this time she let him hold her—*"May I hold you?" Jesus!*—and they did the Deed of Darkness and she's still up there, rutting around like a sow.

No. *Thank God.* She knew her parents were coming today, she wanted to see them, to show them how far she'd come, she'd told him that. And Banner wouldn't dare keep her up there. He wasn't completely nuts, no matter whether he was still sticking things up his nose from time to time. He'd have to know people would be looking for her.

So?

So she went up there. Maybe he invited her, maybe he didn't, but she went up there. . . .

Why would she go up there if he didn't invite her?

There's too darn much pain in the world.

Marcia. She went up there to plead Marcia's case, to get Marcia's job back for her.

And?

She had said what she had to say, and maybe Banner said yes, maybe no, but she started back and . . .

What?

Never got here.

Why not?

Because she couldn't.

What does *that* mean?

She just couldn't.

That's bullshit. That . . .

Oh my God!

Preston switched off the light, walked to the window, opened it, climbed out and began to run.

The sound floated over the still night air, clarion clear. If a security guard had been patrolling in one of the electric golf carts, he couldn't have missed it. But perhaps he would have fled, convinced he was fantasizing or being tantalized by the spirit of some long-dead child.

The voice was high and soft, not wistful or unhappy but placid as a little lake in a forest glen. But a lake without life, as if killed by acid rain.

The sound chilled Preston, made the hair rise on his arms and the back of his neck.

> *"The itsy-bitsy spider*
> *Went up the waterspout.*
> *Along came the rain,*
> *And washed the spider out.*
> *Along came the sun,*

And dried up all the rain,
And the itsy-bitsy spider
Went up the spout again."

He came over the sand rise, the erosion bulwark at
the farthest point of their walks, and stood looking down
at their hiding place.

She had dug a pocket in the sand and lay in it, staring
up at the moon, with the fingertips of one hand climbing
her other forearm in time with the song.

". . . the itsy-bitsy spider
Went up the spout again."

She stopped. Without moving, without seeming to
see him, she said, "Hello, Scott. I've been hoping
you'd come."

He skidded down the face of the bulwark and sat
beside her. He took one of her hands and held it. It felt
as if all the muscles had been removed. Like holding a
lamb chop.

"Are you okay?"

"The itsy-bitsy spider went up the waterspout. . . ."

"Priscilla?"

"Did you know you can't kill yourself by eating
sand? You get full too fast."

Very slowly, he lay her hand across her stomach and
lifted her shoulders and drew her into his lap, so her
head rested against one of his thighs. He stroked her
hair. It was as gritty as if she had been boiled in a wave
and slammed against the ocean floor. He saw in the
moonlight that her bottom lip was split and puffy, and
there was a bruise on one of her cheeks.

"Can you tell me?" he said.

"Is that Eloise?" she asked, pointing at the sky.

It took nearly four hours for him to learn what had happened. The moon was down, and her constellation, Eloise, hung directly overhead.

Weeping seemed to pull a plug that allowed her to cleanse herself. She had been singing, and tracing the outlines of Eloise, and telling him that sand bugs tickled when they crawled over you—for she had lain buried in the sand, with only her face exposed, for all of today's daylight hours—when suddenly, in the middle of a sentence, tears had erupted and her throat had caught and she had begun to sob in the spastic, strangulating way of a chastised child, clutching one of his arms so tightly that after a while her fingers cramped and he had to help her pull them off, one by one.

After that, she was quite coherent.

Preston's deduction had been on the money: She had decided to go up to Xanadu to demand—to plead, to beg—that Banner reinstate Marcia and Dan. She had been convinced that Banner had nothing to do with their dismissal. No one who had been through drug addiction, no one who had felt the frailty of the human spirit, who had known the loneliness of the black hole, could fault another for seeking love and accepting it gratefully—from whomever, wherever, however.

The decision must have been made by a board of detached, self-righteous racists.

When she arrived, Banner was there, but not there—drifty and dreamy one minute, edgy and twitchy the next.

He was delighted to see her, had fixed on her as a

gift from God, some sort of manna sent down to liberate him from whatever demon had gripped him.

He asked if he could hold her.

She said no, she had come to talk about Marcia.

He didn't know what she was talking about, didn't know who Marcia was. That made her feel better, confirmed her assumption of his innocence. All she had to do was explain the injustice to him, and he would correct it.

He offered her a drink.

She said what did he think she was, suicidal?

Nonalcoholic, he said. For God's sake. What did *she* think *he* was, crazy?

She said she didn't come up here to socialize.

He said was having a glass of grape juice socializing?

All right, she said, and he gave her what he called no-kick champagne.

But as soon as she took a sip she knew he had lied to her because you can't disguise the warmth it makes going down. There might have been more than alcohol in it, too, because as much as she felt angry at him, as much as she wanted to throw the glass at him and walk out, those feelings seemed to be separated from her, like someone else's, and deep down inside *her* she didn't care. About anything.

That was the last thing she remembered until the next morning, this morning, when she woke up on a couch in the living room. Her first thought was relief at discovering that she was dressed exactly as she had been, but when she moved she realized something was wrong, not just the cuts and bruises, but her clothes didn't feel right. It was the way her sweater bound the sleeves of her blouse.

"What do you mean?"

"You know how when you put a sweater on over a shirt, you always have to shake down the shirt sleeves and straighten them out because the wool grabs the other material?"

Don't ask this question. Don't do this. He couldn't not. "So you think he—"

"It doesn't matter."

"Doesn't *matter*?"

"I thought about it all day, in the sand. It doesn't matter, because they already raped away my soul."

"Who did?"

"Everybody."

She had heard the TV coming from the library. She went in, and there was Banner, watching cartoons in his undershorts and drinking orange juice with probably something in it because it had a pale, watery look to it.

He didn't answer her when she asked him what had happened, just kept watching the Road Runner escape from Wile E. Coyote. He didn't even look at her when she said she was going to report him, just said in a voice that made her think for some reason of an iguana, "Who to?"

She hadn't had time to think, she said, but she was going to tell somebody, maybe the police, because he was a hypocrite and a liar and a bunch of other words that came to her at the time. Even then he wouldn't look at her, and she got so angry she wanted to pick up a fire poker and smash him with it, but at last he turned that big mane of silver hair and sneered at her and said, "Go ahead."

They won't believe you, he said, because you're just a junkie who couldn't take it anymore and went over the hill and got yourself some shit and then fell down a couple times.

They'll believe me, he said, because I'm—and he winked at her as he said it—a saint.

Then he turned back to watch Road Runner.

16

SHE WOULDN'T LET Preston take her to the hospital, wouldn't agree to see the doctor, refused even to have a talk with Nurse Bridget.

"It's okay, Scott," she kept saying in rejection of the several options Preston advanced for vengeance. "It's okay."

As if the weeping had purged her not only of pain but of rage.

As if this were the fate she somehow deserved.

The only thing she wanted was an apple. She was hungry.

What, Preston wanted to know, what was she going to tell Larkin?

"Nothing."

"Then I will. And if he won't do anything, I'll—"

"You will *not*!" she snapped at him. "*My* life is *my* business."

"But you can't just—"

"It's okay," she said, and she smiled and squeezed his hand and started back to the clinic. The rims of the hills to the east were in faint relief against the gradually lightening sky. "Really. It is."

Preston lay down for an hour, hoping to sleep, but his brain played and replayed fantasy scenes of horror at the mountaintop Xanadu. When Kimberly was young, he had had nightmares about her being abducted or murdered or beaten by nannies, and he had pacified himself in the restless dawn by imagining the ghastly retribution he would wreak. Now he conjured a vision of Stone Banner, skinned alive and hanging from a chandelier by his balls.

He found himself trembling with fury, so he got up and took a shower. He was the first one in the dining hall.

Larkin must have intercepted Priscilla on her way to breakfast, and whatever she told him must have satisfied him—Preston assumed that Larkin was so grateful to see her alive, in one piece and not intending to file charges, that he would have accepted a story of her being shanghaied by gypsies—because he went through the cafeteria line right behind her and carried on an animated conversation with the shrink, Frost, while he filled his tray with granola, yogurt and fruit juice.

Preston had saved a place for Priscilla at his table, but she passed behind him and went to a table in the corner, and ate alone.

All day he kept tabs on her—waiting for her after group, barging into line beside her at lunch, cornering her before the afternoon lecture—asking her if she was all right, urging her *please* to see someone, hoping to spark anger or outrage, waiting for the moment when she would take him aside and say she had called the police or that her parents were contacting the board of directors or at least that the redoubtable Preble, Plunkett and Twyne were on the case.

But it was always the same: a blank little smile, a touch on the arm and "It's okay, Scott."

Marcia had accused *him* of victimizing Priscilla, and here she was—victimized? Forget "victimized." *Lobotomized!*—by The Banner Clinic's own holy eponym.

It was okay, was it?

For her, maybe. Not for him.

They say living well is the best revenge? Fuck that. Revenge *is the best revenge*.

What kind of revenge?

Nuclear.

Terminal.

Dream on.

He couldn't work it out alone.

He had hoped to have the meeting at night, during free time, when it might appear to be nothing more sinister than a bull session, but tonight they were scheduled to board a bus for their first off-grounds, civilian A.A. meeting, in the basement of the Methodist church in town.

So they met at dusk, before supper—Preston, Duke, Lupone, Twist, Crosby and Hector. Preston had assembled them carefully, feeling like Lee Marvin in *The Dirty Dozen*, choosing them for their ingenuity, daring, commitment and ability to keep their mouths shut. They gathered on the grass beside the exercise area.

Preston grouped them in a circle, sitting on the ground, creating (he hoped, for the benefit of prying eyes) a tableau of an impromptu discussion of Fifth Step priorities or individual approaches to long-term sobriety.

He told them what he knew, including his assumptions about the blanks in Priscilla's memory.

"That stupid fuck," Lupone said when Preston had finished.

"Fat lot *you* talk," said Twist. "You and Raffi, you the guys gave him the blow."

"A guy's got a gun, don't mean he hasta shoot somebody. A guy wants to stick shit up his nose, fine with me, I'll sell him all he wants. But that ain't a license to fuck up little girls. Uh-uh."

"Or throw people off mountains," said Hector.

"We don't know that," said Crosby.

"Chuck knows," said Duke. "Unless the tooth fairy's giving out Porsches."

"Anyway," Lupone sighed, "it's no big deal."

Preston said, "No big *deal*?"

Lupone shook his head like a disappointed parent forced to discipline a child. "I call Raffi, Raffi checks with the don. We whack Banner. Have to. He's bad news."

"No," said Preston.

"What you mean, no?"

"All that'll do is make him a martyr."

"Bull*shit*!" said Twist. "What it'll do is make him dead. He won't mess with Gloria no more."

"But nobody'll know why," Preston argued. "There'll be testimonials to him. Plaques. People will revere his memory. You want that?"

Lupone said, "We'll put a fuckin' note on his chest. You know your problem, Scott? You don't wanna whack *no*body. You're one a them liberal pussies can't see the virtue of capital punishment.''

"Nobody'll believe it, Puff! He says he's a saint, and to a lot of people he *is*."

Lupone chuckled. "So let's burn him at the fuckin' stake.''

"It'll make you people look bad, put a lot of heat on the clinic. No more drying out juicers. No more helping junkies.''

"I say bull*shit*!'' Twist shouted. He was about to shout again, but he saw Crosby looking over his shoulder and raising a hand in warning, so he stopped.

Just Mel was strolling by on his way to Peacemaker, and Twist's expletive had made him veer this way. "Hi there, fellows,'' he said. "Everything copacetic?''

Lupone glared at Just Mel and was about to suggest that he perform an anatomical impossibility when Preston cut him off.

"Hi, Mel. Boy, this higher-power stuff's a real bear.''

"How so, Scott?''

"Well, Hector was saying that he regards Corazon as his higher power, but Khalil here, he denies that a higher power can be manifested in one human being because if that human being should die, then one would have to conclude that God is dead. . . . Right, Khalil?''

"As rain, Scott.'' Twist was shaking his head to conceal his smile.

"Higher power is difficult,'' Just Mel said, and he crossed his feet and started to drop down.

"Please, Mel,'' said Preston, stopping him by catching his elbow. "We'd like to thrash this one out ourselves.''

"Oh. Right,'' Just Mel said, straightening up. "But

call me if you need a guide. The forest of the higher
power can be pretty dense.''

"For sure, Mel.''

When Just Mel had entered Peacemaker, Twist leaned
forward and said, ''I gotta hurt Stone. No way he gonna
get away with messin' up Gloria. I gotta go up that
mountain and hurt the man real bad.''

Duke said, ''You'll go to jail.''

"Maybe.''

"For ten years?''

"I'll put a stocking on my head.''

"Great. *I* should've thought of that.'' Duke rolled his
eyes.

"Hey, Duke, fuck you!'' said Twist. "You got a better idea?''

"Nobody disagrees,'' said Preston. "But we want to
do it right.''

"How?'' asked Twist.

"I don't know yet.''

There was silence for a moment, and then Lupone
said, ''Forty-eight hours.''

"What about it?'' said Preston.

"You got forty-eight hours to come up with something. If you don't, I call Raffi.''

"And if Raffi don't do it,'' Twist said, "Puff and me,
we will.''

They were shepherded aboard the bus like inmates from
a prison farm. They had been told to wear clean shirts
and comb their hair, and if any of them felt the urge to
speak during the meeting—and Gwen urged them all to
rise and tell their stories and "get in touch with the

higher power of a group of sympathetic souls" if the spirit moved them—they were to *watch their language*.

Preston tried to sit beside Priscilla on the bus, but she had already boarded and was squeezed into a corner by Butterball, who knew nothing about what had happened to Priscilla and nattered on about her plans to start a holistic hair-care center when she got out.

What did he care if Lupone had Banner whacked, or if Twist wanted to go up the hill and maim him? It wasn't his business.

Yes, it was.

Four weeks ago, this had been a good place, staffed by good people who lived by a rule Preston had come to respect: If you help other people, you help yourself. Give, and you will receive. Take without giving, and you will live in the splendid aloneness that leads to self-loathing.

He had taken—a new sense of himself, a new regard for people the likes of whom he had never known existed, and, at least on a day-to-day basis, a clarity of mind he hadn't known since he was a child.

Now the place had gone bad, and it was stinking, like the proverbial fish, from the head down. The head had to be removed, and maybe there would be enough good will left so the body could live.

For lagniappe, of course, there was always the sweet prospect of pure vengeance.

But killing Banner was no answer, maiming him no solution. They had to bring him down and let him crush himself before the world whose adoration was his sustenance.

The problem was, Preston mused as the bus cruised through the twilight toward the dim orange glow on the horizon that signaled the town of Monte Vista, he and the others existed in a vacuum surrounded by a substance about which they knew nothing.

They didn't know what had happened to Natasha. They suspected that Chuck knew, but where was Chuck? Normally, he was ubiquitous, driving Banner here and there, delivering patients to the clinic, subduing the unruly and discouraging the curious.

Nobody had seen him since the blowup with Duke over the Porsche.

They didn't know what had happened to Marcia, except that she had been fired. Where was she? Was she lodging a complaint? Was anybody ever going to look into *any*thing that happened at the clinic?

They didn't know what Banner's soft spots were, where he was vulnerable, *if* he was vulnerable.

Marcia might know. Possibly. If they could find her.

But Chuck was the key. He was Banner's beard, Preston was sure of it. If there was any way to get to Banner, Chuck would know it.

And he was gone. Probably ordered to drive to Canada to break in his Porsche.

The bus pulled up before the church, a forty-year-old run-down replica of the Alamo, and after a final admonition about cleanliness of mind, body and mouth, Gwen and Just Mel permitted them to file off the bus and descend directly into the basement.

Preston thought he had stepped into history, perhaps into an old Eric Sevareid documentary about a *Bierstube* Bund meeting. The low-ceilinged room was a thirty-foot square packed with folding chairs. A folding table held a coffee urn, three boxes of doughnuts and a cereal bowl into which those who chose to dropped change to pay for their coffee. Knots of men and women stood around gossiping and smoking, and their exhalations gathered in a blue layer that hung like fog below the ceiling. A.A. exhortations had been tacked up beside *Sesame Street* posters, children's drawings (the room probably doubled as a day-care center) and a full-length life-size four-color portrait of the Savior sporting what looked to Preston to be the most monumental hangover in the history of Christendom.

Gwen and Just Mel ushered their charges into three rows of seats, then stood against a wall, watching, like warders. Preston felt like a mental patient on an outing at a shopping mall.

A bald man with rimless glasses, checked trousers, a powder-blue polo shirt and two-tone shoes detached himself from his group, walked to the front of the room and stood behind a rostrum made of a milk crate overturned atop a desk. He cleared his throat, and the gossipers quieted down and took seats.

"Hi there," the man said genially. "I'm Walter and I sure am an alcoholic."

"Hi, Walter!" shouted everybody but the contingent from Banner, some of whom mumbled but most of whom looked at the floor.

Gwen, peeved that her lessons had been so ill learned, nudged Crosby with her foot, and like a twitchy frog, he jumped and squeaked, "Yo, Walter . . ."

"We have a couple birthdays," said Walter. "Bessie R. . . . Where's Bessie R.?"

A huge women in a pansy-print dress as large as a king-size bedspread wheezed to her feet.

"Bessie R. has been sober for . . . sixty days!"

Everybody applauded—everybody but the spoilsports from Banner.

Gwen kicked Crosby, who yelled, "Yeah, Bessie!"

"And here's a whop-doozer," said Walter. "Lester V. Where you at, Lester?"

Preston heard a chair scrape somewhere behind him, and a voice say, "Rahcheer."

"Lester V. has been in God's platoon, sober as a judge, hasn't had a drop, for three thousand, six hundred and fifty days . . . that is *ten years* today!"

People whistled, applauded, stamped, and Preston thought, I will never be sober for ten consecutive years. Not if I live forever.

"Did you ever think you could go ten years, Lester?" asked Walter.

"Never did," said Lester. "Just go one damn day at a time, though, and them suckers do pile on up."

"Come see me after," Walter said. "We got a cake for you, and we'll all sing 'Happy Birthday.' "

"Look forward to it," said Lester, and he sat down.

" 'Course, we could do the cake now"—Walter grinned—"but I 'spect with all our fine young friends from The Banner Clinic, theren't be none left for you, Lester." When his thigh-slapper didn't receive the uproarious laughter he evidently expected, Walter coughed and continued. "Which reminds me: You all prob'ly know but I'll remind you anyways, tomorrow night Stone Banner's gonna receive the President's own special medal for contributions to humanity and a drug-free America."

Preston had been barely paying attention, had let his mind begin to drift. Now he froze and focused.

"It'll be over to the civic center in Promised Land.

They gonna be all sorts of celebrities there and dignitaries, they say maybe even Dick Van Dyke—he's a personal favorite—and the television'll cover it so you can go home and see yourself on TV. Anyhow, we're all invited, and it's important that we get a real good turnout for our very own Stone, so I hope to see you all there. Tomorrow night. Seven o'clock.''

There is no justice in the world.

''Better get there early, though,'' Walter said, trying another joke, ''else all the Banner people gonna get the good seats and get *them*selves on TV.''

Preston looked at Gwen. She was beaming and applauding, forcing the rest of the audience to applaud with her. She caught him looking at her. He raised his eyebrows and pointed to himself: Are *we* going? She winked at him and nodded vigorously.

Well. There's *something to chew on.*

Preston felt that someone was looking at him. He turned his head. Halfway down the row, Lupone was leaning forward and staring at Preston, and when he saw that he had Preston's attention he extended a fist and shot him a thumbs-up sign.

''Okay,'' Walter said, ''who wants to get things rolling?'' He looked over the room. ''How 'bout one of the folks from Banner?''

Sixty people held their breaths at once. Sixty pairs of eyes tried to drill holes in the floor.

''Maybe later, then. Somebody? Nobody? Hey listen, folks, I'll tell my story till I'm blue as a dead calf, but I know you're all sick to pukin' over it.''

A man in the second row stood up. He was thin as a pencil and had hair to his shoulders. ''I'm Ferlin,'' he said, ''and I'm one sorry sumbitch of a drunk.''

Walter led the room in a chorus of "Hi, Ferlin!"

While Ferlin ambled into his story (he was the son of a waitress and a pass-through cowboy; his mama fed him whatever she could scrounge from the café where she worked, which turned out to be mostly beer), Preston pondered their options.

They could try to get to Banner before the ceremony, could knock him out and tie him up, prevent him from getting there.

What would that accomplish?

Nothing.

They would be escorted to the ceremony, put in their seats and watched over like serial murderers. What could they hope to do? Produce secret placards and face them toward the TV cameras, proclaiming Banner to be a hypocrite?

Banner would make a joke and they'd all be thrown out of the clinic.

They could place anonymous calls to the TV stations and feed the reporters their suspicions.

The reporters would check out the rumors, find them baseless and ignore them.

They had to make Banner destroy himself.

And they couldn't.

Nobody could.

Except maybe Chuck.

And he had disappeared.

Preston was distracted by a light breeze on the back of his neck. The outside door had opened. He half-turned in his seat and looked at the door.

Marcia.

She saw him, and she gave him a tiny nod, and what

struck him was that she didn't smile or wave or look the slightest bit surprised to see him.

It was as if she had known he would be there, as if she had come to the meeting to speak to him.

How could he speak to her? He couldn't just get up and walk back there and sit beside her. Gwen of the Gestapo would knock him down and stomp him to death. Maybe he could hang back after the meeting, pretend he had to go to the john, meet her in a hallway or upstairs in the apse. (He wasn't sure what an apse was, it was a crossword-puzzle word, but he had always fancied meeting somebody in one.)

No. Just Mel would be on toilet detail, would follow everybody into the john, probably check specimens for controlled substances.

He *had* to talk to her.

Ferlin had concluded his story, counting off ten days, twenty-two hours and seventeen minutes of continuous sobriety, and now someone else was telling how he had convinced himself that booze was God's elixir since if Christ's blood had been turned into wine, why then all he had been doing all his life was taking nonstop communion.

The guy finished, to laughter and applause, and suddenly Preston—without knowing what he was going to say but positive that this was his only chance to make contact with Marcia—jumped to his feet and heard himself say, "I'm Scott and I'm an alcoholic."

"Hi, Scott!"

Duke looked at him as if he had rabies.

Lupone was so startled that he bounced on one of his chairs and splayed its legs.

Gwen smiled at him like a proud mother at a potty-trained child.

I said it! Preston felt that his brain was unspooling, like a videotape on fast-forward. *I said it in public and nobody laughed! What have I been scared of? Sonofabitch!*

He almost said it again, to see if it felt as good in reruns. But that wasn't why he was on his feet.

"I was born . . ." he began, and stopped. Born where? Poor and black in Mississippi? Born on a farm in Nebraska? Born to lose? He wanted to send a signal to Marcia, but he couldn't deviate too far from the truth or Gwen would manacle him and bundle him off to a rubber room.

"That's a start, Scott," Walter said, and people laughed.

"I was born into a family where problems weren't discussed. Standards were set, and you were expected to toe the line, and if you didn't there was a lot of silent disappointment, but nobody ever actually said anything."

Good. Close enough to the truth. Now: throw in a ringer to get her attention.

"There were three of us—my sister . . ." *A name. Think of a name!* ". . . Penelope, my brother, Charles—we called him Chuck . . ." *Yes. That should do it. "Chuck" ought to sit her up straight. If she remembers that I'm an only child.* ". . . and me. We idolized our father. He could do no wrong. Of course, if he had done anything wrong, nobody would have talked about it."

Enough back story. Get some drinking in here. Now!

"Anyway, I started drinking when I was about fourteen, but nobody said anything. It was almost as if they didn't want to notice.''

He glanced down and saw Twist looking at him with a worried frown on his face, as if he was debating whether it would be a kindness to subdue Preston and give him a shot.

Preston gave Twist what he thought was a reassuring smile.

''Over the years, Chuck drifted away, and I haven't been able to find him, and I *need* to find him now . . . because I've just learned something pretty terrible and I feel I have to share it with him.''

Twist whispered something to Duke, and Duke whispered back, and they were both about to come out of their seats when Lupone put one of his giant hands on Duke's thigh and pressed him down into his chair.

Thank God. Puff has got it.

''What I've learned is that all along our sainted father has been abusing people—maybe Penelope, too—and it's critical to my recovery that I tell Chuck and see if we can work it out together. . . . That's all I have. Thanks for listening.''

Preston sat down.

Walter said, ''The Program isn't in the lost-and-found business, Scott, but never mind. We know what kind of courage it takes to stand up for the first time, and we're with you!'' He clapped, and a bunch of other people clapped along with him.

Walter then called on a handsome woman in jeans, riding boots and a sweatshirt, who said her kids wanted her to go white-water rafting with them but she was happy staying here and raising her mastiffs, and though she didn't want to tick off her kids, because she enjoyed their company, or at least their attention, there was no way she was going to be able to spend a week sitting in a raft without a little liquid comfort to get her through the rapids of their bickering.

And that led to a roundtable discussion of what was more important, sobriety or family, leading to the inevitable conclusion that without sobriety there *was* no family.

When the meeting was over, the contingent from Banner was instructed to stay in their seats until the room had cleared.

"What are we," Duke asked Gwen, "contagious?"

"There are dangerous people here," she said.

"There are?"

"Like that . . . Ferlin. People who haven't been sober as long as you have. How do I know he's not carrying or using or even dealing?"

"He looked okay to me."

"The devil has a large wardrobe, Duke. Always remember that."

As they lined up to board the bus, Preston murmured to Lupone, "Think Marcia got it?"

"The spade lady? She was there?"

"You didn't see her?"

"Hell, no."

"What'd you think I was doing?"

"Pulling their chains. What else?"

On the ride back to the clinic, Gwen held forth from the front of the bus and explained the different abuse patterns reflected in all the different stories they had heard. She praised Preston for having spoken and said she could see that God had made a little crack in his armor, and if he kept opening that crack a bit more every day, there was still a chance he would receive his medallion, after all.

Something woke Preston. He looked at the luminous dial on his watch: two-thirty. He heard Twist making sounds like a bear with asthma, and he vowed (as he did every time Twist's snoring woke him) that this morning he would ask Guy Larkin to requisition a pair of nose clips for Twist.

He threw off the covers and stood up and was about to bend down and clamp off Twist's nose—which usually forced Twist to grumble and change position and bury his face in his pillow, which usually stopped the snoring for a while—when he heard a faint scratching on the window.

It might have been a branch blowing against the windowpane, but there were no trees beside the window and he had never known a breeze to blow here at night.

He padded softly to the window. He saw nothing, so he opened the window and stuck his head out.

Something touched his arm. He lurched backward and struck his head on the window frame.

It was Marcia, flattened against the wall. She pointed to the far end of the building, where a cigarette glowed. They waited—Marcia against the wall, Preston leaning on the windowsill—until the tiny orange light vanished around the corner of the building.

She gestured for him to follow her, so he pulled on his trousers, climbed out the window and tailed her across the sand.

Her car was hidden in a hollow a hundred yards from the building. Its tires were almost flat, for she had driven across the desert and had let most of the air out so she could maintain traction on the shifting granular ground.

"You did good," she whispered when they were far from the clinic. "No wonder all you Yalies went into the CIA."

Before he could say anything, she opened the back door and gestured inside the car and said, "Got a present for you."

Someone lay on the back seat, breathing deeper than sleep. Unconscious. Or comatose. Preston leaned in and looked.

Chuck.

17

IT WAS LIKE trying to close an overstuffed suitcase. Big slabs of Chuck kept flopping out—an arm, a leg, his head—until the three of them pushed together and finally crammed all of him into the shower stall and turned on the water and shut the door.

Preston and Marcia had barely been able to roll him out of the car, couldn't possibly have lugged him all the way back to the clinic, so Preston had woken Twist, and they had half-carried, half-dragged him across the sand and squeezed him through the window.

Now he lay curled up in the shower stall, a great mass of reeking meat, and they waited for the hot water to steam him back to consciousness.

"What's he on?" Preston asked.

"Smorgasbord," said Marcia. "Little bit of everything."

"I'd say juice, mostly," said Twist. "Christ . . . *smell* the man. I wonder where he was tryin' to get to."

"Oblivion," Marcia said. "Looks like he made it, too."

298

Dan had urged her, begged her, to try to get their jobs back for them, so though she knew from the outset that the hope was vain, she had tried. She tried to see Lawrence Tomlinson and was refused an appointment. She drove up to Xanadu to see Banner, but Chuck turned her back at the gate, nicely—reluctantly, embarrassedly—but obviously he had been instructed to keep her away from Banner, on pain of losing his own job.

She lodged a protest at the county level, then with the state, but found herself swimming in a sea of procrastination and buck-passing. She made inquiries at the various associations of mental-health professionals, but they all refused to take a case based only on innuendo and inferences drawn from Tomlinson's carefully crafted letter.

She was angry enough to go public with a charge of racial discrimination, but a friend of a friend, a woman who was going out with one of Tomlinson's flunkies, let her know that silence would be the course of wisdom: No, the Banner board wouldn't write letters of recommendation for her and Dan, but on the other hand, if she kept her mouth shut they wouldn't pour poison in the ears of the administrators of the other thousand or so clinics across the land.

She had applications out to sixteen rehab centers, from New Jersey to California.

Dan, meanwhile, was taking a course in fixing transmissions so he could work at AAMCO. He had always liked cars.

She had started doing volunteer work with a "Just Say No" program, cruising around, making friends with kids, shooting the breeze, finding a basketball if they wanted to play, convincing a merchant to permit them to put a hoop up in his parking lot. That kind of thing.

That's how she had begun to see Chuck, just hanging around. At first, she had thought he was Twelfth-Stepping—keeping his own memory green by spreading the word—and she had stayed away from him so nobody could deduce a conspiracy of grown-ups.

Then he had shown up in that red Porsche, and she had smelled rot. He gave everybody rides, let some of the kids drive it even, and it was like he was some sort of Pied Piper, always with a knot of kids around him.

She stopped him on the street a day or two ago and let him know that the Porsche was spreading the wrong message, it was bad news, because what it was telling the kids was: Happiness is money. And these kids knew only one way to get money. For crissakes.

And Chuck—nice Chuck, friendly Chuck, Chuck who had known so much pain of his own but still seemed to feel her pain when she was fired—had told her to fuck off and mind her own business. With eyes whose pupils were the size of pinpoints, as if light—the tiniest atom of light—hurt. With a voice that came from somewhere deep in his guts, and a tongue that lagged a fraction behind every word it wanted to utter.

Last night she had seen the Porsche parked in a courtyard of a half-finished condo complex. Its hubcaps were gone, and someone had bent the radio antenna in half.

Today, driving back from the unemployment office, she had seen it parked behind a roadhouse. She went inside, and in the dark, sour-smelling bar was Chuck, smashed out of his mind, lurching with a list, playing darts for money with two truckdrivers. As she watched, he lost and couldn't pay up, had run out of money, so the two truckdrivers slammed him up against the dart board, and while one of them held him, the other threw darts at him. They didn't have to hold him, though, because Chuck thought the game was hilarious. He ducked the first two darts, but the third one hit him in the chest, in one of those pectoral muscles the size of a standing rib roast. He pulled it out and tossed it back to the truckdriver and said something like "Try again, asshole, I bet you can't hit me in the eye."

She tried to get the bartender to stop it, but he said, "Are you crazy, lady? I don't need to have my place turned into a pile of matchsticks. Besides, they're having fun, no harm done."

By now she figured she had to find out what had gone wrong, what had pushed Chuck over the edge, this guy whose sobriety was as precious to him as his soul—hell, he used to say his sobriety *was* his soul.

She couldn't go to the clinic, knew nobody there would take a call from her.

Then she remembered the schedule, the A.A. meeting, and decided to go. Maybe it would be a waste of time, maybe she wouldn't learn anything. But it was better than sitting alone in a pasteboard condo, wishing she had a drink and listening to a symphony of flushing toilets.

Afterwards, once she had received Preston's message, she had no trouble finding Chuck. The red Porsche was in a ditch beside a vacant lot. She found a couple of kids who helped her roll him from his car into hers.

Now that they had him, what did Preston need him for?

Preston told her everything he knew, then said, "I don't know, though. Suppose Banner's already fired him."

"I doubt it," Marcia said. "That's the great thing about us chronics: You're humble enough, there's always another chance." She thought for a moment, and a look of loathing leavened by sorrow passed over her face. "How's Priscilla?"

"Shitty," Twist said.

"Living somewhere else," Preston said, "in some twilight zone. Going through the motions."

Marcia nodded. "You see it in abused kids. Something inside them tells them they have to get away or they won't survive. It's usually a real mess, a lot of irrational guilt, a sense that they deserved it, but whatever it is is intolerable. They can't escape physically, so they run away mentally. They create a secret safe place, and that's where they live."

"What brings them back?"

"Time, if you pull them out of the situation and give them *real* safety. If you don't, sometimes they don't come back. They keep going."

Preston could feel the pulse in his temples. "Where to?"

"New people. They'll create a new person. The brain can't deal with the real person, can't take the overload of shit, so it creates a new person that doesn't know anything about it. Remember *Three Faces of Eve?* Remember *Sybil?*"

"Jesus . . ."

Marcia put a hand on his arm. "We're not there yet. We'll make her safe."

There was a crash in the bathroom, and the sound of

the plastic door panel exploding out of the shower stall, and a roar of an enraged hippopotamus.

Preston and Marcia jumped. They stood between the beds, looking at each other.

Twist smiled. He rolled off his bed and pulled the table between the beds out from the wall and unplugged the brass lamp. Glass broke in the bathroom, and there was the sound of Chuck falling and cursing and struggling to his feet. Twist very calmly removed the shade from the brass lamp and unscrewed the bulb and wrapped the cord around the base of the lamp and gripped the lamp by its slender neck and tested its heft.

When he was seven years old, Preston had seen the original version of *The Thing*, and after he peed himself he went up the aisle and stood by the usher, who had seen the picture probably a hundred times.

He recalled it now, for standing in the bathroom doorway was The Thing incarnate, hulking, staggering, dripping wet and grunting with a lust to inflict grievous injury.

Twist shouldered past Preston and Marcia and stood facing Chuck, swinging the heavy lamp at his side.

"How you doin', Chuck?" he said.

"Bhaaa . . ." said Chuck.

"Know what you mean. You must have a head 'bout the size of a fuckin' Buick."

"Bhaaa . . ." Chuck said again, and he swung a random punch that did nothing but cause him to lose his balance and carom off the doorjamb.

"Now, Chuck," Twist said, "here's what it is. You're a big motherfucker, I'll give you alla that, but lemme tell you what. Scott here, and Marcia, they gonna dance around you and hassle the shit outa you, like mongooses, till I get inside and fetch you upside the head with this here heavy sumbitch, which gonna make your head feel even worser. So what say we cool right down, Chuck, and have us a talk?''

Chuck said "Bhaaa . . ." once more and tipped backward and sat down on the floor with a thud that made the toilet seat jump.

"Atta boy." Twist turned to Preston and said, "All yours."

Preston asked Twist to fetch some coffee from the brewer in the common room. Then he sat cross-legged on the floor outside the bathroom door and talked to Chuck. He told him what Lupone had said about Banner. He told him what had happened to Priscilla. Then he repeated it all twice more, hoping that fragments would pierce the fog in Chuck's head and somehow assemble themselves, like a jigsaw puzzle, into a comprehensible picture. He deferred asking any questions until Chuck had had two cups of coffee and washed his face and run some toothpaste around his mouth and drunk about half a gallon of water.

When Chuck was cleaned up, they took him into the bedroom and sat him on Twist's bed. Marcia offered him a cigarette. As he reached for it, his hand trembled so badly that he shook his head and clasped his hands together and dropped them into his lap. She lit the cigarette for him and put it between his lips.

He smiled bitterly and said, "You know what I am? A—"

"A human being," said Marcia. "And it's no damn bargain."

Chuck talked then, unprompted and uninterrupted. As much as Preston wanted to edit him, wanted to urge him to cut to the chase and tell them what he knew about Natasha and Banner and about the details of the award ceremony, he knew that Chuck had to talk in his own way, at his own pace (perhaps with some gentle guidance if he strayed too far into the backwaters of his childhood), if he was to resolve his conflicts and come to the conviction that he would help them.

And need him they did, for without him they would be helpless to bring Banner down.

Chuck recited the familiar facts about his career in the NFL and his discovery of the ephemeral joys of cocaine.

Preston was smoking a cigarette and barely listening when, at the end of that chapter, Chuck said, ''Nobody knows this, but I was s'posed to go on trial when I got outa here, possession with intent. Stone said he could do a deal with the court if I'd come work for him, stay under his supervision. What did I want, serve three-to-five or drive a car for him? Shit, that was an *easy* choice.''

For the first year, there were no problems. About halfway through the second year, he asked Banner how long he'd have to work for him, thought he'd like to move back to the Philadelphia area and get an outdoors job in construction or something, he didn't really like the desert. Banner blew up at him and said he was to stay until Banner decided he didn't need him anymore and if he took a hike he ought to keep in mind that Banner could have the charges revived anytime, the indictment was still valid and he was a friend of the judge. Chuck was a prisoner.

He figured, well, he shouldn't piss and moan too much, he *had* been in possession and he *had* had intent, so his conviction was as sure as sunrise, and three-to-five in the desert wasn't half as nasty as three-to-five in "Q" or someplace.

Then Banner began to lean on him for more than just driving, like getting some inside information from some of his old NFL buddies that Banner could pass on to his friends, and taking Banner to Tahoe and Reno and other places and dealing with a bunch of Eye-Ties in shiny suits about cleaning up after Banner and keeping it quiet, and, over the past few months, ferrying girls and shit—and sometimes just the shit itself, hidden in Pringle's potato-chip cans—up the hill to Xanadu.

Even that he could deal with, could rationalize, because recovery is a one-man job, and no matter what Banner was doing to himself, he—Chuck—was keeping himself clean one day at a time, and that was all that counted. He tried to talk to Banner a couple of times, offered to help him, even be his private sponsor and get him clean again, and Banner just kissed him off like he was a worm. So Chuck figured, Fuck him. Every man for himself.

Then came the Natasha business.

She had heard talk about Banner, maybe she overheard one of Don Ciccio's parasites bragging at a prize-fight or some showbiz stand-around, and she decided to pay him a visit. No warning, no nothing.

First thing Chuck heard about it was when she called him at home and asked him to pick her up at the airport and drive her up to Xanadu.

It was in the car that she told him she had heard bad news, and she asked him if it was true.

"I didn't say dick," Chuck said, "and I told her why I wasn't about to. She accepted that real nice. She was in fine shape, all pretty like in the pictures, in control. Said she was gonna lay it out for Stone, plain and simple: He cleaned up his act or she was gonna blow the whistle. She wanted him to go back into treatment, said she'd even go with him if he wanted.''

Chuck stopped.

"Then what?" Preston said.

"Don't know. Don't know if I ever will. I parked the car and went 'round to the slaves' quarters to get Cook to make me a sandwich. 'Bout an hour later, I was there havin' coffee and a smoke, Stone came in and said he had to see me. He looked *bad*, all shaky and shitty.

"We get back in the main house and he says, Something's wrong with Natasha, she up and run away. He musta seen in my eyes that I had trouble swallowin' *that*, 'cause he started off on how he could tell the minute she walked in the door she was on somethin', she was all frazzled and didn't make sense. When I didn't chime in right away and agree with him, he said, Of course, it would've been hard for you to know because you were in the front of the limo and she was alone in the back and she never was a big talker to . . . He couldn't bring himself to say what he meant—servants or the masses or something—so he let it tail off. I made a mistake and told him right then that she sat in the front seat, not the back, and she talked the whole way. If I had a brain in this fuckin' coconut of mine, I woulda saved that for the sheriff.

"I wanted to go outside and have a look for her, and he told me not to bother, she had called a cab. Then he said, No, she had run out and said she was *gonna* call a cab. He didn't know what he was talkin' about. When I said I had to look for her, he brought up the indictment crap again. So I never did see the hole in the fence, not till . . . after.

"Five o'clock the next day, the motherfuckin' German whore of a flame-red car shows up outside my condo."

Chuck put his head in his hands.

Marcia said, "How did you deal with that?"

Chuck looked up at her and smiled. "Shit, you the one found me."

Preston said, "What do you *think* happened?"

"Gun to my head, I guess he fed her somethin', like you say he did Priscilla, and she prob'ly had no tolerance—I mean, she'd been clean for damn near a month—and she went apeshit. Maybe she run outside and fell over the edge. Maybe he got scared and followed her. Maybe he pushed her. Strikes me, it don't matter. One way or other, he *did* her."

Marcia lit another cigarette and handed it to Chuck. "What now?" she said.

"I made my deal," Chuck said after he had sucked half an inch off the cigarette, "and I lived up to my end. But that prick, he gone and changed the rules. What you told me, he's not just a sick fucker anymore. He's *dangerous*. What you got in mind?"

Preston asked about the award ceremony. Chuck said he knew about it, that Banner was real excited, had had invitations engraved and sent to just about the whole of *Who's Who*.

"You're driving him?"

" 'Spect so."

"He hasn't fired you?"

"I don't guess he'd dare. We got each *other* by the short and curlies."

Preston told him what they had in mind.

Chuck thought about it, got up and walked to the window. After a moment, he turned around, and there was a big grin on his face.

"That would be real nice," he said.

18

"CLARISSE'LL KILL ME," Duke said. "She'll kill me, and then she'll cut me up in little pieces and feed me to the buzzards."

"You were the one wanted to napalm the place when Marcia was fired," said Preston. "You were all for—"

"Yeah . . ." Duke was squirming, embarrassed. "But that was talk. Now you're *serious*."

"It's up to you." Preston didn't want to push him. "If we're careful, there's no way we'll get caught."

Duke's meeting with Clarisse had gone better than he had dared dream it could. If he graduated, she'd take him back. "I don't know what love is," she had said. "You're a slippery bastard, but I miss you." She might even consider having kids. But if he got thrown out, forget it. She'd take the house, the cars, the furniture and the bank accounts and leave him with nothing but the payments on the home equity loan.

"I can't do it," Duke said, looking wretched. "I just can't." He had a cigarette going, but he lit another one anyway.

"Fair enough."

Hector said, "Me too. I got my future to think about. Pretty soon they gonna make me graduate. Couple weeks on the streets, I find me another joint, no sweat. But they throw me outa here, somethin' like this, I'm blackballed every joint in America. Haveta find me a joint in fuckin' Canada. Who needs that shit?"

"Okay," said Preston. He wasn't surprised. This was pretty much the way he had thought it would go. *Hoped* it would go. Too many players could screw up the game. But everybody had to be given a chance. "That leaves me and Puff and Twist and Clarence. I think to protect—"

"I'm out," said Crosby, ripping blades from a patch of grass in the exercise area where they sat. "They'll never let me play again, not in the bigs. My boy'll never see me stroke another one. I can't handle that. He's only six."

"Right." *That's the core. No more defections. Please.* He looked at Lupone.

"I made the call," Lupone said. "Raffi still wants to whack him, but he'll give you your shot."

Before Preston could turn to Twist, Twist said, "Chuck's set. He makes the pickup at the deli, same as always, swings by the place you told him, then goes to get Stone at six-thirty."

Preston nodded. He smiled at Twist. "How you feeling?"

"Not too nasty. But I got that funny feeling, y'know, like"—Twist grinned—"like I'm comin' down with somethin' *bad*."

"Me too."

* * *

They planted the seed after lunch. Preston and Twist went to Gwen and begged off the afternoon lecture and group, both claiming to feel nauseous, sweaty and strange.

She looked from one to the other, like an avenging angel imagining deeds so vile as to defy description, and said sternly, "What have you been doing?"

"Breathing each other's air," said Preston.

"In your room, both of you," she said. "I want you fit as fiddles for tonight's affair."

"Absolutely," said Twist.

"Wouldn't miss it," said Preston.

They slept until five o'clock. Twist laved his eyes with soapy water, then rinsed them and looked in the mirror.

"Nice," Preston said. "You look good in pink."

They went to see Gwen again.

Preston coughed noisily and wiped his mouth with a handkerchief.

"I don't know what this is," Preston said. "Plague, maybe. There've been cases out here."

Gwen said, "If you didn't smoke so much—"

"I keep tellin' him," said Twist. "Sucker's poisoned me." He made a hideous sound into a tissue.

"We're going tonight," Preston insisted. "I just wanted your permission to get some cough medicine."

"And infect Liza Minnelli? Maybe even Mary Tyler Moore? The only place you're going is to see Nurse Bridget. Perhaps she'll take you with her and isolate you in the back of the hall."

Oh-oh.

They went into the common room, to the coffee brewer, and while Preston stood watch, Twist poured coffee into two small specimen containers he had clipped from the bathroom next to the infirmary.

"Is it hot?" Preston said. "It's got to be hot."

"Hot?" said Twist. "Shit's like to melt the plastic."

They stood outside Nurse Bridget's office. Preston raised his hand and popped one finger, then two, then three. On three, they poured the coffee into their mouths and buried the containers in the sand of a standing ashtray.

Preston felt the roof of his mouth begin to sear, like when hot pizza cheese sticks up there and clings.

Nurse Bridget was hanging up her phone. "Speak of the devil," she said, and she reached into a beaker of alcohol and pulled out two thermometers.

Preston swallowed.

Twist's eyes watered, and he moaned.

Nurse Bridget slipped the thermometers into their mouths, and she pushed the stopwatch button on her watch.

For three minutes, she recorded data in a patient's file. Then her watch beeped at her, and she pulled the thermometers out of their mouths and looked at them.

"Gracious!" she said. "Let me take some blood, then off to bed with you. As soon as Doctor gets back from the ceremony, I'll ask him to look at you."

By then, Preston thought, he'll be too busy to care if we're dead.

He rolled up his sleeve.

I hope.

The bus came for the patients at six o'clock.

Before she left, Gwen looked in on Preston and Twist, who lay in their beds, covered with blankets, shivering.

"What's that for?" Gwen pointed to the wastebasket Twist had placed on the floor beside his bed.

"Just in case," Twist said weakly.

At 6:05, when they heard the bus pull away from the roundabout, Preston and Twist got out of bed and tried to yank the wrinkles out of their jackets. Preston wore his lightweight suit, a white shirt and a dark blue tie.

Twist wore Preston's blue blazer, blue shirt and striped tie, a pair of his own black jeans and black motorcycle boots. He couldn't button the collar of the shirt, and the sleeves of the jacket rode so high that his huge forearms made the brass buttons stand at attention, like shiny warts.

"Nobody gon' believe me," he said.

Preston thought Twist looked like a commercial for anabolic steroids. "Nobody who values his life will challenge you."

At 6:08, they climbed out their window.

Twilight still came early, so the shadows were already long, giving them cover to the farthest corner of the building.

At 6:12, they stepped out of the shadows and sprinted to the drainage ditch that bordered the road. They ran in the ditch, skidding and tripping in the loose sand, trying to keep their heads below the surface of the road.

They had ten minutes to cover the half mile to the abandoned gas station.

Preston hadn't run half a mile in twenty years, and Twist, with his long legs and easy lope, quickly pulled far ahead.

The trunk of the limousine was already open when Preston arrived. Chuck, wearing a white shirt, black tie and black chauffeur's trousers, had removed the spare tire and was helping Twist curl up in the trunk.

Preston leaned against the car and caught his breath. "Any problems?" he said when he could speak.

"Not a one," said Chuck. "Smooth as silk."

"What is it, you know?"

"I don't hafta know. I just hafta know where to put it."

Preston entered the car head-first, and Chuck folded him into the niche on the floor before the front seat. He covered Preston with a dark gray blanket, then put his chauffeur's jacket atop the blanket and his hat atop the jacket.

"You can breathe," he said, "but if you cough, might's well keep on bendin' and kiss your ass goodbye." He shut the door and walked around the car and climbed in.

"He never sits up front, does he?" Preston asked as the awful thought occurred to him.

"You kiddin'? Up front's nigger country."

Chuck started the car and pulled out from behind the tumbledown gas station.

"You know what I feel like?" he said as he accelerated toward the road up to Xanadu. *"Mission Impossible."*

"I hope you're right," Preston said, his voice muffled by the covers. "The good guys always win."

19

THE LIMOUSINE REACHED the top of the hill, leveled out and came to a stop.

Chuck said, "You want to snort or cough, get it over with. You got about two minutes." The car door slammed.

Soon, a rear door opened. Preston held his breath. He felt the limo's springs sag. Mushy. That was the trouble with Cadillacs. He'd heard of people actually getting seasick in the back of Cadillac limos. For a long ride, you want a Mercedes or a Daimler.

Chuck's door opened, closed again, and the car started and pulled away.

From the back seat, the sound of ice rattling around in a bucket, cubes dropping into a glass.

A smooth ride on a flat road, like floating over an oily sea.

Banner's voice: "I don't appreciate your taking off like that."

Chuck: "Sorry, boss. I had a fever 'bout a hundred and thirty. I was like in a fog the whole time."

"I thought maybe you'd gone off the deep end."

"Me? No way."

"Well, call next time."

"Sure thing."

Silence. The limo braked, turned, straightened out and accelerated again.

"Big night," Chuck said. "All your friends flyin' in."

"Awards . . . People give awards so *they'll* feel good. Makes them think they're doing something. I've only begun to pay back what other people've done for me."

Getting the false modesty down pat.

Again the sound of ice cubes rattling.

"Still, must make you feel good."

"We do what we can, Chuck. Some people more than others, that's all."

"Yeah, but if anybody deserves it, you do."

What's he doing, baiting the man?

Two metallic snaps, like a briefcase being opened, then papers being shuffled around.

Banner mumbling to himself. Memorizing his speech. Preston picked up bits and pieces.

". . . on behalf of everybody who has ever known the agony of addiction . . .

". . . if I cannot help my brother, I cannot help myself . . .

". . . as my friend Liza says, life is a cabaret, and I'm here to tell you, it's a lot more fun sober than stoned. . . ."

The limo slowed, turned a couple of times, stopped.

"Where are the Certs? Don't tell me you forgot the goddam Certs."

"In the thing there, boss, on your right. Two packs."

"Oh."

Chuck's door opened, the car bounced, the door closed again. Then the back door opened.

Chuck said, "You want I should pour you a settler, bring it along?"

"Uh-uh. I'm tuned up fine." Banner paused. "But bring along the emergency kit, in case of . . ." He laughed. "I guess that's why they call them emergencies!"

The door closed. Footsteps fading away on pavement.

Preston waited, counting to fifty. Other cars pulled in and parked. Voices jabbered.

He threw off the covers and slowly raised his head above the dashboard and peered through the windshield.

The civic center looked like something designed by one of Frank Lloyd Wright's less talented disciples. On drugs. Donated to the town of Promised Land by one of the suddenly rich—perhaps one of those couples who hit it big with a chain of hotels cutely named after the two of them, as in Sonny plus Esther equals Sonesta. It had wings and fins and a few cupolas, and was lit up like the spaceship in *Close Encounters of the Third Kind*. The parking lot encircled the monster, and people swarmed toward it like myriad black bugs.

Preston lifted the floor mat on the driver's side and found the keys where Chuck had stowed them. He got out of the car, walked around to the back and, checking to make sure no one was watching, opened the trunk.

Preston froze. *Jesus! He's dead!*

Twist was curled into a fetal ball, eyes closed, mouth slack. There must have been a leak in the exhaust manifold that poured carbon monoxide up into the trunk compartment.

Twist snored.

Preston exhaled and reached into the trunk and shook Twist's shoulder. Twist opened his eyes.

"Your threads is mussed," Twist said. "All I'm gonna pass for is a bag lady." He climbed out of the trunk, stretched and stared at the civic center. "Damn thing looks like it's got a disease."

They didn't bother to hide on their way across the parking lot. They were just another pair of penitent rummies come to worship the saint of sobriety. They passed a phalanx of rented limousines and, at the curb beside the building, the Banner bus.

A television crew had set up at the main entrance, and a reporter was interviewing names. Preston and Twist hugged the wall out of the pool of light cast by the TV floods, and as they hurried by they heard some marcelled bird in a full-length sable orating about her higher power.

"Where's he gonna be?" Twist said when they were again in the safety of shadows.

"Chuck says there's a stage. If there's a stage, there's a backstage. And if there's a backstage, there's a stage door . . . I dearly hope."

It was an unmarked metal door in the back of the building. Unlocked.

They walked down a lima-bean-green hallway lit by fluorescent panels overhead that gave the place the warmth of a morgue. There were doors on either side of the hall—dressing rooms, probably. They climbed a circular steel staircase at the end of the hallway.

The second story was the size of a barn but tightly

packed with ropes, pulleys, backdrops and suspended sandbags.

A bald man in a windbreaker sat before a complex lightboard, smoking a cigar and doing the crossword in a paper.

"Help you?" he said.

Preston pulled his wallet out of his jacket, flipped it open, waved it at the man, snapped it closed and said officiously, "Stone Banner."

"Over there." The man pointed to a dark patch of the barn. "Behind those curtains."

"Right."

"You wouldn't know a four-letter word for a small case."

"Etui," Preston said over his shoulder, and he spelled it.

"Hey, much obliged."

As they walked on tiptoe to the dark corner, they could hear the rustling and murmuring of a thousand bodies, softened by three or four layers of thick curtains.

They pulled back the first curtain and stood between the layers, out of sight of the lighting man.

They heard Banner walking back and forth, reciting his lines. His footsteps came very close, stopped and turned, then receded.

Preston gripped the edges of the remaining curtains and peeked around them. Banner was walking away, across the wing of the stage toward Chuck, who sat at a small wooden table. Beyond, Preston could see the stage, unadorned except for a podium and microphone, and a sliver of the audience.

He wondered where Priscilla was sitting, how she would react when the fun began.

This is for you . . . so you don't flee forever to the misty isles of unreality.

Banner was looking down at his script, gesturing with one hand, so Preston dared shake the curtains to get Chuck's attention.

Chuck looked up, saw Preston.

Preston made an "okay" sign at Chuck, then pointed at Banner.

Try it. Try it now. Let's see what happens.

Chuck raised his eyebrows: You kidding?

Preston nodded, made a fist. *Do it.*

Chuck shrugged and reached into his jacket and pulled out a pewter flask. He put it on the table.

"Boss?" He pointed at the flask. "You sure?"

Banner shook his head. "The hell you think I want? Make a horse's ass of myself?"

"Only tryin' to help. You lookin' kinda ragged."

"I need your help, I'll ask for it. Just keep your mouth shut."

Damn. Preston let the curtain fall as Banner turned back his way. It would be better all around if Preston and Twist never had to make an appearance. They were there as a fail-safe. Twist looked like an escapee from Boys Town. Banner would never believe him. *This is insane. We're all going to jail.*

The lights dimmed and came up again. The crowd fell silent as a man rose from the first row of the audience and climbed the stairs at the side of the stage and went to the podium. He was tall and slender, dressed in a three-piece blue pinstripe suit. His black hair was gray in such strategically perfect places that it might have been done by a paint-by-the-numbers artist. His buffed fingernails twinkled in the spotlights.

He pulled a stack of three-by-five cards from his inside pocket and placed them before him on the podium.

"My name is Lawrence Tomlinson," he began, "and as some of you know, it has been my honor to serve as chairman of the board of trustees of The Banner Clinic." He looked down at his first card. "Very few of us are lucky enough to be able to make a difference, but the man we are honoring tonight . . ."

As Tomlinson embarked upon an apparently endless voyage across an ocean of encomia, Banner dropped his script on the table, put his hands behind his back and paced in circles, practicing facial expressions. With his lizard-skin boots and tuxedo jeans (a blue silk stripe down the side of each leg) and fringed calfskin jacket filigreed with spangles, with his rhinestone-studded ascot and diamond-studded Rolex, he looked like Elton John imitating Liberace imitating Elvis Presley trying to walk like Prince Philip.

Tomlinson was in mid-ocean, awash in adjectives like "selfless" and "dedicated" and "loving." There was no way to tell when he would reach the far shore.

They had to try again. Now.

Preston peeked around the curtains and gestured to Chuck.

"Y'okay, boss?" Chuck whispered. The flask was lying on its side. Chuck set it upright. "Lookin' jeeby."

"Shut up!" Banner said.

Okay. Preston looked at Twist and nodded. *If this doesn't work, if we have to throw him down and do it to him, we're all bound to die. Or at least have to move to Bhutan.*

He tugged at Twist's sleeves, which had gathered up beneath his elbows. He buttoned his own jacket and checked his tie. His mouth felt full of flaking paint.

He stepped out from behind the curtain. Twist stepped after him and stood behind him.

"Mr. Banner," Preston said in a voice he hoped would demand respect. A whisper would have signaled undue deference; full volume would have been audible to Tomlinson.

Banner's head snapped up. "What? Who're you?"

Preston whipped out his wallet, flashed it. "I'm Agent Barnes. This is Agent Noble. Need to know when you'd like the President to make his remarks, before you or after."

"The Pr—? The Pr—? He's *here*?" Under his makeup, Banner's color was fading like that of a day-old bass.

"Outside. Don't want to bring him in till we have to." Preston gestured at the ropes, wires and sandbags. "Didn't have time to sweep the place."

"No. . . . Sure." Banner smiled, and his color came back.

"He wanted it to be a surprise, but . . . you understand."

"It *is*! It is a surprise. I'm . . . I'm flattered. I'm—"

"So what do you think? I'd recommend after. Give you time to say your piece, then the President'll come on and sort of be the capstone to the evening."

"Yes. Right. Good idea." Banner's hands touched his hair, his ascot, smoothed his jacket.

"Fine. We'll go get him." Preston took a step back and landed on Twist's foot. Twist jumped. "You do good work, Mr. Banner," Preston said, covering. "I heard the President say you're a source of comfort and strength to him.''

"We're a family here, Agent . . . Barnes, is it? That's what it's all about . . . love.''

Preston and Twist stepped behind the curtains, took a couple of noisy steps, then returned on tiptoe.

"Hear that, Chuck?'' Banner said, and they could feel him grin. " 'Source of comfort and strength.' Jesus!''

Preston peeked. Chuck wasn't saying anything, just sat there with his hand on the flask, turned so it caught the light and glittered.

Lawrence Tomlinson was coming in to port. ". . . never in my broad experience have I known so much to be done for so many by one man. And so it is with the greatest of pleasure . . .''

Do it! Do it, damn you! . . . DO IT!

Banner said, "I can't remember . . .''

Chuck said, "You don't look so good, boss.''

"I think this is an emergency, Chuck.''

"I agree, boss. I sure do agree.'' Chuck unscrewed the cap and passed the flask to Banner.

Banner tipped the flask back, and Preston saw his Adam's apple bob. Banner closed his eyes and waited. The recollected feeling swept over Preston: the creeping suffusion of warmth and comfort.

Thank you.

Then Banner tipped the flask again and took another draft, deeper this time.

My God! They'd better evacuate the women and children.

Chuck's eyes were as large as cue balls as he reached to take the flask from Banner.

". . . ladies and gentlemen," Tomlinson said, "your friend, my friend . . . Stone Banner!"

Banner popped a big breath and marched out onto the stage. The audience rose to its feet, cheering and applauding.

Preston and Twist eased from behind the curtains and walked over to stand beside Chuck.

Banner and Tomlinson embraced. Tomlinson draped a gold-colored medal on a silk ribbon around Banner's neck. The applause grew louder. Tomlinson shook Banner's hand, descended the steps and returned to his seat.

Banner stood alone at the podium and bathed in the waves of adoration.

There was a peephole in the curtains at the side of the stage, and Preston looked through it and scanned the audience. In the first few rows he recognized a couple of athletes, a U.S. senator, some television actors and a rock singer wearing a T-shirt emblazoned with his own name.

The patients from Banner were in the sixth and seventh rows. Priscilla sat between Duke and Crosby. None of them applauded. Priscilla's face as she looked up at Banner was a blank, a death mask.

Don't go yet. I beg you, stay awhile.

At last, Banner raised his arms, and gradually the applause subsided. A couple of people coughed, and then there was silence.

Banner put a hand on the podium and smiled at the audience. He looked fine, cool, in control.

"Before I begin," he said, "I hope you'll all join me in the Serenity Prayer. It's my rock, as I know it is for many of you." He closed his eyes and extended his arms, as if holding hands with the congregation.

"God grant me the serenity to accept the things I cannot change . . ."

The sound of a thousand voices was like surf on a rocky shore.

". . . the courage to change the things I can . . ."

Suddenly Banner's eyes opened and he pointed at the ceiling and said—not alarmed, not panicked, just commenting—"Wow! Flutterbugs at ten o'clock!"

Here we go. Preston felt his heartbeat double. *Did anybody hear him?* He looked through the peephole at the audience. A few people were startled, two or three gazed at the ceiling, but most were immersed in the prayer and deafened by their own voices.

Duke had heard it, though, and Crosby. They looked at each other, Duke grinning, Crosby frightened.

Preston couldn't tell about Priscilla. Her expression hadn't changed, but her eyes, wide and cold, were fixed on Banner.

By the time Preston looked at Banner, his eyes were closed again, his arms outstretched.

". . . wisdom to know the difference."

Banner opened his eyes, dropped his arms and started to smile. Then, as if he had forgotten something, he frowned. One of his hands flew to his throat, and he tore off his ascot and threw it on the floor.

"Hot mama tonight," he said.

Preston heard scattered murmurs from the audience.

Banner shuddered, shook his head and began to speak. "I accept this award, humbly and with gratitude, on behalf of everybody . . ." He stopped. He looked down at his ascot. His eyes bugged, and he shouted, "Hey!" He stomped on the ascot, first with one foot, then with the other, then with both, grinding it into the stage. "Who let them in here?" he yelled. He turned to the audience, grinned and said, "Lucky thing I was on duty."

There were some awkward laughs, as if they thought they should appreciate a joke that had eluded them.

"Tyrannosaurus Rex," Banner said. "The most dangerous woman in London." He giggled. The giggle evolved into a whinny, then into a chain of deep, spasmodic sobs that brought tears and coughing and, finally, hysterical, high-pitched, wailing laughter. Banner leaned on the podium and gestured at the audience, willing them to share the fun.

People were no longer murmuring; they were talking out loud.

Tomlinson got to his feet and started for the steps.

"Ringo!" Banner said, jolting upright and staring at Tomlinson. He held his arms up as if clutching a dancing partner, and began to tango across the stage, away from Tomlinson, singing at the top of his voice, "Whatever Lola wants, Lola gets, and little man, little Lola wants you. . . ."

At the far side of the stage he halted, bent over and kissed the air. He looked up and winked at a man in the front row. "I sure could use some pussy," he said. "How 'bout you?"

Tomlinson was on the stage. Guy Larkin was running down an aisle. A man in a sports jacket—Walter, from the A.A. meeting—started up the steps on the other side.

Banner saw that he was surrounded. He backed against the curtain. His eyes narrowed, and his head snapped from side to side. He was General Custer or Davy Crockett or Audie Murphy. He reached for his pistols and yelled, "Don't give an inch, men!" He fired two phantom shots, and when neither Walter nor Tomlinson fell, he holstered his pistols and charged at Tomlinson, shrieking like an amok.

Tomlinson threw his hands up to protect himself, took a step backward, turned to flee . . . and stumbled off the edge of the stage and sprawled onto a chubby woman, who screamed.

The entire audience was on its feet now, many rushing for the doors at the back of the room, many more staring in fascination.

Larkin shouted, "Chuck! Get out here!"

Deep in the shadows backstage, Preston shook Chuck's hand and said, "Tell him you were in the john."

Chuck handed Preston the flask and ran out onto the stage.

Through the peephole Preston saw Priscilla. Her expression was no longer blank. Her eyes sparkled, and a slight sly smile played across her face, as if wonderful news had at last reached the faraway land she was visiting.

Banner spun and faced Larkin, Walter and Chuck. They were spread before him, and they advanced slowly, pressing him back against the lip of the stage.

"It's okay, Stone," Larkin purred. "It's okay. Just let me—"

"Stand back!" Banner unzipped his fly and reached in his pants and grabbed his penis and pointed it at them.

They obeyed, as if facing a machine gun.

"Don't worry, Mr. President," Banner said over his shoulder. "I've got them covered."

Mention of the President seemed to alter Banner's hallucination, for he faced the audience, snapped to attention, saluted with one hand and gripped his penis with the other, and said, "Ladies and gentlemen, the President of the United States."

Then he began to pee.

Chuck, Walter and Larkin charged.

Preston emptied the last of the liquid onto the floor and set the flask—engraved with a steer's horns and the initials *S.B.*—on the table.

"Let's go," he said to Twist.

20

IT MADE THE late-night telecasts, of course, and by midnight CNN's Headline News Network had bought the tapes and was broadcasting Banner's performance worldwide. Although the incident was not of cosmic import, so sensational was the footage that the next morning, the *CBS Morning News, Today* and *Good Morning America* all led their newscasts with it and followed up with roundtable discussions with celebrity substance-abusers.

The producers of the Phil Donahue show, Oprah Winfrey and Geraldo Rivera called the clinic and let it be known that if Stone Banner would appear exclusively, he could name his fee.

But Banner was being held incommunicado in a detox unit in Santa Fe. Reports leaked out—via a ward nurse who was behind in her payments on a Jeep Cherokee and was thus susceptible to having her palm greased—that Banner recalled nothing about the evening at the civic center in Promised Land, a symptom typical (according to reliable sources) of users of PCP or Ketamine. His mood was said to be swinging wildly between violent hostility and a manic congeniality during which he was offering to buy drinks for one and all.

The police were waiting to question him further about the circumstances of Natasha Grant's demise, for a routine search of his premises had turned up chemicals that would normally be found only in the possession of psychiatrists or circus veterinarians.

The board of trustees of The Banner Clinic resigned *en masse*, as did the clinic's chaplain, its resident psychotherapist and two of its counselors, Gwendolyn Frye and Melvin Crippin, who declared their intention to marry and go into missionary work among the Guaraní Indians of Paraguay.

The governor of New Mexico considered closing the clinic and transferring patients to other facilities. But the waiting list at other reputable rehab centers—"reputable" meaning any that did not practice aversion therapy, under which patients were forced to consume large quantities of ethyl alcohol and were then given pills that made them convulsively allergic to ethyl alcohol, or revelation therapy, under which patients were browbeaten with religious messages until, supposedly, they were visited by a revelation of Christ or the Virgin or a charismatic figure of their choosing who commanded them forever to keep their noses clean—was between three and six months long. And so, in consideration of the many patients whose treatment was at a critical phase and who might relapse immediately if they were exposed to the temptations rampant in an America propelled by engines of instant gratification, he permitted the clinic to continue operation with a skeleton staff.

Lobbied hard by a committee of patients surprisingly well versed in manipulation of the media, the governor prevailed upon one Marcia Breck, who was said to have left the clinic because of a disagreement over treatment policy, to accept an appointment as senior staff counselor.

Lupone hung up the phone. "Raffi," he said. "Sends you his best wishes. Hopes you make it."

"I don't think I want to know," Preston said, "but did he ever tell you where he got that stuff?"

"It's a batch the don's been tryin' to move to the government."

"The U.S. government?"

Lupone nodded. "Thinks it'd be great stuff to send to Nicaragua, pump in the Sandinistas' water."

"Jesus!"

"Yeah. The don's very into foreign policy."

Preston had put on his suit and had shined his shoes, for he and Duke were graduating. Twist would graduate tomorrow, with Hector, who didn't mind leaving because he had gotten bored with the desert and it would be a while before enough people came to Banner to make it interesting again. Marcia had already alerted a rehab center in New Hampshire to expect a call from Hector within the month, and Hector was looking forward to it. He'd heard New Hampshire was pleasant in the summer.

Preston and Lupone had a cup of coffee and waited for Marcia to assemble the other patients and begin the ceremony.

Priscilla entered the common room, moving soundlessly, seeming to hover a few centimeters off the floor.

She saw Preston and came over to him and smiled and touched his head and said, "You look nice," and moved along, drifting toward the water fountain.

She was almost back now, lingering on the border between this world and her private world of secret safety, as if not ready quite yet to take the final few steps. Marcia wanted to keep her for two more weeks, to escort her tenderly back into the realm of reality.

Preston had had one brief coherent conversation with her.

"What will you do?" she had asked him.

"I don't know. I have no wife, no place to live. I think I still have a job." She looked sad, so he added, "The good thing is, whatever I do I'll do it sober."

"Will we . . ." she began, but the question vanished, like steam.

"Nobody can know. Best not to plan. When you're better . . ."

"I'll look at Eloise every night," she said with a smile. "She'll tell me how you are."

When all the patients had gathered, Marcia sat Preston and Duke in straight-backed chairs in the center of the room. She spoke of her impressions of them when they had arrived, described them as hard cases who knew it all, denied everything and thought treatment was a waste of time, told of her bets with Dan that neither of them would make it. Then she talked about how she thought they had changed, how they had come to know themselves, to tolerate and appreciate others, to realize that they couldn't survive on their own, that the world of recovery was one of caring and commitment.

She urged them not to become "dry drunks"—

solitary soldiers for whom every day was a lonely battle against the bottle because they would not take solace from their fellows—but to get with the Program and stick with it.

Everybody said a few words about Preston and Duke, nothing memorable, really, except perhaps Lupone's offer to find them work if they fell on hard times and Twist's confession that hanging out with Preston had taught him one thing: It might not be a bad idea to learn how to read, *really* read, not just comic books and road signs.

Duke said these four weeks had been a real adventure and now that Clarisse was going to give him another chance, he was sure he'd make it.

Preston hadn't thought about what he was going to say. He stood and looked around the room and his eyes lit upon an A.A. poster.

"I've been thinking," he said, "how nice it'll be to be in a place—any place—where every picture on every wall doesn't say 'One Day at a Time' or 'Easy Does It,' where every minute of every day isn't taken up with warnings about how not to get drunk.

"But now that it's about to happen, you know what? I'm going to miss those things because I'm scared. Those things work. They keep me thinking, let me know that I'm just one little glass of clear shiny liquid away from where I was when I came here. And that's a place I do not want to be."

He paused, because for some reason his throat felt thick.

"But as scared as I am," he continued, hurrying to finish before some emotional thread could unravel and embarrass him, "I have one thing that's like armor, and nobody can take it away from me. It's my higher power. I never thought I'd have one. You know what it is?'' He looked at Marcia. ''It's people. It's people who understand, people who care, people who . . .'' He felt a weird sensation, as if he were drowning. ''I think I'd better shut up,'' he said, and he did.

Marcia presented them with their medallions.

Then everybody hugged everybody.

21

CLARISSE WASN'T THERE.

Lupone and Twist had accompanied Preston and Duke to the lobby and waited while they checked out and carried their bags to the curb by the roundabout. There had been more hugs and pats on the back, more pledges that they'd keep in touch and would try to get together at least once a year. Then Lupone and Twist had gone in to lunch.

"She knew we got out at noon," Duke said, looking at his watch. It was twelve-fifteen.

"She probably got hung up with a client," said Preston.

"Yeah."

"She could've had car problems."

They sat on the curb and reminisced about the day they arrived, about Duke's rabbit suit and how scared Preston had been.

At twelve-thirty, Duke said, "You don't have to wait around."

"I can't go anywhere without Chuck. He's performing surgery on the limo." Preston lit a cigarette. "Besides, my plane isn't till three."

They talked about what would happen to Banner. Preston bet he'd go to jail for a while, maybe a token sentence. Duke thought Banner had so many contacts that he'd get off with probation and community service.

That gave them a good laugh.

At twelve forty-five, Chuck pulled up in the limousine.

"Come on," Preston said. "We'll drop you in Emerald City. It's on the way."

"Suppose she shows up and I'm not here. She'll go off like a Roman candle."

"If we pass her coming this way, we'll stop. There's only the one road."

Duke considered. He looked awful. "Okay," he said, and they climbed into the Cadillac.

"One of her buddies prob'ly got sick," Duke said as Chuck slowed on the outskirts of Emerald City, a hamlet that existed only as support structure for the spa, a turquoise-and-gold neo-Moroccan fat farm. "She had to fill in, didn't have time to call."

Bitch! Where are you? Don't do this to him. "Exactly," Preston said. "Makes sense."

"Where you want I should drop you?" Chuck asked over his shoulder.

"Anywhere." Duke looked out the window. "Here. Here's fine."

Chuck pulled over and stopped.

Where are we? Preston looked. There was nothing here, nothing but a shoe store, a dress shop and across the street . . . a bar and grill. Villa Margarita.

Preston held his breath. He turned to Duke. "Duke . . ."

"What?" Duke wouldn't look at him.

"Don't."

"Don't what?" He was blushing.

Preston tipped his head at the saloon. "Don't do it."

"I gotta sit somewhere, don't I? Can't just go in and stand around the lobby there, waiting for her."

Preston paused. "Okay," he said. "I'll go with you."

"You'll miss your plane."

"Piss on the plane. There are other planes. What've I got to rush home for? Let's go. We'll have a Pepsi."

Preston reached for the door handle. Duke stopped him. "Remember I told you, I never said I wanted to quit. Not really *quit*."

"Duke! Are you nuts? Four weeks, you didn't learn anything?"

"A lot. I learned what I can handle, what I can't. Hey . . . something's wrong, Scott. She didn't show, something's wrong. I can't handle that. I gotta have one, just one. Then I can deal with it."

"Chuck," Preston said, "turn this thing around. Take this stupid bastard back and lock him up till he—"

"Fuck you!" Duke shouted, and he grabbed his little overnight bag and flung open the door and jumped out. "You think you know everything. You don't know *dick*!" He began to run.

Preston started after him, but Chuck was out of the car now, and he put a hand on Preston's shoulder and stopped him.

"You can't," Chuck said.

"I got to!" Preston struggled, but his feet were off the ground.

"You can't. Oh, we can drag him outa there and lock

him up, but in a day or a week, whenever, he'll find a way.'' Gently, Chuck allowed Preston's feet to touch the ground. ''Thing is, Scott, if a man don't want to do it, he ain't gonna do it. And there ain't a thing on God's green earth we can do about it.''

They watched as Duke dodged a car and cursed the driver and, without once looking back, marched into the dark and soothing bar—the anteroom to the abyss.

Chuck put an arm around Preston's shoulder and led him back to the limousine.

''You okay?'' Chuck said as he handed Preston his suit-case and closed the trunk.

''I keep thinking—''

''Don't. Thinking sucks. First while out, you gotta shut off your thinker. Only one thing matters, and that's you. Imagine everybody else died and took their prob-lems to heaven. Want me to hang with you till the plane comes?''

''No, I'm okay.''

They embraced and shared a joke about sending each other tapes if another impossible mission called for their special skills. Then Preston hefted his suitcase and walked into the airport.

The air-conditioning was broken. Technicians had roped off an area and were working on the machinery, while mothers comforted squawling infants and college kids lolled on the marble floor and businessmen fanned themselves with newspapers.

Preston passed the bar. It looked cool and dark, and the overhead lights made the bottles arrayed against the mirrors shine like jewels.

Its scent reached him: beer and peanuts and stale

smoke, leather and cleanser and bourbon. He felt himself salivating.

Maybe he'd stop in and have a glass of soda water.

Maybe he wouldn't.

But, Lord! was it hot in here! Had to be a hundred and ten. At least.

Then something occurred to him: There he was, dressed in a suit and tie, carrying a heavy suitcase, walking through this oven . . .

And he wasn't sweating.

Not a drop.

He laughed softly and kept walking.